WHAT PEOPLE ARE SAYING ABOUT
Speak to Me of Love

"Robin Lee Hatcher's novels always speak to my heart, sending me off to find tissues before the story soars to a joyful and redemptive finish—this one especially so. How I do love a Bad-Boy-turned-hero like Drake! Tender, touching, and romantic, *Speak to Me of Love* is the kind of novel you can't wait to start reading . . . and can't bear to have end."

› **LIZ CURTIS HIGGS** ›
author of Thorn in My Heart

"Stupid me. I thought I'd outgrown a good old-fashioned romance, but Robin Lee Hatcher proved me wrong in this tender story of faith, renewal, and healing love. *Speak to Me of Love* tells the timeless tale of two wounded souls touched by the grace of God and the love of one another. Robin's graceful pen continues to enchant the heart and soothe the soul and will do so, this reader hopes, for years to come."

› **LISA SAMSON** ›
best-selling author of The Church Ladies *and* Women's Intuition

"In a dying town populated by lonely misfits, love comes calling. Robin Lee Hatcher brings fiery-haired Faith Butler together with mysterious rancher Drake Rutledge in a tender story that will warm hearts and remind readers of God's divine power to heal and restore. A delight!"

› **CATHERINE PALMER** ›
author of Love's Proof

"*Speak to Me of Love* is a beautiful tale of second chances. I fell in love with the characters in the first chapters of the novel and was sorry to leave them behind when I turned the final page."

› **DEBORAH RANEY** ›
author of A Scarlet Cord *and* Beneath a Southern Sky

romance the way it's meant to be

HeartQuest brings you romantic fiction
with a foundation of biblical truth.
Adventure, mystery, intrigue, and suspense
mingle in these heartwarming stories of
men and women of faith striving to build
a love that will last a lifetime.

May HeartQuest books sweep you
into the arms of God, who longs for you
and pursues you always.

Speak to me of Love

ROBIN LEE HATCHER

Romance fiction from
Tyndale House Publishers, Inc. Wheaton, Illinois
www.heartquest.com

Visit Tyndale's exciting Web site at www.tyndale.com

Check out the latest about HeartQuest Books at www.heartquest.com

Copyright © 2003 by Robin Lee Hatcher. All rights reserved.

Cover illustration copyright © 2003 by Richard Farrell. All rights reserved.

HeartQuest is a registered trademark of Tyndale House Publishers, Inc.

Edited by Traci L. DePree

Designed by Zandrah Maguigad

Scripture quotations are taken from the *Holy Bible,* King James Version.

ISBN 0-7394-3682-1

Printed in the United States of America

To Peggy and Joanne

MY IDAHO SHAKESPEARE FESTIVAL BUDDIES

All the world s a stage,
And all the men and women
merely play ers.

AS YOU LIKE IT, II, VII

———•—

Rather let my head
Stoop to the block than
these knees bo w to any
Save to the G od of heav en . . .

Part II of KING HENRY THE SIXTH, IV, I

1

THE physician shook his head as he slowly straightened and raised gray eyes to meet Faith Butler's anxious gaze. "It's not good, Mrs. Butler," he said, his tone gentle and solicitous.

Faith glanced at her daughter, lying so still on the bed. Her heart twisted with grief and fear. Becca's skin was nearly transparent. Even her lips were colorless. Her frail body—small for a five-year-old—seemed to cause barely a wrinkle in the blanket that covered her. As Faith touched the child's brow, brushing limp strands of hair away from Becca's face, she felt apprehension slice through her.

"I believe it's her heart," Dr. Telford continued. "You say she was diagnosed as having rheumatic fever some time ago?"

Looking up, Faith nodded, the lump in her throat making it too difficult to speak.

The doctor removed his glasses and rubbed his eyes with the thumb and index finger of his right hand. "Did you understand rheumatic fever is a chronic disease, Mrs. Butler?" He met her gaze again, not waiting for a reply. "Of course, I'm not an expert on diseases of the heart, but I believe, if your daughter is able to rest and get the proper care, she may recover from this episode. It will take a great deal of time, and you mustn't delude yourself into believing she'll ever be strong."

Faith's own heart felt as if it would give out. Becca couldn't die. She had to get well. She simply had to.

Dr. Telford continued grimly, "You must understand this, Mrs. Butler. If you put your daughter back into that wagon, she won't live out the week. She can't take any more jouncing around on rough roads. She must have complete rest and decent nourishment. She hasn't the constitution for such a vagabond existence."

Faith sank onto the chair beside the bed, fighting despair. "But what am I to do? The stage is how I make my living. Acting is all I know. If the company must go on without me ..." Her voice trailed into painful silence.

When sorrows come, they come not single spies
But in battalions.

Shakespeare's words echoed.

"Well," Dr. Telford said with a note of disdain, "if you must go on, there's a home in Cheyenne for orphan children. I suppose my daughter-in-law might agree to keep the child until she's well enough to send to the orphanage."

"No!" Faith shot to her feet. "I'm not deserting my daughter." She stiffened her back and lifted her chin. "I'll stay here as long as it's necessary. I'll do whatever I must to take care of Becca."

The doctor cleared his throat. "That's very commendable, Mrs. Butler."

For an actress, she could almost hear him thinking. No doubt he also wondered if there actually was a Mr. Butler.

There wasn't. At least not anymore.

She shoved away thoughts of her ex-husband, George, and the hurt and anger that came with them. She hadn't time to indulge herself in those emotions. Or in self-pity either. She had to take care of Becca and Alex.

Mentally, Faith added up the money she'd tucked away during this most recent tour. There wasn't much, and Raymond Drew, the company manager, wasn't likely to part with any of her unpaid wages if she left the troupe without notice, especially out here in the middle of nowhere.

She shoved away thoughts of Raymond Drew as quickly as she had those of her children's father.

"Dr. Telford, perhaps you could suggest where I might find work in Dead Horse and where we might stay until Becca is able to travel?"

He raised an eyebrow. "I'm afraid there aren't many opportunities for employment here, Mrs. Butler. As you could see when you came into town, there's little left of Dead Horse these days. The stagecoach quit coming through nearly two years ago. The bank closed its doors six months after that. Folks've been moving out ever since. It's a wonder this hotel's still open. Wouldn't be if my son didn't believe the railroad will come north through this valley soon." He scratched his temple. "About all that's left hereabouts are the cattle ranches, and those are few and far between. Of course, women are scarce, too. If you're looking for a husband, you might find a cowboy or a rancher who is—"

"I don't want a husband."

"Well, then, I don't know what there might be for you. The general store isn't hiring; the Golds have their six children to help them." He squinted as he gave the matter more thought; then he said, "I suppose Stretch Barns over at the saloon might have work for you."

"A saloon?" Her heart sank. She knew what the work was like

for women who dressed up in revealing costumes and served drinks to already drunken patrons. At least onstage she was protected from pawing hands and other unwelcome advances. "There must be *something* else."

The doctor seemed to hear the note of desperation in her voice. He reached out and patted her shoulder, his attitude suddenly changed. "It just might be you could get work up at the Rutledge place. Can't be sure, of course. I heard their cook quit earlier this spring. Don't know that Mr. Rutledge has hired anybody new yet. Even if he has, he's got that big house up there on the hill and a large crew working cattle for him on his range. Maybe he needs himself a housekeeper, too. There'd sure be plenty of room for you and your children. I know the ranch foreman. Parker McCall. He's an honest, hardworking fellow. I imagine he'd put in a good word for you if I asked him to." He gave his graying head a shake. "Never have met Mr. Rutledge myself. Don't know anyone in town who has. But I hear the cowhands like working for Parker. I think you'd do all right there."

A housekeeper or a cook. She could manage that. Not that she'd had much experience with keeping a house. She'd lived her entire life out of a trunk—traveling in wagons, staying in hotels, living in tiny rooms above theaters for a week or two at a time. As for her cooking...well, it left something to be desired, but at least she had some experience. She could make coffee over a campfire, and she could fry most foods without burning them. Surely she could cook well enough to satisfy a bunch of hungry cowboys.

After all, it wouldn't be for long. Only until Becca was well enough to travel. Then they could all go back East, and Faith could find work with one of the theater companies in New York.

Of course, if she had been able to find work in New York City, she would be there now instead of in a wide spot in the road appropriately called "Dead Horse."

Tis true that we are in great danger;
The greater therefore should our courage be.

"*You must trust Jesus,*" Fannie Whitehall would have said. "*You've made Him your Savior; now you must trust Him, no matter what.*"

Oh, how she wished Mrs. Whitehall, the elderly wardrobe mistress, hadn't left the theater troupe last month. Faith could have used her advice. Her own faith in Christ was still so new and her understanding so small.

Lord, show me what to do.

Faith drew a deep breath, looked at the doctor, and asked, "How do I find Mr. Rutledge?"

"I've got a patient to see at the Jagged R tomorrow. I'll take you along if you'd like." He took his black leather bag in hand and crossed to the door, then glanced over his shoulder. "I'll be by first thing in the morning to check on your girl. My daughter-in-law, Nancy, can come to stay with her while we're gone."

"I'm most grateful, Dr. Telford."

He left, but before the door could close behind him, Alex slipped through the opening.

"How's Becca?" Concern creased her son's brow. Faith could see that he was trying hard to be strong for her, and she fought new tears as she observed his bravado. He was only seven, but every so often she caught glimpses of the young man he would soon become.

What will I do if—?

Faith sank onto the chair a second time and motioned for Alex to join her there. When he did, she put her arm around his back, pulling him close against her side. Then she took hold of Becca's hand and looked down at the sleeping girl.

"Becca's going to be all right," she whispered. "She needs rest, so we're going to stay here for a while."

"I'll help take care of her, Ma."

Faith gave her son a squeeze. "I know you will. You've always been a big help to me." She kissed his cheek. "Would you tell Mr. Drew I need to talk to him?"

Alex nodded, then hurried to do as she'd asked.

After the door closed behind the boy, Faith leaned forward and placed a kiss on her daughter's feverish forehead. "Jesus," she prayed, "please help Rebecca Ann. Please, Lord. I couldn't bear to lose her."

Faith loved both of her children equally, but she'd always worried more about Becca. Rebecca Ann Butler had nearly died at birth, and her health had remained fragile. But she was perfect in every other way. As an infant, she'd rarely fussed, always smiling and cooing, never any trouble to care for. Even as a toddler she'd been well behaved, obeying her older brother, both of them sitting quietly behind the scenes during rehearsals and performances.

"Lord, there is so much I want for her and Alex. I want them to have the home I never had. I want them to know security instead of fear. I want them to know You while they're young instead of waiting until they're my age. I want—"

Her words were interrupted by another knock, and the door opened to reveal Raymond Drew.

"How's she doing?" The company manager nodded toward the bed as he entered.

"She's sleeping." Faith moistened her lips. "The doctor said Becca can't travel again until she's better. It's going to take time. Weeks. Maybe months. The children and I will have to stay in Dead Horse."

"Stay *here?* Great Scott! And do what, Faith? We've got a show in Cheyenne next week. You can get another doctor to have a look at her once we're there. This one doesn't know anything. What kind of doctor can he be if he's living in this forsaken place? He probably doesn't know what's wrong with her. He's nothing more than a quack, if you ask me."

"Look at her, Raymond. You don't have to be a doctor to know he's right. It will kill Becca if I put her back in that wagon. If we were in Green River City and I could take her by rail ..." She shook her head and met his gaze with a determined look of her own. "You'll have to go on without me."

"And where do you suggest I find an actress to replace you? We have a contract, Faith Butler, and I mean to hold you to it." His tone became harsh, menacing almost.

She drew back, feeling as defiled as if he'd slapped her. Softly, she said, "She's my child, Raymond. What would you have me do?"

He swore and spun away. "All right, then. Stay here, if that's what you want. Christine can do your part as well as her own until I find someone else." He jerked the door open. "Just don't come looking to me for another job when you're ready to work again. You're not that good, you know." He disappeared into the hall, muttering something derogatory about actresses.

Faith slept little during the night that followed. Each time she drifted off, she awakened with a start of fear only moments later. Fear for Becca, fear for the future.

What if Mr. Rutledge wouldn't give her work? She'd already told Raymond to leave her behind. The troupe would be gone by morning, and then it would be too late to change her mind. What would she do if she couldn't get work? What would happen to Becca and Alex then? Would she save Becca's life only to watch both of her children starve?

By morning, there were dark circles of worry beneath Faith's eyes. Her body ached with a weariness that went beyond the physical. One look in the mirror told her it wasn't likely Mr. Rutledge would want to hire her. She didn't look strong enough to lift a frying pan, let alone run a household.

She dressed with care, all the while sending up little cries for help. She could scarcely call them prayers, but they were heartfelt. Mrs. Whitehall had said God always listened to His children. Faith hoped so, for she needed Him to hear.

It was midmorning when she and Dr. Telford left Dead Horse in his buggy, headed south.

"That's where we're headed." He pointed. "That's the Jagged R Ranch."

A three-story house sat on a high bluff about five miles outside of Dead Horse. It seemed severely isolated, cut off from the rest of the world and the small town below. A terrible loneliness swept over Faith as she stared at the house in the distance.

What sort of man sought such solitude? she wondered, a shudder of trepidation racing along her spine.

When they drew near the top of the bluff, Faith realized that the Rutledge house was larger than she'd at first thought. It was painted gray, all of the windows framed by charcoal-colored shutters. There were numerous outbuildings—some large, some small. There was also a corral holding about a dozen horses, all of them sturdy, well-fed animals.

As they came into the yard, the front door opened and a man stepped onto the front porch. He tipped his hat back on his head and leaned against the post as he waited for the buggy to stop.

"Is that him?" Faith asked the doctor.

"No. That's Parker McCall, the ranch foreman."

She was disappointed. There was something kind and friendly about Mr. McCall's leathered face and the half-smile tipping the corners of his mouth.

"Howdy, Rick. What brings you out this way?" The foreman's dark eyes slipped to Faith's as he stepped down from the porch.

"I'm here to remove Gertie's stitches." The doctor inclined his head toward his passenger. "This is Faith Butler. Mrs. Butler, Parker McCall."

Faith nodded. "How do you do, Mr. McCall?"

"I do right fine, ma'am."

Rick continued, "She'd like a word with Mr. Rutledge."

Parker raised an eyebrow, his smile disappearing. "See Mr. Rutledge?" He rubbed his chin. "The boss don't receive company. You know that, Rick."

"But I *must* see him," Faith blurted. Then, embarrassed by her frantic outburst, she clenched her hands in her lap, drew herself up straight, and said with as much dignity as she could muster, "Mr. McCall, I've come to seek employment. I have two children to support, and we are unable at present to travel elsewhere to look for work. The good doctor has given me to understand Mr. Rutledge may be in need of a cook and a housekeeper. I should like to apply for the position."

Parker McCall glanced at the doctor. "A cook and a house-keeper?" He was silent a moment; then his gaze returned to Faith. "Might not be a bad idea at that." A moment later, he grinned. "In fact, I think it's a mighty fine idea. You come on with me, Mrs. Butler."

Nervously, Faith took hold of Parker's proffered hand and stepped down from the buggy.

"I think Gertie's in the barn," the foreman called over his shoulder to Dr. Telford as he led Faith away.

Upon entering the house, Faith found herself cloaked in a dim, gray light. The windows in each room had been shrouded by heavy draperies, shutting out the sunlight that was so abundant in a Wyoming summer. Faith wondered if someone had recently passed away, then thought not. There was a permanence about it all, a look that said little had changed here in years. An ominous feeling shivered up her spine, and she wanted nothing more than to turn and leave.

Cowards die many times befor e their deaths.

Parker stopped and rapped on a door.

"Yes?" a deep voice called from the other side.

"Got a minute, Drake?" Parker didn't wait for a reply. He turned the knob and opened the door, drawing Faith with him as he entered the room. "This little lady is Faith Butler. She'd like a word with you." He gave her elbow a squeeze, then stepped back into the hallway and closed the door.

As in the rest of the house, this room was bathed in shades of gray and black, these windows, too, hidden behind heavy draperies. Faith could see she was in a library. The walls were lined with shelves and shelves of books. The only light came from a lamp, turned low, on the desk. Beyond it, she made out the form of a man seated in a chair, out of reach of the lamp's light.

Drake Rutledge rose. His shadow appeared exceedingly tall and threatening. "What is it you want?" He sounded angry.

Her mouth went dry, and she feared her knees would buckle.

"Well?" he demanded.

Don't get stage fright now, Faith. Remember why you came.

"Speak up, madam, or get out."

She drew a quick breath. "Mr. Rutledge, I've come to seek employment as your cook and housekeeper."

"I have no need of either."

"But *I* have need of a job." She stepped forward, determination driving out fear, if only temporarily. "Mr. Rutledge, my little girl is sick. The doctor says if she travels, she could die. No, he says she *will* die. I must find work and a place to live until she's well again. Please, sir, I'm desperate. I'm not asking for charity. I'll work as hard as anyone else on your ranch."

A long silence followed. Then Drake Rutledge stepped around the desk, coming toward her with intimidating strides. His sheer height made her want to draw back from him, but she held her ground.

"I don't believe you belong here." His voice was low, resentful.

She tilted her head, staring up at him.

His shoulders were broad. She could see that he wore a suit, as if dressed to go out for an evening. His hair was dark—black, she imagined—and long, reaching his shoulders. His face, bathed in shadow upon shadow, seemed harsh and frightening. In the anemic lamplight, she saw that he wore a patch over his right eye.

Like a pirate. She subdued a shiver.

For a long time neither spoke, neither moved. Faith's heart pounded a riotous beat in her chest. Never in her life had she felt such rage as that which emanated from this man. It was as palpable as a white-hot fire, singeing her skin.

Finally, he took a step back from her. "I think it's time for you to go, Mrs. Butler."

"But... but what about the job? You haven't told me if you'll hire me."

He leaned forward. "Do you *want* to work for me, madam?"

She managed to hold her ground once again. "No, but I have no other choice. I'll not let my daughter die for lack of a roof over her head or food on the table. And I won't have my children living over a saloon, which seems to be my only other choice of employment in Dead Horse." Suddenly, her courage evaporated, replaced by desperation. Tears flooded her eyes as she extended a hand in supplication, nearly touching his chest. "Please, Mr. Rutledge. Becca's only five years old. Please help us."

There was another lengthy silence; then he cursed softly and stepped around her, heading across the room. "You're only cooking and cleaning until your daughter's healthy. Tell Parker to give you and your children a couple of rooms on the third floor." He yanked open the door. "And stay out of my way, Mrs. Butler, for as long as you're here."

Then he was gone.

Faith drew in a deep breath and let it out slowly, scarcely able to comprehend what had happened. She'd achieved that for which she'd come. She'd found a place to live and a way to support her children until Becca was well again.

Thank You, Lord.

She left the library and walked toward the front of the house. When her fingers alighted on the doorknob, she paused and glanced behind her, halfway expecting to find Drake Rutledge standing in the shadows, watching her.

He was a man, take him for all in all,
I shall not look upon his like again.

But she *would* look upon him again, and instinct told her he was *not* like any man she'd known. She felt another shiver, this one of apprehension for what the next few weeks might bring.

From the landing on the second floor, Drake listened to the closing of the front door. Then he moved to the window overlooking the yard and surreptitiously pushed the draperies aside so he could peer down.

Faith Butler appeared a moment later, out from beneath the porch awning. She stopped when she reached the buggy and looked back at the house.

Her hair was red, the color of hot coals before they turned white. Red without a hint of orange, bright in the morning sunlight. Her bustled gown was striped in shades of gold and brown. She was small and perfectly shaped.

And she was beautiful.

His fingers tightened on the draperies.

He'd known she was beautiful, even in the dimly lit library. Even her fragrance—soft, tantalizing, womanly—had been exquisite. But he hadn't known the extent of her loveliness until this moment.

What had possessed him to tell her she could stay at the Jagged R? He didn't need a cook or somebody cleaning up after him, and he certainly didn't need a woman in his house, causing him grief. Experience had taught him that women, particularly beautiful women, weren't to be trusted.

Yet there'd been something about the way Faith Butler had stood before him—afraid but not fleeing—that had kept him from sending her away. There'd been something courageous in her stance that had given him reason to pause. But it had been the quiet note of discouragement in her voice that had been his downfall.

Just then, Rick Telford, Dead Horse's doctor, strode into view, coming from the direction of the barn. Although they'd never met, Drake recognized Rick from his previous visits to the ranch. With scarcely a word to Faith, the doctor helped her into the buggy, then climbed up beside her, took the reins in his hands, and slapped the leather straps against the horse's rump. The buggy jerked forward, quickly carrying the beautiful woman with the fiery red hair out of sight.

Drake let the draperies fall into place, closing out the light and leaving him in familiar gloom.

She won't stay long. He turned from the window. *I'll see that she doesn't.*

Faith's heart still raced as she opened the door to her hotel room.

Nancy Telford rose from a chair, looking none too happy. "Well, *finally* you've returned." She reached for the basket that held her embroidery work.

"How is Becca?"

"Fine. Never a peep out of her."

Even with Nancy's words of assurance, Faith wasn't satisfied until she crossed to the bed and touched her daughter's cheek. Relief flooded her as she felt the coolness of Becca's skin. The fever had broken. Turning, she said, "Thank you for staying with her, Mrs. Telford. I don't know what I would have done if—"

Nancy made a sound of dismissal, waving away Faith's thanks with a flick of her wrist.

"Mr. Rutledge gave me the position," Faith offered.

The other woman's eyes widened. "I don't believe it."

"Neither do I, but it's true." She smiled.

"You actually *met* him?"

"Yes." Faith removed her hat pin, then lifted the small straw bonnet from her head and set it on a nearby dresser.

Nancy stepped forward, her face alight with anticipation. "Well? What was he like? Tell me everything."

Angry. He was very angry. She kept the thought to herself, not wanting to betray the mysterious man who'd given her employment and a place to live. "I'm not sure, really. He's . . . not the least bit talkative. Our meeting was brief."

"I've always believed he must be running from the law. Why else would he hide up there in that house and never come into town? Mark my words. He's probably a murderer. You'll be sorry you went up there. No one but a fool would have taken my father-in-law's suggestion. No doubt you'll all die in your beds at the hands of a mad-man." With a toss of her head, she swept from the room.

Faith stared after Nancy, the woman's parting words echoing in the silence. *No doubt you'll all die in your beds at the hands of a madman.* Faith remembered the subdued rage that had been present in the Rutledge library, and she wondered if Nancy Telford might be right. Had Faith made a mistake? Was she taking her children into danger?

A sudden calm fell over her, erasing her doubts. She needn't fear. She could trust God with their future.

She turned to her daughter, leaned over, and brushed wisps of strawberry blond hair from Becca's forehead. The girl's eyes fluttered open.

Faith's heart tightened, then soared. "Becca, darling?" She sat on the side of the bed.

"I'm thirsty, Mama."

Quickly, Faith poured water from a nearby pitcher into a glass and held it to her daughter's lips, supporting the girl's head with her other hand. Becca took a few sips, then closed her eyes again, slipping into sleep as quickly as she'd awakened.

"We're not going to travel anymore, Rebecca Ann. Not until you're completely well. Mama has taken a job in a big, beautiful house. No more theaters or hotel rooms. Just lots of fresh air and sunshine." She thought of the tall, shadowed man who was her new employer. "Mrs. Telford is wrong about Mr. Rutledge, Becca. I think he must have a kind heart to help us this way. A very kind heart, indeed."

Drake Rutledge rarely found sleep until the wee hours of morning. For years, he'd spent his nights prowling the house or sitting on the porch as the hours marched toward dawn. There were comfort and peace in the darkness.

But tonight he didn't feel comforted or peaceful. He felt hollow, tense, and he knew what was coming. He tried to summon anger, rage, bitter fury—old, familiar feelings, trustworthy companions—but even those failed him tonight.

Standing at the edge of the porch, he stared at the tiny lights of Dead Horse in the distance. Moonlight reflected off the ribbon of river that cut a swath across the valley floor. It was a serene scene, one he'd gazed down upon countless times in the years since he'd purchased this house on the bluff. One he'd been satisfied to view from a distance—and alone.

But I have no other choice. . . . Please help us. He heard her voice, sweet and frightened. He saw her face, beautiful and uncertain.

He berated himself for listening, for allowing himself to respond. Faith Butler would bring grief to the Jagged R Ranch. He should never have said she could come here to live. He should send Parker into Dead Horse right now to tell the woman he'd changed his mind. He didn't want her at the Jagged R. He didn't want any woman there. But her words still echoed.

He stepped off the porch and headed for the corral. He had to get away. He had to escape the memories that were pushing in, crowding him.

In a matter of minutes, he had his gelding saddled and bridled. He mounted and turned the pinto away from the river valley, heading out onto the sweeping plains. He gave the horse his head, trusting the animal's night vision far more than his own. Soon they were speeding across the range. The wind—cool and bracing—whipped against his face. It was a mad gallop to outrace things better forgotten. Horse and rider followed a familiar path, for it was a race they had run before.

It was a race they had never won.

2

EVERAL days later, as the team of horses followed the road out of town and up to the Rutledge ranch, Faith sat in the back of Joseph Gold's wagon, cradling Becca's head in her lap and trying not to think about what she might face in the days ahead.

Dr. Telford—who had insisted she call him Rick, as everyone else did—drove the borrowed wagon slowly, for which Faith was grateful. It didn't matter that the doctor had said Becca was improved enough to make the trip. Faith was still frightened by every bump in the road, each jar of the wagon wheels, remembering only too well what harm he'd warned travel could cause.

Alex didn't share his mother's trepidation. After too many days of confinement, he was eager to reach the ranch. He was full of questions about where they were going to live and would he be able to ride horses and would he meet any real cowboys.

"Will we see Indians?" he asked next, obviously hoping his mother would answer in the affirmative.

"I don't know, Alex."

Not satisfied, he addressed the man beside him, "Will we see any Indians, Dr. Telford?"

Rick muttered some sort of reply that Faith couldn't quite hear.

Becca opened her eyes. "Mama?"

"Yes, darling?"

"Will there be Indians?"

Faith smiled as she stroked her daughter's forehead, comforted that Becca's fever had not returned. "I don't think so. And if there are, I'm quite certain they'll do us no harm. You remember seeing Buffalo Bill's Wild West Show, don't you?"

Becca nodded.

"Those Indians didn't hurt anyone. It was all just for fun, a show. Remember?"

Her little girl nodded again.

"Then, there's nothing to be afraid of, is there?"

Becca shook her head and closed her eyes.

Faith wished she could be reassured as easily. Not about wild Indians, but about her new employer. She'd tried not to think about Drake Rutledge in the days since he agreed that she and her children could come to his ranch to live. She'd tried and failed. It had been impossible to erase his dark image from her mind. Impossible to avoid the questions that plagued her.

What did her future hold, working as his housekeeper? Would she be able to cook and clean to his satisfaction? Would he turn them out before Becca was well again? Worse yet, could Nancy Telford's dire prediction be true? Would they die in their beds at the hand of a murderer? Was Faith making a horrible mistake?

The Lord holds our future. . . . The Lord holds our future. . . . The Lord holds our future.

She clenched her hands into fists, then opened them as she let out a deep breath, trying to relax. She reminded herself that this job was

God's providence. Each day the Butlers remained in the hotel, their small savings had dwindled further. Faith had eaten little, giving what food she'd purchased to her children, fearing what would happen if she ran out of money before the doctor agreed that Becca could be moved.

Now, Faith gazed up at the gray house on the ridge and subdued a shiver. *It's only for a short time. When Becca's well, we can leave. We won't be there for long. God will make a way.*

"'When I was at home,'" she quoted softly, "'I was in a better place: but travellers must be content.'"

"What's that, Mrs. Butler?" Rick asked, interrupting her musings.

She met the doctor's eyes, surprised he'd heard her. "A line from a play."

"Shakespeare?"

"Yes."

"My wife always liked Shakespeare's plays." A frown furrowed his brow as he turned his attention to the road before him. "I never cared for them much myself. Too difficult to understand the way they spoke, if you ask me." He paused, then added, "Esther loved it, though."

There was something in his final words—a melancholy tone— that told Faith he wished he'd not spoken. She swallowed her reply but welcomed the sudden flood of memories his comment stirred to life.

To Faith, William Shakespeare had almost been a member of the family. From early childhood she'd memorized his plays, come to know his characters as if they were her friends. In truth they'd been her only friends, for she'd known few other children.

After her parents—both Shakespearean actors—were divorced, Faith had lived with her father, who constantly moved around the country. She'd been raised backstage, in hotel rooms, in wagons, and on trains. She'd had her first role at the age of ten and had been performing ever since.

Perhaps my whole life has been one long performance. Perhaps none of it's real.

She frowned at the uncomfortable thought and quickly rejected it. Her life was as real as anyone's. She'd always admired great actresses like Sarah Bernhardt and Helena Modjeska. She'd wanted to have the same stage presence that her mother, Nellie Fields, had displayed. Faith had never envisioned anything for herself other than the life she'd known.

No, that wasn't true. Once she'd dreamed of hearth and home, of the kind of life others led but she could only imagine.

A momentary loneliness squeezed her heart, but she drove it away with ruthless determination. She wasn't lonely, and she didn't want a life different from what she had. She was content. She had everything she wanted or needed—the Lord, her children, and her work. And when Becca was well, she would be happy to return to the stage. Acting was an honorable profession. As honorable as any other as long as she lived according to God's will. As honorable for her as tent making was for Saint Paul, according to Mrs. Whitehall. Faith would do well to remember that.

***

Drake stood at the window of his second-floor bedroom and watched Rick Telford lift the little girl from the wagon bed. She was a frail-looking child. Drake felt his heart soften at the sight of her. A few moments later, Faith Butler—and the young boy whose hand she held—accompanied the doctor and Parker into the house. He heard the front door open, listened to their voices and footsteps as they made their way up the stairs to the third floor. It was the most noise and activity the house had heard or seen in seven years, and it left Drake feeling unsettled.

Raking his fingers through his hair, he turned from the window and strode across the room to the door. He opened it, then stepped into the hallway.

"Ma, can I go outside?" he heard a young voice ask from the floor above.

"Not yet, Alex. Come back into the room. We must get settled first."

"But, Ma—"

"Alex."

Silence followed, then the closing of a door.

Drake set his jaw. He wouldn't have a moment's peace as long as Faith and her children were here. Not one solitary moment of peace!

He descended the stairs and stalked into his library, closing himself in where he could be alone—and undisturbed.

"You let me know if you need anything, Mrs. Butler," Parker McCall said from the doorway. "Take your time with settlin' in. We're used to mostly doin' for ourselves. You take care of the little lady there, and when you're ready, I'll show you around the place, give you the lay of the land, so to speak."

"Thank you, Mr. McCall."

He set a dusty hat on his head. "I reckon you'd better call me Parker."

"Then you must call me Faith."

He grinned, his sun-bronzed skin crinkling around his dark eyes and at the corners of his mouth. "Be right pleased to do so, ma'am."

"Faith," she reminded him, returning his smile.

"Faith."

The warmth of his smile lingered with her as he closed the door.

Perhaps it wasn't going to be so bad here. Parker McCall made her feel welcome. Maybe the others—

"Look, Ma. There goes Dr. Telford on his way back to Dead Horse. Look how high up we are!"

She turned to find her son hanging halfway out of the window, barely visible beyond the draperies. "Alexander Butler!" She grabbed hold of his shirttail before he could topple headfirst out the opening. "Lord, I could use a bit of help here," she muttered as she yanked her son back into the room.

Alex tried to wriggle free.

"Hold still, young man." She placed her index finger beneath his chin and tipped up his head. "Alex, I already have my hands full with your sister. I won't have you breaking your fool neck. Is that understood?"

He looked as chagrined as a seven-year-old boy full of vinegar could manage. "Yes, ma'am."

"Do you know what many folks think of us? They think actors and actresses are charlatans, people of low character. They think we don't know how to properly raise our children. They don't believe we know good manners. I won't have you confirming their suspicions." She knelt on the floor. "I know this is exciting and new, Alex, but you must be on your best behavior, at least until I can prove myself as housekeeper to Mr. Rutledge."

This time his apology was earnest. "I'm sorry, Ma. I promise not to cause any more trouble."

It was Faith's turn to feel bad. "I know you won't." She gave him a tight hug. "You've always been a good boy. I'm proud of you, Alex. I've always been proud of you. But I'm going to need your help now more than ever." Releasing him, she rose and looked about. "Since Mr. McCall told us these are our rooms, shall we have a look at them?"

In a flash, Alex forgot the scolding, curious to discover all he could about his temporary home.

Their two rooms—as gloomy as all the others in this house—had a connecting doorway between them. This first room, where Becca lay sleeping, had two narrow beds and a small fireplace. A window—the one Alex had nearly fallen out of—was set into a steeply pitched roof. Once Faith removed the draperies that covered the window, she found its northern exposure gave them a clear view of the valley and the town below.

"There." She dropped the dark fabric to the floor. "That's much better."

The second room, she discovered, was larger than the first and had both a bed and a sitting area with a sofa and two chairs. There were two windows in this room, one on each side of the fireplace, which looked out upon the bunkhouse, barn, and corrals.

The draperies were promptly removed from these windows, too, allowing morning sunlight to spill into the room, chasing gloom from the corners. The light also revealed dust motes floating in the air, reminding Faith she had a job to do. She'd been hired as a housekeeper, and she didn't suppose that meant just cleaning her own living quarters.

"Alex, I want you to sit with your sister while I find the kitchen and see about fixing us something to eat. Then you may go outside for a while, but only where Mr. McCall says you may. Understood?"

Her son nodded.

"Good." She opened her trunk and withdrew the new apron she'd purchased at Gold's General Store with funds she could ill afford to spend. Pushing away her concerns about money, she tied the blue-green apron around her waist. With a quick glance in the mirror, she checked her hair to make certain it was tidy, then left their quarters and descended the stairs to the ground floor.

"Mr. McCall?" she called softly.

First, she looked into the parlor. It was sparsely furnished, the windows darkened, but she recognized the familiar shape of a piano in the far corner. She wondered if her mysterious employer played the instrument, but she found it difficult to imagine that the heart of a musician could beat within such a man.

With a shake of her head, she crossed the hallway and looked into what was obviously the dining room. Despite the drapery-shrouded windows, she could see a long table in the center of the room, surrounded by numerous chairs with tall backs.

"Parker?"

Still no reply.

Well, the kitchen can't be too far from the dining room.

Squinting in the darkness, she saw what appeared to be a door at the opposite end of the room. Certain it must lead to the kitchen, she headed toward it—and smashed her toe into the leg of a chair set askew at the table.

"Ooh." She doubled over, the pain making it hard to breathe. "Ooh." She glared at the black skeleton of the chair, then sent an even harsher glance toward the window coverings that blocked out the light. She straightened, muttering, "If this place weren't as dark as a mausoleum, a body wouldn't find herself running into things."

Limping slightly, she continued toward the back of the dining room, moving much more slowly this time to avoid more unpleasant surprises. When she pushed on the swinging door, she discovered herself in a narrow hall containing a table and a service window to the pantry. Beyond the passage was the kitchen.

Here, for the first time, she found a room not bathed in darkness. The kitchen had windows facing the south and west and a doorway that opened onto a small veranda. There was a black cookstove in one corner. In the center of the room was a long table with benches on both sides and a chair on each end. Along the outside wall was a large cupboard, an icebox, and a counter with a sink and a pump handle. The connecting pantry was enormous, but the shelves were almost empty. Another door led to the back hall, a second stairway, and a third entrance, this one opening onto a porch.

It was there she found Parker McCall, leaning his hip against the rail while he talked to a tall, slender cowpoke with a dirt-smudged face and sweat-darkened shirt and trousers. Parker turned as Faith stepped onto the porch.

"Here she is now." He motioned Faith forward. "Faith, I'd like you to meet Gertie Duncan. Gertie, this is Faith Butler, our new housekeeper and cook."

Gertie removed her hat, revealing a riot of short chestnut curls. "Howdy, Miz Butler. It'll be nice to have some decent grub for a change. Parker here's a lousy cook."

Faith tried not to reveal her surprise as she returned the greeting, but she doubted she was successful.

Gertie laughed. "If it makes you feel any better, Miz Butler, you're not the first t'be taken aback when they see I'm a woman. 'Course, most folks seem t'forget it quick enough." She slapped her ragged hat onto her head. "I'd better get back t'work. Them horses ain't gonna break themselves."

Faith watched the tall woman stride away. She knew she was staring, but she was unable to keep from it.

"Gertie's one of the best wranglers I ever worked with," Parker said.

"I'm afraid I was rude. It's just I—"

"Gertie's used to it. She's got feelin's as tough as rawhide. She doesn't hurt easy. Wouldn't've lasted ten minutes around here if she did."

Faith watched the woman disappear around the corner of the barn, hoping the foreman was right but feeling sorry for her bad manners all the same.

Parker pushed off from the railing. "Well, let me show you around the kitchen, for starters. Like Gertie said, I'm a lousy cook and everybody's already glad you came."

"I'm going to do my best." Praying she didn't appear as nervous and unsure of herself as she was, Faith rubbed her palms on her crisp new apron.

A trickle of sweat wound its way down the back of Faith's neck as she dipped the last strip of salt pork into the cornmeal and dropped it into the melted fat in the skillet. While the meat browned, she opened the oven to check on the potatoes baking in their jackets. Just a few more minutes and they would be ready.

Straightening, she said a quick prayer of thanks for Wiley Pritchett, the crotchety old stage driver who'd hired on with Raymond Drew's company last year. Wiley had taught her how to fix this rather simple but tasty meal. Not to say she'd ever cooked it all by herself, but she'd helped Wiley often enough to feel a measure of confidence. Luckily the Jagged R smokehouse was full of meat, and by some miracle she'd found the remaining necessary ingredients for the meal in that woefully stocked pantry.

But what about tomorrow?

Pot roast. She could fix a pot roast. And fried chicken. She knew how to make good fried chicken. Well, edible, anyway. And her rice pudding was passable.

But then what?

She glanced quickly about the kitchen. What she needed most of all was a cookbook with recipes even *she* could follow. If there wasn't one to be found here, she would have to go into Dead Horse and buy one at the general store.

Catching herself woolgathering, Faith remembered the meat in the frying pan just in time to keep it from burning. Quickly she removed the strips of pork, then drained off all but a couple tablespoons of fat. To this she added flour, browned it while stirring well, then mixed in some canned milk and let it simmer into a thick gravy before returning the strips of meat to the pan.

Finally, she leaned forward and tasted the concoction. Her eyes widened. It was good! She'd done it. She'd prepared her first meal without burning a thing and without anyone's help. Grinning like a schoolgirl, she scooped the pork and gravy into a large blue bowl.

"Mmm, mmm. Somethin' shore smells good in here, and it's been callin' t'me t'come see what's cookin'."

She glanced toward the back door to find a grizzled cowboy standing in the doorway.

He whipped off his hat, spit on his hand, and smoothed his graying hair back on his head. "M'name's Dan Greer, and you must be Mrs. Butler."

Before she could answer, more cowpokes came pouring through the back door, forcing Dan Greer into the kitchen before them. Faith looked from one man to the next, growing increasingly nervous at the sight of them.

"All right. All right." Gertie Duncan pushed her way through the crowd of dusty cowboys. "Give 'er a break, boys. She ain't the first filly you ever laid eyes on." Her gaze met Faith's. "You ready for us t'be in here, Miz Butler? If not, say the word, and I'll run the lot of them out."

Faith nodded, then shook her head, and finally swirled about, gasping, as she remembered the baking potatoes. She grabbed a towel to protect her hand and yanked open the oven door. Fortunately, she wasn't too late.

"I'm ready for you," she said with a relieved sigh.

While she pulled the potatoes from the oven, she heard the ranch hands taking their seats among plenty of good-natured jostling and joking. She recognized Parker's voice and felt a flash of comfort, knowing she had at least one friend amid all the strangers.

She smoothed the strands of hair that had pulled loose to straggle about her face, then brushed her hands over her apron. The newness of the fabric had already disappeared beneath splatters of grease and a dusting of flour.

I must look a sight.

But she wasn't on the stage, she reminded herself, and those hungry men behind her hadn't come to look at the cook. They'd come to eat.

After setting aside portions to serve Becca and Alex later, Faith picked up the serving platter stacked with potatoes and the bowl of salt pork and gravy, then turned to face the waiting crew.

Except for Gertie, they rose in unison from their chairs. The men grinned as Faith approached the table.

Dan Greer jumped forward to pull out a chair for her. "You sit here, ma'am, by me."

"Oh, I don't know, Mr. Greer." Her gaze flicked to Parker. "Perhaps I—"

"Go on and sit down, Faith," the foreman said. "You gotta eat, too. Besides, everyone wants t'get to know you. Can't think of a better time than now."

"Well…"

The boy to her right—perhaps fifteen or sixteen, Faith thought—held his hat against his chest and nodded in her direction. "The name's Johnny Coltrain. Please t'meet you, Miz Butler."

"I'm Will Kidd," said the man beside Johnny.

Across the table, a giant blond fellow said, "They call me Swede." His thick, rolling accent told her why. "Swede Swenson."

"And I'm Roy Martin," said the man to Swede's left. "We're right glad you've come to work at the Jagged R, ma'am. Right glad."

The last remnants of nervousness vanished as she looked at them. "Thank you." She smiled, then added with a laugh, "I'm right glad, too."

With an impatient sigh, Drake slammed the ledger closed. He'd been staring at the same column of figures for over half an hour without really seeing them. He leaned back in his chair and gazed at the ceiling, trying to ignore the muffled voices beyond his closed door.

The cowpokes had come in for lunch an hour before, as they did every day. But this day was different because they'd lingered instead of eating quickly and getting back to work. And he knew it was because of *her*.

His fingers tightened on the arms of his chair as he squeezed his eyes shut.

He'd heard her laughter, light and airy, drifting to him from the kitchen. The men's laughter had been louder, more boisterous, and it was easy for Drake to imagine them all preening and vying for her favors.

He rose abruptly and began pacing the room, feeling caged, wishing it were night so he could saddle up his horse and outrun the restlessness. When he heard the rap on his door, he snapped, "What is it, Parker?"

The door opened. "It's not Mr. McCall. It's Mrs. Butler. I've brought you something to eat."

He whirled around. "What are you doing in here? Didn't I tell you to stay out of my way?"

She didn't turn and flee as he'd expected. Probably because she couldn't see him clearly in the dark room. Probably because she didn't know the man who'd hired her, know what he could do when pushed.

Lowering his voice, he said, "Come in." He returned to his desk. "Put the tray on the table over there."

With his back still to her, he turned up the lamp, allowing light to spill into virgin corners of the library. He heard Faith's hesitant footsteps as she entered the room, taking the tray of food to the small table near the fireplace. Then he turned and watched her.

Before she looked up at him, her face was serene. He realized he'd failed to judge the full extent of her beauty. But her serenity shattered when her gaze lifted toward him. He recognized her surprise. He knew what she saw—the wretchedly scarred face, the black patch over a sightless eye—and he knew what she felt.

She felt what Larissa Dearborne had felt. Revulsion. Loathing. Disgust.

But her voice didn't reveal any of those things when she spoke. "Your food is getting cold, Mr. Rutledge. Why don't you sit down and eat? I'll return for the tray later." She walked toward the door, then paused and turned to face him. "I . . . I want to thank you again for hiring me. I'm going to do my very best to prove myself an excellent cook and housekeeper." Her smile was soft, gentle, perhaps even courageous.

Unable to return the smile, Drake turned his back to her, reaching out to the lamp, turning it down. The room plunged into familiar darkness. A moment later the door closed, leaving him alone—just as he wanted.

Once outside the room, Faith's calm demeanor disappeared instantly. She leaned against the wall, pressed her hands against her chest, and consciously slowed her breathing.

She didn't know what she'd expected. She'd known her employer was an angry man. She'd known he wore a patch over his right eye. She'd known he was tall and strongly built. But she hadn't expected to feel a sharp jab of sorrow pierce her heart when she saw him clearly for the first time. She hadn't expected to feel the stranger's pain as if it were her own.

She closed her eyes and recalled his image. His hair was black as a raven's wing, worn long, like Buffalo Bill Cody's. He had a neatly trimmed mustache above a grim, unsmiling mouth. His chin was squared, stubborn, strong. A narrow white scar cut his right eyebrow in two, then disappeared beneath his eye patch and appeared again on his right cheek.

She'd felt a strange urge to reach out and touch him, to offer some sort of comfort. But why?

"Faith?"

She gasped and her eyes flew open.

"Sorry," Parker said. "Didn't mean to startle you. You all right?"

She nodded as she straightened, glancing quickly toward the library door. Then she headed to the kitchen.

Parker followed. "Maybe I should tell you a bit more about Drake."

"That isn't necessary."

"I think maybe it is."

She felt again that sharp pain in her chest—pain that belonged to another. "Another time, perhaps," she whispered. "I need to check on Becca."

Like a coward, she fled up the back stairway. But she couldn't escape the memory of Drake Rutledge or the curious sense that her life would change because of him.

3

ERTIE Duncan leaned against the top rail of the corral and watched the white stallion as he paced the width of the enclosure, tail held high, nostrils flaring. The wild horse was a beauty—or would be as soon as she was able to take brush and curry to him. If there was one thing Gertie knew, it was horseflesh, and this stallion was one of the best she'd seen.

"You might as well get used t'me, fella. We're gonna spend a lot of time together. We're gonna get to be good friends, you 'n' me."

The stallion snorted and tossed his head as he whirled and pranced away from her.

"Wow! Look at him."

Gertie glanced down to find a young boy standing beside her, staring wide eyed through the fence rails. She grinned. "He's somethin', ain't he?"

"Is he yours?"

"Nope. Shore wish he was, though. He belongs to Mr. Rutledge."

The boy tore his admiring gaze from the stallion and looked up at her. His eyes widened even more. "You're a *girl!*"

She laughed. "Yeah, but it ain't fatal. The name's Gertie. What's yours?"

"Alex."

"Miz Butler's your ma?"

He nodded.

Gertie tipped her head toward the corral and the pacing stallion. "I'm the Jagged R wrangler. That means I take care of the horses here. This one, we just brought in off the range. I've been tryin' to catch him for three years."

"He looks wild."

"He is." She watched the horse again, studying his fine lines, well-shaped head, intelligent eyes. "He's smart, too. What he's gotta learn first is to trust me. The rest'll come easy after that."

Alex climbed onto the fence for a better look. "Could I be a wrangler when I get bigger?"

Gertie pushed her hat back on her head and glanced at the boy a second time. "I don't know. You like horses?"

He nodded again.

"How old're you?"

"Seven. But I'll be eight come September."

"You ever had a horse o' your own?"

Alex shook his head.

Grabbing the boy beneath his arms, Gertie lifted him off the fence and set him on the ground. "Come on. I got somethin' t'show you." She didn't shorten her long strides or look behind her to see if he followed. If Alex wanted to learn, Gertie figured he'd keep up.

The doors at both ends of the barn were thrown open to the afternoon sunlight. The cavernous building smelled of straw and hay, leather and manure, dust and sweat—familiar scents that made Gertie feel at home. She'd always been more comfortable with horses and other animals than with people. Kids were different, though. She liked kids. Maybe because they didn't think she was some sort of freak like most grown folks did.

Stopping at one of the stalls, she looked inside at the buckskin mare. "This here is Sugar," she told Alex when he stopped beside her. "She's got a bad cut on her left front fetlock, and I've got to doctor it twice a day. I've also got to keep her stall mucked out so it's nice and clean for her. And she needs walked a bit so she don't stiffen up. You think you could help me do all that?"

"Sure!"

She grinned at his enthusiastic response. "Well then, I guess it's up to your ma. If she says it's okay with her, then it's okay with me."

"I'll go ask her." With that, he darted off.

Gertie chuckled as she watched him disappear through the barn doors. Too bad Parker thought the Butlers would be at the Jagged R just a few months. Gertie figured it was going to be a plea-sure having them around. The lunch Alex's ma served today was a whole lot better than anything Parker had whipped up lately. Faith Butler was nice and friendly, to boot, even if she was prettier than a newborn heifer in a flower bed.

Turning her gaze toward the buckskin mare, Gertie remem-bered the way all the cowpokes had removed their hats and slicked their hair with the palms of their hands as soon as they'd laid eyes on Faith. Gertie couldn't think of a time when any man had looked at her like those boys were looking at that red-haired housekeeper. It hadn't surprised Gertie when she learned Faith was an actress. She was surefire too pretty to be hidden away on a Wyoming cattle ranch cookin' grub for a bunch o' mangy cowpokes.

Gertie took off her hat and ran her fingers through her unruly mop of curls. She wondered what it would be like to have hair as shiny and pretty as Faith's. She wondered what it would be like to be small and shapely and have men staring at her like she was the first water hole after five days on the desert.

Slapping her hat against her thigh, she snorted in disgust. As if she needed a man of her own! She worked with a couple dozen of them, day in and day out, year in and year out, and she didn't see that there was much call for having one all to herself. More trouble than they was worth, the lot o' them. And since she didn't seem to have any of the qualities that men wanted in a woman, it must have been she wasn't meant to belong to anybody in particular. That suited her just fine.

Turning on her heel, she headed back to the corral and the things she did best.

In the valley below, Dead Horse was a mere wide spot on the old stage road—a few houses, a few businesses, and a smattering of green-leafed poplars, no doubt planted when the town was born. Not far beyond Dead Horse was the river, running high on its banks this time of year, a ribbon of life-giving water winding its way south in the high desert country. And in the distance, to the east and to the west, rose mighty mountain ranges, purple peaks and pine-covered slopes, a sight of great beauty that left her breathless.

Faith stood on a chair before the parlor windows. Minutes before, she had removed the draperies, dropping them into a pile on the floor. Now she was washing off the accumulated grime from the windowpanes with a mixture of vinegar, water, and plenty of elbow grease. When a good portion of the glass was clean, she paused to admire the view.

In the valley below, Dead Horse was a mere wide spot on the old stage road—a few houses, a few businesses, and a smattering of green-leafed poplars, no doubt planted when the town was born. Not far beyond Dead Horse was the river, running high on its banks this time of year, a ribbon of life-giving water winding its way south in the high desert country. And in the distance, to the east and to the west, rose mighty mountain ranges, purple peaks and pine-covered slopes, a sight of great beauty that left her breathless.

Pushing loose strands of hair from her face with the back of her wrist, she returned her attention to the task of cleaning the large windows, wondering as she did so why anyone would want to shut out the spectacular view with draperies and gloom.

But she suspected she knew the answer. Her employer was hiding from the world. Was it because of his scar? Because of the blindness of one eye? Or was there another reason for his seclusion?

She recalled again the moment Drake Rutledge had turned up the lamp in the library. He'd wanted to frighten her. Why? So she would leave? If that was what he wanted, he could fire her, turn her and her children out. Would he have her believe he was a hard, cruel man? If so, he'd failed. He'd given her and her children a place to live when they'd so desperately needed one. Nothing he did could eliminate that one act of kindness, no matter how gruff and unpleasant he tried to be.

I can best thank him by getting this house in order and letting in the sunlight. With renewed vigor, she began scrubbing another pane of glass.

Suddenly, her son barreled into the room. "Ma! Ma!"

Fear pierced her heart at the sound of his voice. Then she realized his cry was one of excitement, not pain or panic. She glanced down. "What is it, Alex?"

"Gertie says I can learn to be a wrangler just like her, if it's okay with you."

"A wrangler?"

He nodded. "That's the cowboy who takes care of the horses. Can I, Ma? Can I?"

"Oh, Alex, I don't know. Mr. Rutledge might not like—"

"But Gertie said it's okay. Please, Ma."

Faith released a sigh as she stepped down from the chair. "I suppose it might be all right, but I need to talk to Miss Duncan first." She wagged a finger at him. "And you, young man, remember your manners. You're to call her Miss Duncan, not Gertie. Now I want you to go upstairs and check on your sister. I'll come for you there."

Alex opened his mouth to argue, then appeared to think better of it. With hands shoved into his pockets, he left the parlor.

"A wrangler," Faith whispered to herself as she removed the kerchief from around her hair. She could only imagine what sort of trouble her son might get himself into. "O Father-God, however shall I see Alex properly raised?"

With another sigh, she headed toward the back of the house and out the rear door. She found Gertie inside the corral with a pacing white horse, his eyes wild and his nostrils flared.

"You might as well settle down, fella," Gertie crooned. "I ain't goin' nowheres. Come on now. Settle down. That's right. Easy, boy. Easy."

The horse stopped suddenly. He bobbed his head up and down, then stomped his right hoof, stirring a cloud of dust that drifted across the enclosure on the light breeze.

"Thatta boy. I ain't gonna hurt you."

The horse snorted and tossed his head, then burst into motion, resuming his restless pacing.

Gertie laughed.

"Miss Duncan," Faith called softly, uncertain if she should interrupt or not.

Gertie glanced over her shoulder, then turned and walked across the corral. "Alex didn't waste no time, did he?"

Faith shook her head.

"Didn't think he would." She grinned. "You got a nice boy there, Miz Butler."

"Thank you." Faith returned the smile. "Miss Duncan, are you certain you don't mind? About this wrangler business, I mean. I don't expect others to be watching after my son. I know he can get underfoot at times."

"I don't mind. Really I don't. And nobody calls me Miss Duncan. I'm just Gertie."

"You'll be Miss Duncan to Alex. I'll not have him showing disrespect for his elders."

Gertie hooted with laughter. "Don't think I've been called anybody's elder before." She scratched her head. "Not sure I care for the thought much."

Faith didn't know how to respond. She was no stranger to odd characters. She'd known more than a few during her lifetime in the theater.

But Gertie Duncan was quite different from anyone else. Everything about the wrangler's appearance was masculine, from her lean but muscular build to her shirt, trousers, boots, and hat. Her face had been browned and freckled by the sun, despite the wide brim of her Stetson. She wore her hair shorter than many men, and there was nothing feminine in the way she walked or talked.

Although her appearance was unusual, something about the woman appealed to Faith, something that made her want to be friends with Gertie Duncan. Maybe it was the ever-present twinkle she saw in Gertie's dark blue eyes or the oft-used smile that revealed the slight gap between her front teeth or the laughter that seemed to come to her so easily.

With a fluid motion, the wrangler stepped onto the fence rail, then swung her legs over the top and dropped to the ground beside Faith. She removed her dusty hat and combed her fingers through her mop of hair. Her smile was gone as she met Faith's gaze. "Listen here, Miz Butler. Parker told me about your little girl bein' sick and all. You got yourself plenty on your platter t'handle. I guess I can keep an eye on one small boy now and agin."

Faith felt a sudden welling up of tears. She looked away, her vision blurred. "Everyone has been so very kind," she whispered around the lump in her throat.

"Folks here take care of one another. Got to. This is hard country. Nobody can make it all on their own."

Faith nodded, still unable to look at Gertie.

Nobody can make it all on their own. She wasn't alone, of course. Jesus was with her. Jesus had promised never to leave her. Still, there were times Faith longed to lean on another person. Sometimes it seemed she'd been making it on her own all her life.

Her father, Jack Fields, hadn't wanted the responsibility of raising a child, but he'd been so infuriated by his wife's request for a divorce, he'd refused to let Nellie see her daughter again. Faith had tried to be a good daughter; she'd tried to take care of Jack, to make him happy. She'd failed. He'd deserted her before her fifteenth birthday. If not for Raymond Drew keeping her on with his traveling troupe, she might have starved—or worse.

A few years later, Faith had met George Butler. She'd believed everything would be perfect from then on. She'd tried to take care of her husband after they were married. She'd tried to make him happy. But she'd failed. George had deserted her, as her father had before him. With his mistress in tow, George had divorced Faith. A few months later, he'd deserted his mistress, too, this time to marry a woman with money—or so Faith had heard.

Once upon a time, she'd entertained a lovely dream of what her life would be like. Once upon a time, she'd been in love and believed in her husband and—

Gertie's fingers alighted on Faith's shoulder. "I'd be obliged if you'd let the boy help me, Miz Butler."

A wry laugh escaped Faith's lips. "I don't know if he'll be much help, but he does seem to want to learn about what you do."

"He'll help, all right." Smiling broadly, Gertie slapped her hat back onto her head. "I'll see that he does."

"Mr. Rutledge won't mind, will he?" Faith glanced toward the house.

"No reason he should." Gertie stepped forward, her gaze following Faith's. "Never have figured what Rutledge is doin' out here. He don't seem t'take much interest in the place. I've only talked to him a half-dozen times in the years I been here. Always closed up in that back room o' his. 'Cept when he takes his horse out for one of their midnight rides."

"Midnight rides?"

"I seen him once. Like he was runnin' from the hounds of hades, racin' that pinto across the plains. A wonder he didn't end up with his fool neck broke. And his horse, too." Gertie shook her head, her eyes downcast. "Powerful sadness in that man. Powerful sadness."

"I know," Faith whispered, remembering what she'd seen when Drake turned up the light on his desk. Remembering also the strange way it had made her feel. Earlier that day, she'd run from those feelings, refusing to listen to Parker when he'd wanted to tell her about their employer. Now she wanted to know. "What happened to him?"

"That scar and his eye, you mean? Don't know. Parker does, I reckon, but he's never said an' I never asked."

Faith nodded again, even though she hadn't been inquiring about the scar. It was something much more intangible that tightened her heart whenever she thought of Drake Rutledge.

"Well..." Gertie cleared her throat. "I'd best be gettin' back t'my work. Rutledge don't pay me t'stand around jawin'." She stepped onto the bottom rail of the corral. "You send that boy out t'me when you can spare him, Miz Butler, and I'll see he does what he's told."

"Thank you, Gertie. And please, call me Faith."

The cowgirl responded with another one of her broad smiles. "It's gonna be right nice havin' you around the place, Faith Butler." Then she swung over the fence and approached the white stallion, talking softly as she went.

The house fell into silence with the coming of night, and at last, Drake felt free to leave his library.

Anger and frustration had warred within him for the better part of the day, and he blamed it all on the new housekeeper. Faith Butler was the reason he'd felt trapped in his library with his books and ledgers and dark, restless thoughts. If not for her . . .

With a sound of disgust, he strode down the hall. But he stopped abruptly outside the parlor, his uncovered eye widening in surprise. Moonlight, spilling through the large window, silvered the room. The clean tang of vinegar lingered in the air.

He took a step into the parlor, surprised to find the room had warmth and appeal. The chairs and sofa had been rearranged, grouped near the fireplace, a silent invitation to sit and converse. The piano had been polished to a high sheen, and a sheet of music had been set out, beckoning whoever entered the room to create a melody on the ivory and ebony keys. Knickknacks and bric-a-brac that had been packed away in the parlor's closet sat on the shelves after so many years of neglect and glittered in the moonlight.

She had done this. In one day, she had done all this.

Blast her!

He didn't want her meddling with his house. He didn't want her coming in here and rearranging things. He didn't want a cozy home. He wanted a refuge—a refuge from women like *her!*

Muttering to himself, he strode out of the parlor. He yanked open the front door and stepped onto the porch, dragging in a quick gulp of crisp night air as if his life depended on it. Only when he heard a soft gasp did he realize he wasn't alone.

He turned and glared toward the porch seat as Faith rose to her feet, her hands smoothing the folds of her dress.

"I . . . I hope it's all right that I sit out here," she said. "I needed a moment of quiet before retiring for the night."

"You must be tired. You've made yourself busy today." He'd meant it as an insult. He'd meant to call her a meddlesome busybody. But he saw her smile in the silvery glow of moonlight. It was a smile that could have lit up the night by itself.

She lifted her left hand and brushed back loose strands of hair. "Yes, it's been an eventful day, but it feels good to have accomplished so much."

Drake wanted to tell her to leave his house alone. He wanted to tell her to let the draperies be, to let the dust accumulate, to keep things as they were, as they'd been for years. But just as he'd been unable to deny her a place to live, it seemed he was unable to deny her whatever had brought about her smile.

Obviously unaware of his inner turmoil, she stared down at the distant lights of Dead Horse. "When Dr. Telford brought me to your ranch the other day, I couldn't imagine why anyone would want to build a house on this ridge. But tonight, I understand. It's so peaceful here." Her voice changed slightly. " 'Every man shall eat in safety / Under his own vine what he plants; and sing / The merry songs of peace to all his neighbours.' "

When she recited those words, they painted an image in his mind, in his heart. He almost believed in such a place. He almost believed in such a peace.

"Well, I'd best be to bed," she whispered as she turned and walked to the door.

Although he didn't glance behind him, he somehow knew she paused there and looked over her shoulder.

"Mr. Rutledge . . . thank you again." Another pause, then, "Good night."

"Good night, Mrs. Butler."

He heard the door open and close. He felt her going like a sudden chill upon his skin.

. . . and sing / The merry songs of peace to all his neighbours.

Drake didn't know his neighbors. Hadn't wanted to know them. Had intentionally remained on this ridge and watched as the town faltered, as family after family moved away. What was it to him whether Dead Horse was there or not? If it disappeared tomorrow, it wouldn't change his life one iota.

It hadn't always been so. Once he'd enjoyed a vast array of friends. At least he'd thought they were his friends.

But that was long ago, and the young man he remembered had been someone else entirely.

The cry of a lone coyote floated on the night air. A cooling breeze rustled the leaves of the tall aspen that grew at the corner of the house. In the corral, a horse nickered softly; another snorted.

Songs of peace?

Maybe once. Maybe for others.

He headed for the barn and another late-night race away from memories better left forgotten.

4

HE temperature had climbed into the nineties by early afternoon, rare for June. Rick Telford was more than a little tempted to use the heat as an excuse to visit the Dead Horse Saloon.

What could one drink hurt? a small voice in his head asked.

He knew the answer. One drink would lead to two. Two would lead to more. More would lead him back.

Rick wasn't willing to go back.

He might not be much of a doctor these days, and he might not have much of a medical practice in Dead Horse, Wyoming, but at least he was sober when someone needed him. That was something. Some days, that was everything.

"Father Telford," Nancy called, "are you going to come in and eat, or have I wasted my time cooking for you?"

"Be right there." He tried to ignore the intolerant tone of his daughter-in-law's voice.

Rick had no right to complain. He'd come to Dead Horse with

nothing. James and Nancy had made him welcome in their home even though no one would have blamed his son if he'd turned Rick away.

Rick wouldn't have blamed him, either.

With another quick glance toward the saloon, he rose from the porch swing and entered the house. "Aren't we going to wait for James?" he asked as he watched Nancy set a plate of biscuits on the table.

She shook her head. "No. He said he would eat something at the hotel." She sat down in her usual chair. "Are you certain you'll remember everything that must be done while we're away, Father Telford?" She spread butter on a biscuit, then passed the plate to her father-in-law.

Rick swallowed a sigh. "I think I can manage. Claire has little need of my help. After all, she and her husband built that hotel. She knows all about running it. But I'll be there if she needs me."

"*Mrs.* O'Connell works for us now." Nancy glared at Rick, then jabbed her fork into the broiled ham on her plate. "Although heaven knows, I wish she didn't. We'd have long since moved away if James hadn't bought that wretched building."

"But if he's successful in Green River City, if he can get the railroad to see the profit in bringing—"

Nancy's fork clattered onto the table as she jumped up from her chair. "I hope he fails. I hope no one will talk to him. I don't know why he wants to stay here. If it weren't for you, he wouldn't." Tearfully, she fled from the room.

Rick leaned back in his chair, staring at the uneaten food before him, knowing what Nancy had said was true. If it weren't for him, James might have left Dead Horse long ago. There weren't many places where a man like Rick Telford got a second chance. Because of its desperate need for a doctor—any doctor—Dead Horse was one of the few. James had stayed to lend support and make certain his father got his second chance.

His appetite gone, Rick left the table and headed for the back door. He walked swiftly to the small stable behind the house, where he hitched up his horse and buggy, then set out for the Jagged R, trying not to think about the past, trying not to think about a drink. Trying not to think.

Faith waited anxiously beside the bed as the doctor examined Becca.

"Well, Mrs. Butler," he said as he removed the stethoscope from his ears, "your daughter is doing remarkably well, considering her condition a week ago."

Faith released a sigh of relief. "I was hoping that's what you would say." She smiled at Becca. "Would you allow me to take her outside to sit in the shade? It's so terribly hot up here this time of day."

"I don't think it would do her any harm to be moved, as long as she's carried up and down the stairs." Rick wiped a trickle of sweat from his brow. "I'm sure she would be more comfortable outside where she might feel the occasional breeze."

"Do you hear that, Becca?" Faith sat on the edge of the bed and took hold of her daughter's hand. "The doctor says you may leave your bed for a short while. There are some lovely trees around the house with plenty of shade for you to sit beneath. Won't that be nice?"

Becca's answering smile lasted only a moment, but Faith knew she was delighted by the news.

Rick snapped his bag shut and reached for his suit coat. "I'll ask Parker or one of the other men to come carry her down. I'd do it myself, but I strained my back a couple of days ago." He glanced once more at Becca. "You mind what your mother tells you, young lady, and you'll be fine before you know it."

Unshed tears burned the back of Faith's throat as she watched her daughter nod solemnly at the doctor. She was encouraged by Becca's improving health, but she knew there was a long way to go to full recovery. Becca was frail. Just the effort of a smile seemed to drain her of any energy.

As Becca's eyelids drifted closed, the girl asked, "Will Alex come sit with me under the tree, Mama?"

"Of course he will, darling. Your brother loves to spend time with you."

More tears stung her eyes and throat, knowing the statement wasn't entirely honest. Alex was good to his sister and truly fond of her, but he was restless whenever Faith requested he stay with Becca. It was hard for him to be confined to this room when there was so much to see and do on the ranch, especially for a seven-year-old boy. And he wanted to see and do it all.

"Mrs. Butler?"

At the sound of the unexpected voice, a shiver ran up Faith's spine. She lifted her gaze toward the doorway as Drake Rutledge stepped into the bedroom. It was the first time she'd seen him since their brief encounter on the porch. It was also the first time she'd seen him in the full light of day.

"I came out when I saw the doctor . . ." He seemed almost nervous. "How's the little girl?"

Faith glanced at Becca. "She's doing better."

"The doctor asked me to carry her outside . . ."

Faith realized, with some surprise, that he was a handsome man, despite the eye patch and scar. *His scar. So that's why it's called the Jagged R!* She rose from the bed. "I'd expected Parker." Her throat was tight, her words barely audible.

"I don't mind." He strode toward the bed.

It was on the tip of her tongue to refuse his help. Then he stopped and glanced down at Becca, and a flicker of compassion crossed his face. Others might not have recognized it. Faith did.

"It's like an oven up here," he said.

"I know."

"Perhaps you should move to one of the lower bedchambers." Drake met her gaze.

A short while before, she might have accepted his offer. But suddenly she felt safer in these rooms, a floor away from her handsome, mysterious employer. "Thank you, Mr. Rutledge, but we're fine here." She hoped she sounded convincing. "Alex loves the view from this window, and the rooms cool off quickly when the sun goes down."

Drake didn't say anything in response, only continued to stare at her.

Discomforted, Faith looked down at her daughter. "If you'd carry her outside so she can lie in the shade, I'd be most grateful, Mr. Rutledge."

Drake tried to summon the return of the anger. He'd told himself he wanted to know the girl's condition so he could gauge how long it would be until they left. But the moment he'd looked down at the small child on the bed, his anger had vanished, and even her mother couldn't force its return.

He leaned over and lifted Becca into his arms. She weighed next to nothing. She seemed delicate, breakable. As he straightened, she opened her enormous green eyes, met his gaze, and smiled.

"Are you going to carry me downstairs?" she whispered.

"Yes."

She leaned her head against his chest and released a trusting sigh. "Thank you."

An odd warmth spread through Drake. His heart constricted even as his arms tightened around the child. He didn't allow himself to remember how long it had been since he'd held another person, how long it had been since he'd allowed himself to feel anything other than rage and bitterness. He tried not to acknowledge the protective feelings that surged to life within him.

It was better to feel nothing. It was always better to feel nothing.

Avoiding looking at Faith—knowing he would be sorry if he did—he turned and carried the little girl down the back stairway, in a hurry to be rid of Becca and the unwanted feelings she and her mother caused within him.

Once off the rear porch, Drake stopped beneath the leafy canopy that stretched overhead.

There were numerous trees, as well as a narrow swath of lawn, around the circumference of the house. Now, in late June, the yard provided a cool green oasis, an inviting escape from the summer heat.

Faith stepped past him, blankets and pillows in her arms. "Just a moment while I lay these on the grass." She paused to look about her, then pointed. "Let's go over there where Becca can see the horses."

Drake watched as Faith knelt near the trunk of a tall cottonwood. She spread the blankets on a thick carpet of grass beneath the massive tree. As she straightened, she glanced over her shoulder and met his gaze.

For a moment, he stood riveted. Although aimed at Becca, the tenderness in her eyes spilled onto him, and he felt it touch some hidden place deep inside. A place that hadn't been touched in many years.

Faith stretched out her arm in invitation. "You may put Becca down, Mr. Rutledge."

He gave his head a slight shake to break free of the spell she'd cast over him. Then he moved forward and gently laid Becca on the blanket.

Before he could draw away, the girl opened her eyes, looking directly at him. "It's nice out here, isn't it?"

"Yes, Becca. It is," he said.

She smiled, then turned her head on the pillow, staring toward the barn. "There's Alex. What's he doing, Mama?"

Drake glanced up—and discovered that the three of them had become the focus of attention. Faith's boy, lead rope in hand, stood with a horse near the barn. Gertie Duncan and Rick Telford watched from beside the corral. Parker McCall, wearing an amused expression, leaned against an awning post outside the bunkhouse.

Drake stiffened. The ranch hands rarely saw him, and now here he was a sideshow for their amusement. He hated the stares of others. He felt his anger return with force. She'd done it to him again. Faith Butler had caused him to do something he hadn't intended to do.

"Alex is helping Miss Duncan with the horses," Faith answered her daughter.

"Can I help, too?" the little girl asked.

"Maybe when you're stronger, darling." She looked up. "Mr. Rutledge, you are so kind to us. I cannot thank you enough."

He ignored her words of gratitude. "Next time, get someone else to carry her down," he replied gruffly, then strode back to the house.

But he found no solace inside. Except for his library, daylight streamed into every room. Gone were the draperies that had shrouded the windows. Woodwork had been polished. Floors had been scrubbed. Rugs had been beaten. Intrusive brightness was everywhere. Nothing was as it had been. Nothing was as he'd wanted it.

He stepped into his library and slammed the door behind him.

◆

Faith stared at the back door long after her employer stormed through it.

"Why was he angry?" Becca queried.

"I don't know, darling." She turned toward the bunkhouse. *I don't know, but Parker McCall does.*

Parker knew, and now Faith wanted to know. She wanted to understand more about Drake Rutledge. Suddenly she felt a sharp need to know whatever Parker could tell her.

"I'll be back in a little while." Faith rose and set off across the yard.

As she drew near, Parker pushed his hat back on his head and squinted his eyes against the sunlight. "I reckon I've witnessed some sort of miracle." He grinned. "Can't say the last time I saw Drake outside in the middle of the day. Must be years now."

"Tell me about Mr. Rutledge. I'd like to understand why he acts so..."

"He doesn't frighten you, does he?"

"A little." She gave a slight shrug. "At least, he did at first. But now..." She shrugged again.

He motioned toward a bench beneath the awning. "Sit there where you can keep an eye on the girl, and we'll talk."

Faith moved into the shade and settled onto the wooden bench. Parker followed but didn't sit down. Instead, he leaned his back against the wall of the bunkhouse. Faith watched as he removed his hat and began sliding his fingers around the brim, turning the Stetson in a steady circle.

"I first met Drake up in Montana, oh, 'bout ten, eleven years ago, I reckon. Rich man's son from Philadelphia, playin' at bein' a cowboy. Closest he'd been to a cow was a T-bone steak. Green as peas. All his fancy schoolin' didn't mean nothin' on the range, and he knew it, too." He shook his head, as if remembering more than he was saying.

Faith waited patiently for Parker to continue.

His face crinkled with amusement. "He was a handsome dude, and if there was a female within fifty miles, she'd find him. But Drake didn't have no mind t'get himself harnessed t'any one gal in particular. He was bound and determined t'make himself a cowboy." He chuckled, then sobered instantly. "He did it, too. Earned my respect right quick. If there was any man you could count on, it was Drake."

Faith wasn't surprised. Somehow she'd sensed that about her employer.

"His pa was some important lawyer back in Philadelphia. He was all set on havin' Drake join him in his firm. But that wasn't what Drake wanted. He wanted to stay out West. I think he would've done it, too, if his pa's heart hadn't gone bad. There wasn't much Drake could do when his ma sent for him but go help his family, like they needed."

Parker pushed away from the bunkhouse wall and set his Stetson back on his head. Then he stepped toward the edge of the shade, staring toward the house. "Can't say exactly what went on those couple years he was back in Philadelphia. He wrote once t'tell me he was engaged to a gal named Larissa something-or-other and that he was practicin' law in his pa's firm. Looked like he'd given up on his dream of comin' back. But I reckon he was happy enough, judgin' by his letter. Next thing I knew, he wrote me agin, sayin' his parents were dead. Told me he'd bought this place in Wyomin', sight unseen, and asked if I'd be interested in bein' the ranch foreman." Parker rubbed his fingers along his jaw as he turned toward Faith. "But he wasn't the same when he came back."

Her chest felt tight as she read the compassion in the cowboy's eyes.

"I tried to ask him about it once," Parker continued. "He told me he'd killed his parents."

She gasped.

"Ain't true. I saw the piece that was wrote up in a newspaper. Seems there was a carriage accident. Drake was drivin'. His ma died in it, and that's how he lost his eye. Don't know for sure what happened to his pa. Paper didn't mention him as bein' in the carriage."

"And his fiancée?" Faith asked softly.

Parker shook his head. "Don't know what happened to her, either. Drake never mentioned her again."

She left him, Faith thought with certainty. The girl named Larissa hadn't wanted Drake Rutledge any longer. Because of his scarred face? Because he'd lost an eye? Because she'd blamed him, as he'd blamed himself, for his mother's tragic death? Faith couldn't know for certain, but she knew without question it was because of Larissa that Drake had come to this ranch and cloaked himself in bitter darkness.

"He must have loved her very much," she whispered.

"I reckon he did, at that."

Turning her gaze upon the house, she thought of the dark and angry man inside. She thought of the way he'd shut himself in, closing out the world and everything and everyone in it. She thought of Drake and the girl he once loved, the girl who had left him—and she felt her heart nearly break in two.

> *If thou wilt leav e me, do not leav e me last,*
> *When other petty griefs hav e done their spite,*
> *But in the onset come; so shall I taste*
> *At first the v ery worst of for tune s might,*
> *And other strains of woe, which no w seem woe,*
> *Compar ed with loss of thee will not seem so .*

Faith understood about loss and rejection, more than Parker could know. She'd been betrayed by someone she'd loved. She understood the pain one felt in that secret part of the soul. But she'd found the answer to her brokenheartedness. She'd found the answer in Christ.

The Lord is nigh unto them that are of a broken heart; and saveth such as be of a contrite spirit.

She would pray for Drake Rutledge. She would pray that he would find the answer, too.

"Thank you for telling me what you know, Mr. McCall." She rose from the bench. "I shall keep your confidence."

Faith walked across the yard to sit beside her daughter in the shade of the tall cottonwood, already praying for her employer.

5

Lying on the bed, Alex stared at the ceiling and listened to the rain battering the roof. He frowned as his frustration grew. Why did it have to go and rain today of all days? Gertie—or rather, Miss Duncan—had been going to start giving him riding lessons, and now the weather had ruined everything.

He glowered at his sister. She was sleeping—as usual. It was bad enough he wouldn't get to ride that horse today, but now he was stuck looking out for Becca, too. Their mother had gone into town for supplies with Miss Duncan this morning, before the downpour began. Now Alex didn't know when they would get back.

He silently repeated a few bad words he'd learned from Mr. Drew's stagehands, wanting to say them aloud but knowing he shouldn't. His ma would wash his mouth out with soap if she heard him talking like that.

Getting up, he went to the window and opened it. He leaned forward, turning his face upward and closing his eyes against the cold splatter of rain. In a matter of moments, his head and shoulders were drenched.

Ma would be really mad if she was to see him doing this.

Opening his eyes, he pulled back inside and turned once again toward his sister. Becca slept on. All she *ever* did was sleep. He figured she wouldn't wake up for hours. He'd bet his favorite marble she wouldn't.

Quietly, he moved toward his sister's bed. "Becca," he whispered. No response.

Even more softly, "I'm goin' down for something to eat. You hungry?"

Again no response.

"I won't be long," he mumbled as he headed for the bedroom door.

The Rutledge house was big. Alex hadn't paid much attention to it once Miss Duncan said he could help with the horses. However, with nothing else to do today, this seemed like a real good time to do some exploring.

He liked being on the third floor. It felt like he was on top of the world whenever he looked out the window. He liked racing down the stairs, just to see how quickly he could reach the bottom. If he got up enough speed, he could take three steps at a time without falling.

His mother had told him to always use the back staircase, which suited him fine for running races 'cause it was so steep and all. But today, with no one to see him, he decided to test the perfect curve and pitch of the banister on the front staircase.

The oak railing was wide and winding, an unhindered slope all the way to the entry hall—ideal for sliding down. It had been designed to tempt a seven-year-old boy, bored by a rainy day.

Oh, boy! Ma would tan his hide if she found out.

But of course that thought didn't dissuade him from the adventure. Besides, his mother wouldn't find out. There'd been no sign of her on the road from Dead Horse. She and Miss Duncan were probably holed up at the store, waiting out the storm.

With a quick glance at the floor far below, Alex scrambled onto his stomach along the polished railing, backside first. Then he took a deep breath, leaned forward, and pushed with his hands as hard as he could. Within seconds, he was sliding down the steep decline.

"Whee!"

He gained more speed as he went. Faster and faster and faster, until, all of a sudden, he was afraid. Maybe this hadn't been such a brilliant idea after all.

He squeezed his eyes shut as he prepared to hurtle off the end of the banister and crash against the opposite wall, knowing it was going to hurt. But instead he felt himself yanked away by strong hands. For a moment, he was suspended in midair; then he met with a broad chest. He opened his eyes, glancing upward at his unexpected savior.

The man who held Alex firmly in his grasp scowled at him with his uncovered eye, the other hidden beneath a black patch. "What do you think you're doing?"

Alex trembled, knowing this was Mr. Rutledge, his ma's boss. "I was … I was … I …" His mother would tan his hide for sure. He hung his head in shame. "I … I'm sorry, sir."

"Sorry? You could have killed yourself." He set Alex on the floor. "What's your name?"

"Alex, sir. Alexander Butler. I … I …" His words died abruptly as he looked up. He swallowed the hard lump in his throat and croaked, "I'm real sorry, sir. I won't do it again. I promise."

"See that you don't."

With a nod, Alex scurried toward the kitchen; then, with a safe distance between them, he paused and looked back.

Drake's anger slowly drained from him, an anger born of fear when he'd seen what had surely been a disaster about to happen. He'd done something similarly stupid when he was about the same age as this boy. Except Drake's wild flight down the banister of his parents' Philadelphia home had resulted in a broken arm and fifteen stitches in the back of his head.

"What happened to your eye?"

Drake turned toward the boy whom he'd thought had left.

"Is it gone?" Alex persisted. "Your eye, I mean. Do you just got a hole under that patch?"

"No. My eye is there."

"How'd it happen?"

"Don't you have something you're supposed to be doing? Where's your mother?"

"She's in town with Miss Duncan. How'd it happen?"

The boy was tenacious, Drake would give him that. "I don't believe that's any concern of yours." Drake wanted the silence of his library and a stiff drink.

"I never knew anybody who wore a patch over his eye before. I was just wondering what it was like."

"Why don't you wear one yourself and find out?" Drake replied tersely, then strode into his private sanctuary and closed the door behind him.

Bothersome little brat.

What was it like to be blind in one eye? A nightmare, especially at first. He'd lost his depth perception, and in those early months after the accident, he'd fallen down stairs and run into walls and doors. He'd felt constantly startled by little, everyday things. He'd been afraid and unsure of himself.

He was more used to his blindness now. He'd had over seven years to get used to it, to learn to judge things by shadows, to learn to listen closely to what went on around him.

Is it gone? Your eye, I mean. Do you just got a hole under that patch? Surprisingly, he grinned as he remembered the boy's words. No one in all these years had ever had the courage to ask such a thing.

Leave it to Faith Butler's son to be the one.

"BLAST IT ALL, SON." Clyde Rutledge dropped a sheaf of papers onto Drake's desk. "You're not applying yourself. How will you be ready to take over the firm if you don't take your work more seriously? I'm not paying you to gallivant about town in that fancy carriage of yours. You've got clients to attend to. They need your attention."

Drake stared at the legal documents fanning out before him. The last thing in the world he wanted to do was go over them with his father. Most of the work the firm did was boring, uninteresting, as far as Drake was concerned. How his father had tolerated it all these years, he'd never know.

"Can we talk about this later, Father?" Drake rose from his chair. "I'm supposed to pick Mother up at her dressmaker's in a short while, and then I promised to take Larissa to the Cavanaugh house party."

"I'm counting on you, Drake. You've got to buckle down. This firm needs you."

But it didn't need him. This stuffy old law firm would get along fine without him, and everyone knew it. For a moment, Drake remembered what it had been like to gallop alongside a stampeding herd of cattle—the dust, the noise, the smell, the danger. How alive he'd felt!

Clyde Rutledge sank onto a chair, his hand pressed against his heart. "I won't always be around, Son. When I'm gone . . . well, you know I won't be with you for long. Your mother will need you."

Wasn't it enough that he'd been forced to give up his own dreams? Wasn't it enough that he'd returned to Philadelphia when his mother had sent for him? It wasn't as if the Rutledges needed their son to earn his way or to support them in their old age. They were wealthy enough to live out the rest of their lives in comfort, even if Drake never handled another case for the firm.

And he sure didn't want to sit there and watch his father play out his weak-heart routine.

Drake picked up his gloves, then reached for his fur-lined coat. "I'd better be going. We don't want Mother standing in the cold." He motioned toward his desk. "I'll go over those papers later." Then he escaped before his father could stop him.

He left the law firm of Rutledge and Seever, but he couldn't leave behind the memories his father's comments had brought to mind. As Drake drove his fine pair of matched bays down the street to Madame Celesta's Dress Shop, he couldn't help remembering those brief but adventuresome years he'd spent out West.

His friends in Texas and Montana, and all points in between, wouldn't have been accepted in the upper echelons of Philadelphia society, but Drake hadn't cared. They'd been honest, hard-working men. They'd done their share of good-natured ribbing of the greenhorn among them, but in the end they'd accepted Drake and taught him all he needed to know.

Cowboying had been tough work, but even its worst chores were better than being stuck in an office with a stack of dry, boring briefs. The men he'd worked with on ranches and cattle drives had had little education. Even so, he'd preferred their down-to-earth, *commonsense view of life to the stuffy narrow-mindedness of the men in his father's firm.*

It had always been in the back of his mind to return to the West one day, but then he'd met Larissa Dearborne. Beautiful, exquisite Larissa, who could twist him so easily to her will. After he'd asked her to marry him, he'd known he would never leave Philadelphia. Larissa couldn't survive in the rough and rugged West he'd known. So he'd given up that dream.

And wasn't being Larissa's husband worth giving it up?

That question lingered as he greeted his mother inside the doorway of Madame Celesta's, as he helped Constance Rutledge into his shiny black carriage with its bright green upholstery, as he guided the horses along the quiet streets toward the Rutledge estate.

Perhaps that was why, when they met Teddy Westover at the entrance to the park, he so quickly took up Teddy's challenge for a race. Perhaps he missed the wild and reckless days of his youth. Perhaps it was because he felt everything slipping through his fingers. Because he saw his dull, staid future, and it frightened him.

And so, with his mother in the carriage crying for him to slow down, he raced his team against Teddy Westover's.

He would never know what caused his coach to slide out of control, what caused it to tip and roll. He would never remember the following seconds that changed his life. But he would live with the aftermath forever.

Faith stared anxiously out the window of the general store at the continuing downpour.

"We'll be up to our hubs in mud 'fore we get home," Gertie whispered nearby. "Shoulda known this wasn't a good day t'come into town. Shoulda took one look at the sky and known we were in for a drencher."

"Maybe we should leave now."

"Won't do us no good t'get stuck out in the middle of this storm. We're better off waitin' here. It's gotta let up sometime."

Faith glanced at the woman beside her. "I'm worried about the children. Alex will be restless. We've been gone a long time already. They'll need to eat and —"

"Needn't be worried." Gertie offered an encouraging smile. "Parker'll look in on 'em, see your little girl's okay."

"He shouldn't have to do that."

"Ah, he likes doin' it. From what I've seen, he's right partial to kids. Shame he doesn't have a passel of his own." Gertie removed her hat, then deepened the crease in the crown with the fingers of one hand while holding the brim with the other. "Cowboyin's a lonely business. A man ain't likely to run across a marryin' kind of woman very often. For most of 'em, that don't matter much. Who'd want 'em anyhow? But for a man like Parker . . ." She shook her head, shrugged, then opened the door and stepped out onto the boardwalk without another word.

"Mrs. Butler?" a voice in the back called.

Faith turned toward the proprietress of the general store. "Yes?"

"Is there anything else you'll be wanting?" A heavyset woman with streaks of gray in her brown hair, Sadie Gold watched Faith with an inquisitive gaze.

"No. I believe that's everything for today."

"Well then, why don't you join me in the back for a cup of coffee? I don't imagine there's going to be many customers on a day like this, and we might as well get better acquainted. I've been mighty curious since I heard you'd taken up housekeeping for Mr. Rutledge." She motioned for Faith to follow her. "I hear tell you're an actress."

Sheltered from the rain by a wide awning over the boardwalk, Gertie leaned against the wall of the general store, one knee bent, her foot braced against the wall for balance. The storm was the only thing breaking the silence of Dead Horse. If it weren't for the horses and wagon from the Jagged R standing in front of the store, the entire town would look deserted. Like a ghost town.

Gertie shook her head. It might come to that, too, if James Telford didn't have any luck down in Green River City. The railroad could save this town and the folks who lived here. If it was going to happen, it had better happen soon.

Across the street, she saw the front door of the hotel open and the doctor emerge. She felt a funny little skip in her heart at the sight of Rick Telford.

Odd. It was just Doc.

Rick spied her and waved. Then, with his arm over his head in a useless attempt to shield himself from the rain, he dashed across the muddy street and onto the boardwalk. "What brings you to town, Gertie?" He shook the water from his hair.

"Faith needed supplies."

He glanced through the window into the general store. "How's she working out?"

"Real good. Ain't seen so many just-washed cowpokes at mealtime in all my life."

He laughed at her good-humored sarcasm. "No, I don't suppose you have." He removed his glasses and wiped them dry with his handkerchief.

Well, I'll be!

As if seeing him for the first time, Gertie realized the doctor wasn't a bad-looking man. At least, not for his age, which she figured to be a few years past forty. His abundant hair was the same stone gray as his eyes, but his face wasn't wrinkled much, except for around the corners of his eyes and mouth. He carried himself straight, like a man half his age, and his arms were strong. He was no weakling city-dude sort. Gertie figured he could hold his own against plenty of younger men.

Sometimes when she'd talked with him, she'd thought what a lonely man he was. She understood loneliness. She understood what it was like to be different from those around her. She'd always been different, a bit of an outcast, just 'cause she'd been born female.

But the cause of Rick's loneliness was of a different nature.

Gertie knew all about what happened to his wife, about how he'd been drunk and hadn't cared for her proper when she was sick and how she died. About how he'd pretty much been run out of the town he'd been living in, nobody wanting a drunk for a doctor. It wasn't like any of it was a secret. There wasn't a soul in Dead Horse who *didn't* know the story, not with the way Nancy Telford had of flapping her jaws like a sheet in a strong wind.

Dead Horse had been eager enough for a doctor of its own that the folks here gave Rick the chance he needed. Gertie had to give him credit for what he'd done with that chance. He'd proved himself a good and caring doctor to one and all. As for the liquor, Gertie had never so much as smelled it on his breath since the day he arrived. Not once. Never so much as seen him go near the saloon.

Yes, she'd admired him. But had she really taken notice of him before now?

"How's that arm of yours?" he asked, drawing her from her reverie.

"My arm? Oh, it's fine, Doc. You fixed it up real good."

"Mind if I have a look?"

"Naw, I don't mind." She rolled up her sleeve.

Her pulse did a funny little dance through her veins as Rick cradled her forearm in his hands and leaned forward for closer inspection.

Well, I'll be!

It was unbelievable. It was too incredible for words. But the truth was, she'd give that same right arm he was looking at for him to kiss her.

Doc Telford?

That was crazy!

Ridiculous!

Downright plumb loco!

Doc Telford?

"I guess you won't be needing my services any further." Rick released her arm and straightened.

Their gazes met, and a warm tingling sensation spread through her. Her knees suddenly weakened. She felt herself blush and her eyes widen in disbelief.

Blushing? She'd never blushed before in all her born days.

Her glance fell away as she quickly rolled down her shirtsleeve. "Well, I sure hope I won't be needin' 'em. Can't say I take much pleasure spendin' my hard-earned wages on doctorin'."

When he didn't reply, she dared to look up again. He watched her with a peculiar expression, as if he were seeing her for the first time, too.

He has just about the finest mouth I ever laid eyes on.

How many times in the past few weeks had he held her arm while he'd doctored her wound? Plenty. And not once had she given thought to anything other than making sure her arm healed up so it wouldn't interfere with her work. What on earth was wrong with her now?

She felt her blush grow hotter.

If she didn't do something to stop herself right quick, she was going to give in to that irresistible urge, throw her arms around his neck, and plant one right on his lips. Right here on Main Street.

She sidled away. "Looks like the rain's lettin' up. Think I'll see about loadin' those supplies into the wagon so me and Faith can get on back to the ranch." She reached for the door and yanked it open.

"It was good seeing you, Gertie."

"Yeah. You, too, Doc."

Like a scared jackrabbit, she hurried into the general store and away from the source of her consternation.

✦

"You know, Mrs. Butler," Sadie said as she refilled Faith's coffee cup, "this town hasn't had a proper Fourth of July celebration in three years. Maybe you'd think of doing a Shakespearean reading or something for us." After pouring more of the dark liquid into her own cup, she placed the speckled coffeepot on the stove, then settled onto her chair again. "Treat us to a bit of real culture. It sure would be good for my young'ns."

"I don't know, Mrs. Gold. Independence Day is less than two weeks away."

"Are you telling me you don't have plenty of scenes swimming about in that head of yours?" Sadie waved her hand in dismissal. "I don't believe it for a moment. Besides, the folks of Dead Horse need a bit of cheering up, and I think you're just the ticket. My guess is you're a right fine actress."

Faith felt warmed by the woman's praise. Not once had Sadie Gold made Faith feel ashamed of how she'd made her livelihood. Not once had she so much as hinted that there was any unworthiness in such a profession. Faith appreciated it more than she could say. "That's kind of you, Mrs. Gold. I suppose I *could* find something appropriate to perform, even on such short notice."

"Of course you can. We'll have us a regular festival. See if we don't." Sadie grinned. "Maybe you can even get Mr. Rutledge to come. I swear, sometimes I haven't believed the man is real."

Picturing Drake in her mind—tall, masculine, *disturbing*—Faith whispered, "Oh, he's quite real."

"We'd have us the railroad by now if Mr. Rutledge would lend his support to our efforts," Sadie said. "From what I've heard, he's rich as Croesus. Money like as always gets attention. With all those cattle he's runnin' on his range, he'd benefit from the railroad coming through here as much as anybody."

"Has anyone talked to him about it?"

"They've tried, but he's always sent folks away without seeing them." The older woman shook her head. "If things don't turn out, I doubt we'll be able to stay. I sure would hate to leave Dead Horse. We've been happy here." She sighed heavily. "Starting over isn't easy, especially when you're my age. Me and the mister have done more than our share of starting over."

Before Faith could answer, Gertie appeared in the doorway. "The rain's let up. I think we'd best git while the gittin's good. No tellin' how long it'll take us t'get back as it is. I'm gonna start loadin' the wagon."

"I'll be right there." Faith rose from her chair and offered a smile to her hostess. "It's been a pleasure, Mrs. Gold. I appreciate your kind hospitality."

"The pleasure's all mine. You don't be a stranger now. There's few enough of us womenfolk in these parts. You drop by for a visit anytime. Don't wait until you need supplies."

"I won't."

"I'll be up to see you as soon as we put something together for the Fourth of July. Good heavens! I'm as excited as my children will be when they hear about it."

Still buoyed by the woman's friendliness, Faith walked through the general store, feeling lighter than she had in ages.

6

LAUGHTER, soft and bright, drifted in through the open window of Drake's sanctuary. It wasn't the first time he'd heard the pleasant sounds in the past half hour. This time, however, he rose from the chair behind his desk and followed it.

Two days of rain were only a memory now. Lingering was the fresh scent of an earth washed clean. The blue sky held not so much as a hint of clouds. The mountains seemed nearer and even more purple than usual.

And here, much closer to him, golden sunshine filtered through a web of leaves and branches to cast an aura of light around the mother and daughter resting on a blanket spread on the lawn.

Sitting up, her back braced against her mother's side, Becca wove a long strand of grass between her fingers. There was more color in her face than there had been on the day Drake carried her down from her room. He found himself gladdened by the subtle change.

Faith tenderly brushed aside Becca's strawberry blond hair before kissing the child's forehead. "You should be napping." Her words were full of motherly concern.

"Tell me another story first."

"I have work to do, Becca." She checked the watch pinned to her bodice. "The men will be expecting their supper when they return. I've food on the stove to tend to."

"*Please*, Mama."

Faith laughed again.

Odd, how such a simple scene could bring about a more complex reaction in Drake. He felt something hard and secret inside his chest yield, soften.

"All right," Faith answered Becca. "You may listen as I practice my soliloquy for the Independence Day celebration. Then you must close your eyes and sleep. Agreed, young lady?"

The child nodded.

Faith rose from the blanket. She took two steps away, her back toward the house. For a long time she didn't move, and when she did turn, it seemed she had become someone else right before Drake's eyes.

"'Thou know'st the mask of night is on my face, / Else would a maiden blush bepaint my cheek / For that which thou has heard me speak tonight. / Fain would I dwell on form, fain, fain deny / What I have spoke; but farewell compliment!'"

The brilliance of the midday sun faded to nothing. With only a few words, by the mere magic of her countenance and the lilting sound of her voice, Faith drew Drake into another time and place. With just a few lines from an ancient play, she turned day into night, light into darkness.

Drake leaned forward, resting his forearms against the windowsill, straining to better hear her words, straining to see her more clearly, to watch each subtle expression on her face as she spoke.

" 'Dost thou love me? I know thou wilt say "Ay," / And I will take thy word. Yet if thou swear'st / Thou mayst prove false. At lovers' perjuries, / They say, Jove laughs. O gentle Romeo, / If thou dost love, pronounce it faithfully; / Or if thou think'st I am too quickly won, / I'll frown, and be perverse, and say thee nay, / So thou wilt woo; but else, not for the world. / In truth, fair Montague, I am too fond, / And therefore thou mayst think my 'haviour light.' "

She was beautiful. Everything a fair Juliet should be. The radiance of her flame-red hair. The pale white of her smooth complexion. The earnest, innocent look of love in eyes of blue green. The perfection of her form beneath a dress of buttercup yellow.

" 'But trust me, gentleman, I'll prove more true / Than those that have more cunning to be strange. / I should have been more strange, I must confess, / But that thou overheard'st, ere I was ware, / My true love's passion. Therefore pardon me, / And not impute this yielding to light love, / Which the dark night hath so discovered.' "

The world held its breath for a heartbeat, and Drake held his with it, caught in the wonder of watching Faith as she stood beneath the spreading arms of the tall trees, her own arms outstretched toward her invisible Romeo.

And then her spell was broken as Juliet's line repeated in his head. *But trust me, gentleman, I'll prove more true....*

He straightened and drew back from the window. How easily he'd allowed himself to be drawn into her expertly cast web.

Trust a beautiful woman to be true? Not in his lifetime.

Out of the corner of her eye, Faith caught a movement at the library window. She looked yet saw nothing but the dark draperies, shutting out the daylight.

Closing in the man.

Had he been watching her? she wondered, and felt an odd mixture of emotions to think he might have been.

"Do something else, Mama."

She glanced at her daughter. "No. You promised you would rest, and I must get back to my cooking or I'll have my hands full with a bunch of hungry cowboys and nothing to feed them."

"I wish Alex was here."

"Alex and Miss Duncan will be back later." Faith frowned slightly as she placed her knuckles against her hips. "Close those eyes, little girl, or I'll take you back to your room."

Becca let out a long and pitiful sigh of the oppressed, and Faith nearly laughed aloud at the dramatic display. It would seem Becca had inherited at least some of her mother's talent for theatrics.

Smiling and shaking her head, Faith walked toward the back door of the house.

Thanks to the two days of rain, the kitchen was much cooler than it had been when Faith first started cooking for the Jagged R crew. She knew the respite from heat wouldn't last, but she was glad for it nonetheless. At least she had more confidence in her ability to feed everyone without poisoning them. The cookbook she'd purchased at the general store in Dead Horse was responsible for most of that confidence.

She glanced once again at her watch, then hurried to the stove, where the navy beans were cooking. Fortunately the water hadn't boiled off while she spent time with Becca.

She paused long enough to read over the recipe in the cookbook, left open on the counter; then she removed the kettle of beans and drained the water into the sink. Afterward she poured the beans into a pot and began adding the other prepared ingredients—tomatoes rubbed through a colander, brown sugar, ginger, mustard, black pepper, salt, and dark molasses. The molasses, according to the instructions, was to give a good brown color to the beans. Faith wasn't sure how important that was.

She envisioned young Johnny Coltrain or crusty Dan Greer refusing to eat her beans because they weren't the proper shade of brown, and she chuckled. Not very likely, she thought with an amused shake of her head. The cowpokes who worked at the ranch praised everything she set before them and ate every last crumb. They weren't particularly choosy, but that didn't lessen Faith's desire to do a good job.

The Bible said servants were to serve as to the Lord and not to men. She'd read those very words that morning in the book of Ephesians. It made her feel good to think she was also serving Christ in some small way as she prepared food for the hungry cowpokes of the Jagged R.

With one final glance at the recipe, Faith added strips of bacon over the top of the mixture. Then she placed the pot into the oven, where the beans would bake for three hours, and closed the oven door with a sense of satisfaction. This would be the best meal she'd prepared since arriving at the ranch. Three apple pies were already cooling on the windowsill. Beefsteaks were waiting to be fried, and she'd mastered the art of making biscuits several days before.

She wondered if Drake had noticed the difference in her cooking during this past week. Then she wondered if Drake noticed anything about her at all.

She frowned as she washed her hands and dried them with a towel, recalling what Parker had told her about their employer. Then she considered Sadie Gold's comments about the need for the railroad to come to Dead Horse and the help Drake could have been to the town.

Her eyes widened in sudden realization. *The townsfolk need his help, and he needs theirs, too.*

She turned toward the hallway.

Drake might manage to fool others, but he didn't fool her. She knew he hid a kind heart beneath that gruff, unfriendly facade. He'd shown it by giving Faith and her children a place to live. Now it was time to return the favor. Before she left the Jagged R, Faith would find some way to help him begin living again.

But how?

She stepped into the kitchen doorway and glanced down the hall in the direction of the library door. Closed off from the world. She wondered if she would have chosen the same path of escape after George deserted her if it had been available, if she hadn't been forced to provide for her children. It would have been so much easier to go into hiding, so much easier not to face her own shame, her own failure as a woman and a wife. But she wasn't wealthy. She'd been forced to go on, to—

That was it!

A jolt of excitement shot through her. She suddenly knew how she could help Drake.

She squared her shoulders and smoothed her hair with her fingertips, then grabbed her dust cloth and walked swiftly toward the library.

The three quick raps on the door didn't surprise Drake. For some reason he'd been expecting them—and her.

"Come in, Mrs. Butler."

He watched as she entered and walked across the room, stopping before his desk.

"I'm sorry to disturb you, Mr. Rutledge," she said as she peered at him in the dim light, "but I really must clean the library sometime, and there never seems to be an hour of the day when you're not closeted in here. Why don't you take a break from your work and allow me to dust and sweep?"

Drake leaned back in his chair, away from the low-burning lamp. "I like things as they are. Leave this room alone."

"Fiddlesticks! No one wants to spend a day shut up with dust and grime."

Drake thought her smile brought more of a glow into the room than the lamp on his desk.

Faith turned on her heel and walked straight to the window, drawing open the draperies and allowing in the daylight. "I'm glad to see you aren't totally averse to letting in a bit of fresh air. I'm sure it hasn't done you any harm."

"Mrs. Butler!"

"Yes?" She turned, her eyebrows raised in innocent question.

Blast the woman! As sure as she was standing there, she was daring him to throw her out.

And he found he couldn't do it!

"Nothing," he grumbled.

Once again she smiled. "Did you happen to hear me practicing my Shakespeare a while ago?" Without waiting for a reply, she turned to the nearest bookshelf, pulled a cloth from the pocket of her apron, and began dusting. "Mrs. Gold asked me to do a reading for the town's Independence Day gathering. She said they hadn't observed the holiday in several years. I've chosen a selection from *Romeo and Juliet.*"

And a very beautiful Juliet you make.

"Dr. Telford says he doesn't care for Shakespeare's works," she continued, "but I see you must enjoy them." She ran her fingers lightly over the spines of the books on one shelf. "It must be wonderful to have so many choices of what to read."

"It *would* be wonderful if I had some peace and quiet in which *to* read."

She looked over her shoulder, her mouth curving gently. "It seems to me you have far too much peace and quiet, Mr. Rutledge."

The truth of her words struck him dumb.

"Not that a mother with young children doesn't understand the need for a moment to escape." She paused, then said, "You hide yourself away, yet there's a whole world out there that needs you. Surely God doesn't want you to live your whole life alone, lonely."

Drake searched his mind for something to say, for some rejoinder or even an insult, but nothing came to mind. He seemed helpless to do anything other than watch her as she moved about the room.

How did she do it? he asked himself again. How did Faith Butler manage to destroy with such ease the order and rhythm of his life?

Faith's mind filled with things to say next, but none of them seemed right. She wanted to ask Drake to come to the town's celebration the following week. The folks of Dead Horse needed him, and whether he knew it or not, he needed them, too. The last thing a man like Drake should do was shut himself away like a monk.

That thought brought a blush to her cheeks. The man sitting behind her wasn't the sort she would envision as a monk. He exuded masculine power.

What would it be like, she wondered unexpectedly, to be held by his strong arms? to feel his mouth upon hers? Would his mustache be soft or prickly against her skin?

Her hand stilled as her pulse raced.

What on earth was the matter with her?

"What happened to your husband, Mrs. Butler?"

She sucked in a breath of air, startled by his question.

"Are you a widow?"

She began rubbing with her dust rag again, trying desperately to compose herself before she might be forced to meet his gaze. "No, Mr. Rutledge. I'm not a widow. I…I'm…divorced." Would he no longer treat her with kindness or respect? Or would he turn her out now? She released a ragged sigh. "I…I thought you knew."

She heard his chair squeak as he rose, listened to his footsteps as he crossed the room to the window. She knew without looking that he braced the heel of one hand on the sill as he gazed outside. In her mind's eye she saw him, tall and strong and dark, the patch making his handsome face look dangerous and yet…

"Your daughter is much improved."

Her heart skittered. "Yes."

"I'm glad."

"Thank you."

"Well…" He cleared his throat. "I'll leave you to your cleaning."

He hadn't dismissed her. He hadn't seemed to judge her.

She felt renewed hope and determination as she turned toward him. He looked much as she'd imagined, sunlight adding a hint of midnight blue to his black hair. "Mr. Rutledge, I was wondering if you might take me and the children into town for the celebration next week."

"I don't go into town."

"But why not?"

The moment the question was out of her mouth, she wished it back. That wasn't what she'd meant to say. She saw him stiffen, saw the chiseled lines of his face harden.

"I don't believe that's any concern of yours," he replied in a voice as cold as a Wyoming winter.

"No, you're right. It isn't any of my concern." She stepped toward him. "I apologize, Mr. Rutledge. I hope you'll forgive me."

He offered an abrupt nod, then headed for the door.

Faith whirled about. "Wait!"

Drake stopped but didn't look behind him. "What is it, Mrs. Butler?"

"Please think about my invitation."

Without another word, he opened the door and left.

Faith's disappointment was entirely out of proportion to the circumstances. She hadn't really expected him to join them, had she? What possible difference would it have made? Drake had lived in this house for many years, and no one in town knew him. Nancy Telford imagined him a murderer. Sadie Gold had wondered if he existed at all. Why should Faith's invitation make any difference to him?

It didn't, of course. It couldn't.

Only she'd wanted it to. She'd very much wanted her invitation to make a difference to Drake.

The curtain of night dropped over the earth, bringing with it a cool breeze to rustle the leaves of the tall trees surrounding the house. A quarter moon hung suspended over the mountains and cast a soft light upon the valley below.

One foot on the lower rail of the corral, his forearms resting on the top rail, Drake stared at the horses without seeing them, his thoughts troubled. Troubled because of Faith and her irritating interference.

I don't go into town.

But why not?

It had been hours since she'd walked into his library, opened his curtains to let in the daylight, disturbed the careful order of his life, then asked him to accompany her into Dead Horse. Hours, and the words still lingered in his head.

I don't go into town.

But why not?

Why not? Was she more blind than Drake himself? Couldn't she *see* him with those blue-green eyes of hers? More troubling were her words "Surely God doesn't want you to live your whole life alone." What did she know of such things? Hadn't God put him in this place? And yet he knew in his heart that his bitterness, his despair wasn't God's doing. What was it his mother had always said? "God loves us even when we aren't very lovely." He ran his hand through his hair. He certainly hadn't been very lovely, that was sure. But God must've had better things to do with His time than wait on him.

He heard footsteps and turned his head, relieved to find Parker approaching. Anything to keep his mind off his troubling thoughts.

"Evenin'." The foreman stopped beside Drake. "Nice night. Rains've kept it cool."

Drake grunted a response.

Parker patted his belly. "Sure has been a pleasure havin' a woman to cook for us." Like Drake, he placed one foot and both arms on the corral rails, then stared toward the mountains, dark shadows in the distance. "Be great if we could keep her on after the little girl's well. Sure would. The boys'd all give money to keep her here."

Drake felt like grinding his teeth. He'd wanted to forget Faith, and here was Parker bringing her up within moments. "I imagine she'll want to rejoin her theater troupe."

"I got the feelin' she likes workin' with all of us." Parker turned to stare at Drake. "You think she'd really rather go back to her actin'?"

Drake nodded, although he wasn't at all sure he told the truth.

"You sure about that, Drake?"

"I'm sure."

"Hope you're wrong. We'd all miss her around here."

Drake remembered that afternoon, envisioned Faith as she spoke the lines Shakespeare had written long ago. Her expressions, her movements, were engraved upon his mind. Her melodious voice whispered in his memory, entrancing him again.

Yes, she would be missed around here. Drake would miss her.

"Well—" Parker pushed away from the rail—"guess I'll turn in. Swede and I are headin' up to the north range tomorrow." He started away. "Night."

"Night," Drake returned absentmindedly.

I don't go into town.

But why not?

Why not? Why not go into Dead Horse? He didn't care what the people there thought. What others thought had ceased to matter to him long ago.

Drake turned and stared up at the third-story window through the shadow of tree limbs.

Hadn't it?

❖

Haloed by soft moonlight, he stood alone near the corral.

Faith knew Drake couldn't see her, yet she drew instinctively to one side of the window, one hand flat upon her collarbone. Her skin felt suddenly warm, and she was grateful for the cool night air.

What is the matter with me? Why does he make me feel so strange?

Was it merely his dark and dangerous looks, or was it something more? Was it only because she wanted to help him in repayment for what he'd done for her and her family? Or was it something else?

A need stirred deep inside. A need to be held, to be loved. A need long silenced.

She closed her eyes and leaned against the window casement, her knees almost too weak to hold her upright. Once before she had let herself long for love, but what she had gained was a broken heart and shame. She had loved George Butler with the true simplicity of guileless youth, but he hadn't known how to love in return.

Wonderful, laughing, handsome George.

Was ever book containing such vile matter
So fairly bound? O that deceit should dw ell
In such a gorgeous palace!

Faith turned her back to the wall and slid down until she sat on the floor. She drew her legs up to her chest and rested her forehead on her knees, wrapping her arms around her shins. Hot tears seared her eyelids before slipping free to moisten her cotton nightgown.

She didn't cry for lost love. Those tears had long since been spent. She cried instead for the loss of innocence, for the shattering of dreams.

And, although she didn't realize it yet, she cried for the dark and tortured man who stood in the moonlight beneath her window.

7

JULY arrived in Wyoming on hot, dry winds. The sun beat mercilessly upon the small town of Dead Horse, bleaching the last remnants of paint from the board siding of the saloon and turning the street to a sea of dust. Horses stood with drooping heads, and dogs crawled under bushes and boardwalks, seeking the smallest bit of shade.

Seated on the porch of the Telford house, Rick wiped the sweat from his forehead with his handkerchief while reading the telegram from his son. It was a short message but a hopeful one. James was making some headway with the railroad officials. He and Nancy were leaving for Cheyenne today, but they hoped to be home by the end of next week. James closed by reminding his father to keep an eye on things at the hotel.

Rick folded the telegram and stuck it in his pocket. Keep an eye on the hotel. That wouldn't take much, he thought grimly. If it weren't for the hotel restaurant and Claire O'Connell's cooking, they could lock the doors and forget it. There hadn't been a guest registered since Faith Butler and her children moved to the Jagged R nigh on two weeks ago.

Remembering the Butler family, he turned his gaze toward the ridge south of town, squinting against the bright sunlight. It had been nearly a week since he'd seen his youngest patient. He supposed he should ride up there today, although he was certain his services were no longer needed. Becca Butler was out of the woods. As long as she got plenty of rest, she should continue to improve from this bout of illness.

A cloud of dust rose above the road leading into Dead Horse, drawing the doctor's attention. He stared, too hot to look away, waiting to see which Jagged R cowpoke had decided to come into town for a drink at the saloon.

He licked his lips, his mouth suddenly drier than moments before. Again he wiped his forehead with his handkerchief. The thought of a drink made his belly twist. His hands began to shake. He glanced down at them, eyes narrowing.

When would it stop? he wondered. When would he stop thinking about holding a glass of whiskey in his hand, about staring into the amber liquid, about drinking until oblivion overtook him?

He squeezed his eyes shut and drew his forearm across his forehead. He practiced taking one deep breath, then another, silently rehearsing an old litany that had kept him sober for close to four years now.

If he could make it through one minute without a drink, he could make it through two. If he could make it through two minutes, he could make it through ten. If he could make it through ten minutes, he could make it through an hour and then a day. If he could make it through a day, he could make it through another week and then another month and then another year. He swallowed hard, took another deep breath, then opened his eyes, relieved to find the dreaded moment passing.

He focused his gaze once more on the horse and rider. He recognized Gertie Duncan now. The young woman didn't sit a horse like any man Rick knew. She sat tall in the saddle, with a gentleness in her manner—not feminine exactly, but it spoke of a kindness, a respect she had for her mount. She slowed to a walk at the outskirts of town. A billow of dust and dirt rolled ahead of her, obscuring her momentarily from his view. When the air cleared, she had nearly reached his house.

"Hey, Doc," she called when she saw him on the porch.

"Afternoon, Gertie."

"Hot 'nough for you?"

"It is."

"Same for me." She reined in her lanky dun mare. "You all ready for the Fourth? Miz Gold's been workin' so hard, it's a wonder she ain't drowned in her own sweat."

"I know. Sadie has decided I'm to carry the flag in the parade."

Gertie cocked an eyebrow. "A parade?"

"Right down Main Street. With clowns and music and dogs dressed up in little outfits."

She laughed, a riotous sound coming straight from her belly. "Well, don't that beat all." She dismounted in a fluid motion. "I heard tell there was gonna be fireworks, but this is the first I heard of a parade." Holding the reins in one hand, she stepped toward him, placing a foot on the lower step of the porch. Then she touched the brim of her Stetson with two gloved fingers and pushed the hat back on her head. "Mind if I ask you somethin'?" Her smile had disappeared.

"Of course not, Gertie. What is it?"

"Well, I was thinkin'... I was thinkin' you might like some company at the picnic. I can't cook a lick, mind you, but Miz Butler'll pack me somethin' t'feed the two of us."

Rick's eyes widened in surprise.

"Now don't go thinkin' I'd ask just anybody to join me." A rush of color infused her cheeks. "I just figured, you bein' here alone, without your son an' all, that you might like somebody t'see you're fed right."

"Your invitation is most kind and very much appreciated. I'd be glad to join you, Gertie."

She removed her hat and raked her fingers through her tousled hair, then slapped the Stetson against her thigh, raising a small flurry of dust. "Well, good. Glad that's settled. I just didn't want t'see you alone." She turned and quickly remounted her horse. "See ya on the Fourth." She tapped her heels against the mare's sides and, without a backward glance, rode toward the general store.

Rick stared after her. Gertie Duncan was an odd but thoughtful young woman. She would have made someone a nice daughter-in-law. Him, for instance.

Immediately he was ashamed. James loved his wife. It wasn't up to Rick to be wishing his son had married someone else. It was Rick's own fault Nancy didn't like him. He was the guilty one.

Drake sat beneath the tall cottonwood, staring at the river as it rolled by, his thoughts drifting with it.

Unable to sleep, he'd left the house at dawn and walked to this quiet refuge. There certainly wasn't any peace and quiet in his own home. Not with Faith there. His entire routine had been blithely destroyed by the woman. She'd made him question everything, and he was tired of wrestling with himself, with his past, with God.

And he wasn't the only one affected. His men weren't inclined to get much work done anymore. They loitered around the kitchen and the back porch all hours of the day, talking to Faith, grinning, and making fools of themselves.

Idiots!

That thought had no sooner formed than he heard the crunching of dried twigs. Couldn't he be alone even *here?*

He glared in the direction of the sound. A moment later, Alex pushed his way through the dense underbrush. The boy carried a bucket in one hand, and over his right eye he wore a patch. Just as he reached the river's edge, he stumbled over a rock and nearly pitched headfirst into the water, then toppled sideways instead. Drake stood quickly and grabbed the boy by the arm, pulling him away from the river.

Alex looked up. Alarm momentarily lingered in his expression, then disappeared, replaced by a grin. He pushed the patch onto his forehead. "You were sure right about this thing, Mr. Rutledge. It makes it really hard to see, don't it? I walked into a door yesterday. Almost blacked my eyes. Didn't even know it was there."

"Is that so?"

Alex nodded. "Yeah. Makes me feel funny, too. Like I've been spinnin' around a lot. All dizzy-like. Is that what it's like for you?"

Drake turned away.

"Are you used to it now?" the boy persisted.

"Yes." *Go away.*

"Hey, thanks for grabbin' me just then. I'm not a very good swimmer."

"You're welcome." Drake glanced down at the boy and scowled.

Alex was oblivious of the subtle hint.

"Does your mother know you're here?"

Alex's gaze dropped guiltily to the ground.

"You might have drowned, boy."

Drake knew too well how an accident could snuff out a life, how it could change everything for those left behind. He thought of Faith, imagined her beautiful eyes full of tears for her lost son. The image made his chest ache.

He took hold of Alex's arm a second time. "You don't come down to the river again unless an adult is with you. Do you understand me?"

"Yes, sir."

"See that you mind."

Alex shuffled one foot, kicking up pebbles. "You're not going to tell Ma, are you?"

Drake subdued a groan as he released his hold and sat down again, his back against the cottonwood's trunk.

"Please don't tell her. She's been real happy lately, and I don't want her worryin' about me. Ma's always worried too much, even before we was all alone."

Despite himself, Drake was intrigued. "Where is your father?"

"We haven't seen or heard from him since he run out on us. Don't know where he is." Alex held himself a little straighter, and his tone became belligerent. "But I don't care. We can take care of ourselves. We're doin' all right without him." His voice lowered. "He just made Ma cry anyway."

Drake had the urge to hit the absent Mr. Butler.

The silence grew thick and uncomfortable.

All of a sudden, Alex brightened and said, "Hey, you oughta see what I've learned to do. I can saddle a horse all by myself. Gertie taught me. I'm going to be a wrangler, just like her." He motioned toward the house and barn. "You want to see?" He reached out, as if to help Drake up from the ground.

Drake stared at the small hand, then looked into the pair of hopeful, excited eyes.

The last thing in the world he wanted was to get mixed up in the problems of his housekeeper and her children. The last thing in the world he wanted was to watch this boy saddle a horse in the middle of a hot July day. The last thing in the world he wanted was to leave this cool, serene place by the river.

But for some unknown reason, he took hold of that small hand and allowed himself to be led away.

"Go on, Mrs. Butler," Johnny Coltrain urged. "Do some more."

"Cain't say I like anythin' so much as listenin' to you recite them lines," Will Kidd added.

Seated on a bench near the back porch, Faith lowered the mending into her lap. She glanced from one man to the other. She knew it wouldn't matter what play or scene she chose. She'd found that the cowboys at the Jagged R were easily pleased, whether with her cooking or her acting. Would that all of her audiences through the years had been so.

Drawing a deep breath, she began. "'Let me not to the marriage of true minds / Admit impediments; love is not love / Which alters when it alteration finds, / Or bends with the remover to remove. / O no! it is an ever-fixèd mark / That looks on tempests and is never shaken; / It is the star to every wand'ring bark, / Whose worth's unknown, although his height be taken.'" Tears stung her eyes and longing filled her heart. She imagined Drake Rutledge speaking the words to her. "'Love's not Time's fool, though rosy lips and cheeks / Within his bending sickle's compass come; / Love alters not with his brief hours and weeks, / But bears it out even to the edge of doom. / If this be error and upon me proved, / I never writ, nor no man ever loved.'"

Her small audience began to applaud, drawing Faith abruptly from her thoughts.

"Well," Will said almost reverently, "if that ain't the prettiest thing I ever heard. I could just stand here and listen t'you all day."

She opened her eyes, feeling flushed and embarrassed.

"Me, too," Johnny declared.

Will set his hat on his head. "Now—" he cleared his throat—"if I could just figure out what you was sayin'."

The two cowboys laughed, and Faith laughed with them, pretending a merriment she didn't feel.

"Come on, Johnny." Will slapped the young cowboy on the back. "There's work t'be done."

Johnny touched his hat brim. "Thanks, Mrs. Butler. I sure did enjoy that."

"You're very welcome."

She shook her head as she returned her attention to the mending. She would do well to practice some comedies, she decided. She'd fallen victim to her own performances. She had only been feeling what Shakespeare wanted the audience to feel. Nothing more.

"Pure silliness," she muttered to herself. "I don't want Mr. Rutledge to say any such things to me. Not ever." It wasn't right. No, she had no business thinking such thoughts.

Mrs. Whitehall had once told Faith she didn't understand the real meaning of the word *love*. "It's supposed to be patient and kind, Faith. It isn't jealous or boastful or proud or rude. When it's the real thing, love won't demand its own way or be irritable or keep a record of when it's been wronged. Love's not glad about injustice but rejoices whenever the truth wins out. Love never gives up, never loses faith, is hopeful, and endures through every circumstance. Love'll last forever. That's what the Good Book says."

Is that sort of love really possible, Lord?

Perhaps, she answered herself, but not for her.

Just then Drake strode into the yard, holding the hand of her son. Faith's heart tightened in her chest at the sight. She could hear Alex chattering, although she couldn't make out his words. His face was alight with pleasure as he gazed up at the man beside him. A moment later they disappeared through the open door of the barn.

Curious, Faith laid aside her mending, rose from the bench, and crossed the yard.

The interior was stifling, even with the doors at both ends thrown open to catch any breeze. Earthy scents singular to barns filled her nostrils as she stepped inside. She paused beyond the square of sunlight and gave her eyes a moment to adjust.

"See?" she heard Alex say across the barn. "You gotta be real careful to make sure this strap is laid flat or you could cause a sore right here behind her leg."

Drake leaned his forearms on the top railing of a stall, watching as Faith's son tightened the cinch of a saddle on a buckskin-colored horse.

"Gertie says I'm a quick learner and that I'll make a good wrangler when I grow up." Alex glanced over his shoulder. "You think so, Mr. Rutledge?"

"I suppose so."

"Maybe I can work at the Jagged R. I like it here a lot." Alex caught sight of Faith just then. "Ma, come see what I can do."

She sent her son a smile, responding to his youthful enthusiasm. Then Drake turned, and she felt her heart skip a beat. She walked across the barn, stopping on the opposite side of the stall door, standing as far away from Drake as good manners allowed.

"This is Sugar," Alex told her as he stroked the horse's neck. "I've been helpin' Gertie doctor her leg. See?" He reached down and lifted the buckskin's left front hoof. "She was hurt real bad, but she's almost better now."

"*Miss Duncan*—" Faith emphasized the name—"says you've been a big help to her."

Alex beamed.

"Your son wants to be the next Jagged R wrangler."

Her pulse skipped again as she turned to look at him. *Be careful!* her mind warned, but her heart didn't listen. "I know," she replied softly.

Drake had never seen eyes quite like Faith's. Not blue, yet not truly green. Large eyes, framed by long mahogany lashes. Expressive eyes that seemed to change with her mood.

What was it he read in those unusual blue-green eyes now?

She looked away, as if to keep him from finding the answer to his unspoken question. "Unsaddle the horse, Alex," she said, "and come inside. It's time for me to start preparations for supper, and I could use your help."

"Ah, Ma. I don't—"

"Alexander," she warned softly.

"But—"

"You'd better do as she says," Drake interrupted.

Faith turned to meet Drake's gaze a second time, and he was struck afresh by her loveliness. But there was more, he realized. It went deeper than handsome ancestors and a patrician bone structure.

She has a beauty of spirit, too.

In that moment he forgot his anger, all the many reasons Faith Butler irritated him, all the reasons he had for avoiding a beautiful woman like her. He forgot that she had turned his routine existence upside down. He forgot that he wanted to be left alone in his once dark library. He forgot all about bitterness and loneliness, bad memories and unwelcome tomorrows. He forgot everything except the lovely woman standing before him.

As if she'd seen something that frightened her, Faith took a step back from him. "I'd best see to supper," she said, barely above a whisper. "Alex, come with me." Then she hurried away.

"Don't see why I have to help," the boy muttered. "I got horses to tend to. Gertie needs me to—"

Drake said, "Do as your mother says." Then he, too, left the barn, silently pondering what had just happened and what it might mean in the days to come.

8

THE pewter sky of twilight was broken by pink-stained clouds on the western horizon. Mountain ranges had turned the color of ripe grapes, and tall trees—lodgepole pine and ponderosa, tamarack and quaking aspen, chokecherry and box elder—stood as ebony sentinels over a cooling earth.

With the children in bed and the last of her chores finished, Faith stepped out the back door. She was thankful for a moment to herself, yet her thoughts brought anything but peace.

"I should leave Dead Horse," she whispered. "I should go to Cheyenne and then find a way back to New York."

But she knew she wouldn't go. Not yet.

Becca was better, but she wasn't strong enough to travel. Chances were slim—no, nonexistent—that Faith could find another job that would provide a home and decent food for her children. And Alex was so incredibly happy here. And . . .

She pressed her hands against her stomach, trying to drive away the knot that had formed there earlier in the day and had lingered ever since.

What's wrong with me?

She knew the answer to her own question.

Drake.

"O God, what am I to do with these unwanted feelings?"

She settled onto the stoop, her arms wrapped around her shins, her feet on the next step down. She rested her chin on her knees and watched as the first stars began to wink in the darkening heavens.

God hated divorce, the Bible said. Faith supposed He hated it even more than she did. Mrs. Whitehall had told her that she was forgiven for all of her past sins the moment she'd come to Christ. But Faith didn't *feel* forgiven for this one. She'd failed so miserably in her marriage, and her children paid the price for that failure along with her every day. She and they would always wear the stain of divorce, just as she had worn it because of her own parents.

"If I'd been a better wife, maybe..."

FAITH TINGLED WITH TRIUMPH. *Applause still thundered in her ears as she walked along the darkened streets of New York toward the small apartment she and George had rented for the run of the show. Exhilaration quickened her steps.*

Opening night had been everything she'd hoped it would be. In truth, it had been even more than she'd hoped. Only one thing had marred this night: George's absence. He hadn't come to the theater to watch her.

But Faith refused to think about that now. His mood would change once she told him about the enormous success of the play. Things would be better between them. Things would be as she'd dreamed they would be when they were first married.

Perhaps they'd be able to buy a little house of their own.

George would find a job that he liked, one he would keep, perhaps start his own business. Yes, this play would change things for them. From now on it was going to be better. Faith would become a famous actress, and George would be proud of her. The children would have warm clothes and plenty to eat. George would remember to be kind to her. He would learn to be tender. He wouldn't . . . he wouldn't be so . . . so . . .

A light snow began to fall, and Faith pulled her threadbare coat more tightly about her, fighting a sudden urge to cry.

Why should she cry? Things were going to be wonderful now. There was no more reason to cry.

A few minutes later, Faith climbed the stairs to their fourth-floor apartment and let herself in. The parlor was dark, but she didn't need a light to find her way to the bed tucked in the back corner of the room.

She leaned down and kissed her sleeping children. Alex, not yet five, slept with both arms thrown above his head, taking the lion's share of the thin mattress. Little Becca, barely three, was curled into a ball, her thumb in her mouth. Smoothing their hair away from their foreheads, Faith whispered that she loved them.

She stood gazing at them, imagining the wonderful future she wanted to give them. A house with a yard for them to play in. No more cramped apartments that smelled of cooking grease and garbage. If this play made her famous, the Butlers could have all of those things. They could be a happy family.

She straightened and turned toward the bedroom, where a soft light glowed beneath the closed door. George was awake. He'd waited up for her. When she told him the news, things would get better. She knew they would.

"George," she said softly as she pushed the door open.

She heard him swear, saw him sit up in bed. She watched as

the girl with the flowing golden hair sat up beside him. A blessed numbness spread through Faith, a numbness that seemed to separate her from what was happening, as if she were watching it happen to someone else.

The numbness didn't last.

"George?" Faith whispered. "The children." She glanced over her shoulder. "The children."

"Listen, Faith." Her husband rose from the bed.

She pressed her back against the doorjamb. "Why is she here? How could you, George? How could you?"

He took a step toward her. "I'm leaving. I can't stay here. I wasn't meant to live like this. I was meant for better things."

"But I'm your wife. And the children. What about the children?"

George shrugged. "You're their mother. You'll see that they don't starve. Besides, you're the one who wanted them." He lowered his voice. "I'm getting a divorce."

Faith bolted for the kitchen, where she emptied her stomach into the sink. By the time the retching stopped, George had joined her in the tiny room off the parlor.

"I don't want a divorce," she said, her throat burning.

"Don't get in my way, Faith. You try to stop me, I'll take the children from you and make sure you never see them again. Do you understand me? I can do it. Don't think I can't."

The pain in her chest was unbearable. "I've loved you. We were happy once. We could be again."

The blonde appeared in the parlor doorway, not even feigning embarrassment. "It's time to go, George. Are you finished with her? We've got a train to catch."

"I'm coming." He reached out and touched Faith's cheek. "No hard feelings, honey."

Faith closed her eyes as those words from the past echoed in her head. *No hard feelings, honey.*

Perhaps she'd suspected, even on her wedding day, that George would never stay. But she'd been eighteen and in love with a dazzling man, a charmer. She'd trusted him as only a girl of eighteen could trust, and then she'd mourned the death of her marriage as only the disillusioned and heartbroken could mourn. She'd decided on the night George walked out the door that she would never risk loving a man again.

Faith took a deep breath, driving away the persistent, unwelcome images of Drake Rutledge. She wouldn't think of him. She wouldn't.

As if coming to rescue Faith from her troubled thoughts, Gertie appeared out of the darkness. "Evenin', Miz Butler," the wrangler said. "Nice night, ain't it?"

It was a beautiful night, but Faith had barely noticed.

"I'm not disturbin' you, am I? If I am, just say so an' I'll make myself scarce."

"No, you're not disturbing me." In truth, she was thankful for her company.

Gertie leaned her back against the porch railing, looking up at the canopy of stars now twinkling overhead. "You ever wonder what them stars look like on the other side of the world?"

"Much the same as they do to us, I imagine."

"You ever been to another country?"

"No."

"Me neither. Doc has. I heard him tell once about goin' t'England and Paris and Rome." She grunted. "I ain't been farther east than

Kansas. Don't have no notion how the rest of the world lives. All I've ever known is mountains, plains, and horses."

Faith nodded but remained silent.

"I don't have no education. Don't even speak proper, and I know that for a fact. There ain't nothin' I like better than listenin' t'you, Miz Butler."

"Why, thank you, Gertie."

"I can't read, neither. Leastwise, not much more'n my name." She removed her hat, then turned toward Faith. "You reckon I could learn?"

"I'm sure you could."

"You reckon you could teach me?"

"Me?" Faith shook her head. "I'm not a teacher."

"You're teachin' Alex, ain't you?"

"Yes, but—"

"I won't be no bother."

"I didn't think you would." She smiled gently. "I suppose I could try."

"Thanks." Gertie slapped her hat against her thigh a couple of times, then sat on the bottom step.

Faith had the distinct impression her new friend had more on her mind than just learning to read. "You reckon a fella could ever take notice of a gal like me?" Gertie's voice was hesitant.

So *that* was the problem. A man.

Perhaps a man was always the problem.

Gertie twisted on the step and looked at Faith. "I guess what I'm really askin' is, do you think you could help make me look more ... more like a woman? I know it'd be like turnin' a sow's ear into a silk purse, but I ... I ... well, you see, I invited Doc t'eat with me at the picnic on the Fourth, and ... well, I just thought ..." Her voice drifted into silence.

Hearing Gertie's desperation, Faith couldn't help smiling again.

She leaned forward. "You're no sow's ear, Gertie Duncan, and I'd be delighted to help."

"I don't expect no miracles, mind you."

"It won't take a miracle. Why don't you come to my room tomorrow morning after breakfast?"

"All right." Gertie cleared her throat. "There's one more thing. I know I already asked enough favors. But, you see, I promised Doc you'd fix the lunch. I can't cook a lick, and I'd sure hate t'poison him."

Faith laughed as she placed a hand on Gertie's shoulder. "Of course I'll fix the picnic lunch for you. But only if you will please stop calling me Mrs. Butler. I'm Faith. Remember?"

"Agreed." Grinning, the wrangler rose and set her hat on her head. "Guess I'll be turnin' in."

"Good night, Gertie."

"Night, Faith. And thanks again." She set off with long, yard-eating strides, quickly disappearing around the corner of the house.

Dr. Telford and Gertie. They were an unlikely pair.

As unlikely as Drake and me?

She groaned as the images she'd sought to forget came rushing back. With her elbows on her knees, Faith rested her forehead against the heels of her hands.

"Go away," she whispered. "Go away and leave me alone."

Drake rode again that night.

He began by following the familiar pattern of galloping madly across the plains. But for some reason, midway in his flight, he reined in, drawing his pinto to a halt alongside the river. He stared into the ribbon of water glittering with reflected starlight and thought of his mother. The memory was not of her tragic death and his blame for it, as it had been for years. Instead, he recalled her life, her love of God, her patience, her joy. He thought of the peacefulness of her countenance, of the love she'd shown to everyone, especially to her husband and son.

Let go of your anger and bitterness, Drake, her voice whispered in his memory.

He closed his eyes.

Trust God, my darling son. Don't blame Him for your troubles. He isn't the cause. He's the answer. Accept His forgiveness.

Drake remembered the day his mother had spoken those words to him, although he couldn't remember what the exact trouble had been. Something that would seem minor now, he supposed.

Yet he believed she would say those same words to him again now if she were able.

Drake lifted his gaze toward heaven. *Would You forgive me, God? Even for causing my mother's death?*

And somehow, he knew the answer.

Yes.

Suddenly, he felt as though a great weight had been lifted. He could breathe. Where fury had been for so long there was a sudden and profound peace. And hope.

Yes.

He thought of Faith Butler then. He thought of how his house had changed since the day she'd arrived, how darkness had become light, how his routine had altered, even how his ranch hands were different. But the anger he'd felt for those changes was gone, and even here there was hope, hope for something he'd thought he would never want again.

She was beautiful and talented. There was no reason in the world to believe she might remain at the Jagged R longer than a matter of weeks. But he hoped she would. Drake wasn't a whole man. He was half blind and his face was scarred, disfigured. There was no reason to believe any woman would ever choose to be with him.

And yet the hope remained.

Drake nudged the pinto's ribs with his heels, turning his horse in the direction of the ranch house. After a short while, he kicked the gelding into a gallop.

But this time he wasn't racing from the past. Instead he was riding toward his future.

9

GERTIE looked into the mirror with a mixture of curiosity and horror. Surely that creature wasn't her!

"It's too short, of course," Faith said, kneeling on the floor as she checked the hem of the dress, "but there's plenty of fabric here. We can let it down. We'll have to take it in here and there because you're so slender, but you'll look lovely when it's done."

"Who're you tryin' to fool? I ain't never looked this ridiculous since my ma tried t'put my hair in ringlets when I was knee-high." She turned from the mirror. "Tryin' t'be what I ain't. If this ain't the stupidest idea I ever come up with, then I don't know what is."

"You're wrong, Gertie." Faith stood. "You're just not used to wearing a dress. When we alter it to fit you properly, Dr. Telford won't be able to take his eyes off you."

Gertie wanted to believe everything could be fixed with a bit of sewing, but she couldn't. Not when she only had to look at her reflection to know otherwise. She wasn't cut out to look like a woman, and she knew it. Especially when she stood next to Faith.

"Who said I cared what Doc thought, anyways?" she muttered.

Faith's laughter was soft and airy. "You're not going to lie to me now, are you?"

Gertie released a deep sigh as she sank onto the edge of the bed, her knees apart, her hands clasped between them in the folds of the skirt. "It ain't no use nohow."

"Why not?" Faith sat beside her.

"You think an educated man like Doc would take notice of the likes o' me? I'm just another cowpoke from the Jagged R Ranch, far as he's concerned. He don't even know I'm female." She snorted in derision. "I didn't hardly know it myself 'til I thought about kissin' him." At the admission, heat rushed to her cheeks.

Faith put her arm around Gertie's shoulders and gave her a squeeze. "Looks aren't the only thing that attracts a man to a woman, and if they were, you wouldn't want him anyway."

Gertie cast a sideways glance at Faith, noting the firm set of her mouth and the look of sadness in her blue-green eyes. Briefly she wondered who'd put the hurt there. Then Faith smiled and the sadness was gone, leaving Gertie to wonder if it had been there at all.

"Tell me about Rick Telford," Faith encouraged. "What attracted you to him? Was it merely *his* appearance?"

" 'Course not."

"Then tell me what."

Gertie thought a moment, then answered, "He's smart, for one thing. You don't become as good a doctor as he is without bein' smart. And he's a gentleman, too. Real refined and distinguished-like. I never seen nobody with better manners. I admire him a lot for what he's done, quittin' drinkin' and all." She shook her head. "He sure as all git-out has plenty of patience. Just look at who he's gotta live with. You're too new here t'know, but if you ask me, that there daughter-in-law of his would drive a saint to commit murder. But he's always been kind as can be with her. I don't know how he does it. There's plenty of times I'd like to've punched her square between the eyes, and I don't have t'live with her."

Faith laughed again. "It's good you haven't punched her."

"Yeah. It's not somethin' a lady would do, I reckon. But then, I ain't never been mistaken for a lady." Gertie shrugged. "Or a woman either, for that matter."

Faith rose, then turned and took hold of Gertie's hands, pulling her to her feet. "Come over here." She drew Gertie to the mirror. "Now, I want you to quit seeing yourself as a wrangler or cowpoke or whatever. You *are* a woman, and Rick Telford would be blind not to notice. See how pretty that curl in your hair is, and look at the way it shines in the sunlight after it's been washed. You're lucky to be able to wear it short like that. You don't have to spend lots of time in the morning with a hairbrush and hairpins. And see how slender you are. Why, you'll never go to fat, Gertie. Not in a hundred years. And your eyes are the prettiest shade of blue I think I've ever seen."

Gertie met the other woman's gaze in the glass. "You're a right fine actress, Faith Butler. You almost got me believin' what you're sayin'."

"I'm only telling the truth."

Drake leaned back on his chair, his fingers steepled against his chin as he stared across the desk at his ranch foreman. "In your opinion, what are the chances of getting the railroad through Dead Horse?"

"Without the promised shipment of Jagged R cattle, probably none," Parker answered. "They'll most likely choose another route. But with your support, I'd say the chances are good. The railroad cares about one thing. Making money. If we can show it's more profitable for them to come up our way, they'll do it."

Drake glanced toward the window. "What sort of man is James Telford?"

"Young. Bright. He's a good representative for the town."

"And he owns the hotel?"

"Yeah."

Drake rose and crossed the library. He leaned his right shoulder against the window casing as he gazed across the yard. Two cowpokes stood talking outside the bunkhouse. Another—Johnny Coltrain, he thought—worked a young horse inside the corral. Alex Butler sat on the top rail, observing the training session. Swede Swenson stood in the shade of the barn, shoeing a big white gelding, an ugly animal with pink-rimmed eyes and a deep scoop in his nose.

"It won't matter one way or the other to the Jagged R if Dead Horse survives," Drake observed. "We'll be here no matter what. What's kept the rest of them from leaving before now?"

Parker remained silent.

Drake turned to look at him. He understood Parker's surprise; today was the first time he'd shown any interest in Dead Horse and its inhabitants. No doubt the man was curious about what brought about the transformation. Drake smiled and leaned forward. "I'd really like to know."

Parker joined him by the window. "Well, let's see now. The Golds, Sadie and Joseph, run the general store. They're Jewish and haven't always been welcome where they've lived. They've moved around and know how hard it is to start over. They've got six kids and would like to stay put."

Drake nodded.

"James and Nancy Telford own the hotel. A young couple, just starting out. No children yet. James used to work for the bank, when the town still had one. He bought the hotel after Seamus O'Connell died."

Drake narrowed his eyes thoughtfully. "If James is so bright, why invest in a dying town? Why not move someplace where he'd get a better return on his money?"

"Because of his father."

"His father?" Drake was intrigued. "What about the doctor?"

"Rick needed a place to start over. Dead Horse gave him the chance he needed."

Drake waited for him to continue.

"Rick was a drunk, plain and simple. Didn't have much of a practice, from what I hear tell. Then his wife died. He blamed himself— and I guess so did the folks in the town where they were livin'. So he came to Dead Horse to stay with his son, and he sobered up. After a while, he started practicin' medicine again. When things started goin' bad for the town, James didn't want to move away, pull the rug out from under Rick, so he and Nancy stayed and took over the hotel."

Drake thought of his own father, remembered what it had been like watching Clyde Rutledge grow old before his time, watching his father grieve himself into an early grave, all the while blaming his son. Drake was thankful for God's forgiveness, but he would give almost anything to have had his father's forgiveness, too. But it was too late for that.

"Go on," he told Parker. "Who are the others?"

"Well, there's Jed Smith, the postmaster. He lost a leg back during the war. Only place I've ever seen him is on the boardwalk in front of the post office. Sits there, smokin' his pipe and talkin' to anyone who stops by. Stretch Barns owns the saloon. Beatrice ... hmm, don't rightly know if she even has a last name. Anyways, Beatrice works for Stretch, serving drinks and such. Claire O'Connell— Seamus's widow—she runs the hotel restaurant for the Telfords." He scratched his head thoughtfully. "Oh, yeah. There's the widow Ashley. She calls herself a dressmaker, but I doubt she's had much work the last few years. She's gettin' up in years. Don't suppose she's got anywhere else to go."

While Parker talked, Drake tried to imagine the town and the people who lived there, but he couldn't. Seven years he'd been in this house, and he didn't know those places of business, didn't know the people Parker named.

What did that say about him? he wondered.

He focused his attention on the activities outside his window, realizing he didn't even know the men who worked for him. Oh, he knew their names and what they looked like. But what else did he know?

"Parker," he said without turning his head, "it's been a long time."

After a moment his foreman responded, "Yeah, boss, it has."

"You've been a good friend."

"I've tried to be."

Another silence filled the room.

Finally Drake said, "Someday I'll tell you about it."

Parker didn't ask what Drake meant. He must have known. "When you're ready." Without another word, Parker crossed the library and let himself out, closing the door behind him.

"Show me how to make a *B* again, Mama."

Faith looked across the kitchen table at Becca. The girl's face was wrinkled in concentration as she stared at the paper and chewed on the end of her pencil.

"I don't remember how," Becca added, glancing up. "Show me again."

Faith subdued a sigh. At this rate she would never finish the alterations on Gertie's dress. But how could she complain about her daughter's curiosity? or her improving health? If Becca wasn't feeling so much better, she wouldn't be bored and restless. It was getting more and more difficult to find ways to occupy Becca's time and still make certain the girl got the rest she needed.

Faith put down her sewing and went around to the other side of the table. She took the pencil from her daughter's hand, then leaned forward and drew the letter slowly. "Now you show me."

Becca drew a whole line of *B*s, her tongue sticking out between her lips as she frowned. When she was done, she glanced at her mother with an air of triumph. The smile disappeared a moment later.

Faith followed her daughter's gaze across the room, straightening abruptly when she saw her employer standing the doorway.

"Look who's up," Drake said. "She must be feeling better."

Faith nodded. "Yes."

His gaze dropped to the girl, and then he did something totally unexpected.

He smiled.

Faith knew that he said something to Becca, but she wasn't sure what. She was completely captivated by the curve of his mouth beneath his dark, closely trimmed mustache. His smile had the strangest effect on her.

He moved into the kitchen, stopping on the opposite side of the table. He placed his hands on the back of the chair where Faith had been seated only moments before. "Learning your letters already?"

"I can write my name." Becca looked at her mother, then admitted, "Well, sometimes I forget."

Faith pressed a hand against her abdomen, trying to stop the fluttering sensation inside. "Was there something you needed, Mr. Rutledge?"

He looked up, their eyes met, and her heart skipped another beat.

"Not really," he replied.

"Oh." The word came out as a whisper.

"Mama's helpin' make a dress for Miss Duncan."

"Miss Duncan? *Our* Miss Duncan?" His left eyebrow arched, and the corners of his mouth lifted another notch. "In a *dress?*"

Faith nodded.

"I'd like to see that."

"You can." Why did it seem she had so little air in her lungs? "My invitation is still open."

"Invitation?"

"To join the children and me in Dead Horse for the Fourth of July." She had a sudden vision of the four of them, sitting on a blanket, watching fireworks against a black sky. Her heart raced, and her knees felt ridiculously weak.

Drake stared at her for what seemed an eternity, his dark eyes never wavering, his expression unreadable. Finally he shook his head. "Another time, perhaps." He stepped back from the chair. "But thank you for asking me, Mrs. Butler. I do appreciate it." Then he turned and strode out of the kitchen.

A dozen heartbeats later, Faith whispered, "You're quite welcome, Mr. Rutledge."

"Mama, are you all right? You look sort of funny."

She glanced down at her daughter, then drew a deep breath. "I'm fine, sweetheart. I was just thinking."

Forcing herself to move, Faith returned to her chair and picked up her sewing. As she slipped the needle and thread through the fabric of Gertie's dress, she wondered if she'd told her daughter the truth.

Perhaps she wasn't all right.

Perhaps there was something wrong.

Terribly, dangerously wrong.

With her heart.

10

REVEREND Harold Arnold, the circuit rider who came to Dead Horse once every four to five weeks, was in town for the Fourth of July. His sermon that morning, preached beneath a Rocky Mountain maple behind the hotel, was on the true freedom that came from knowing Christ. The minister then led the small body of worshipers in song, and Faith joined in, her voice full of joy. She had much to praise God for, she thought as she glanced down at Becca.

When the hymn was finished and the service complete, Faith introduced herself and her children to the minister. "It's been far too long since I've heard a sermon preached by an ordained minister, Reverend Arnold. You were most inspiring."

"Thank you, Mrs. Butler. It was a pleasure to see new faces amongst my flock this morning. I suspect several of those men from the Jagged R were here because of you more than me." He grinned. "I hope you plan to remain in Dead Horse."

"I'd like to stay." Realizing what she'd said, she felt a jolt of surprise. *Would I like to stay in Dead Horse?*

The answer was simple: *Yes.*

"That would be wonderful," Reverend Arnold continued. "Perhaps next time I'll get to meet Mr. Rutledge himself." He leaned down and shook Alex's hand. "How about you, young man? Would you like to stay in Dead Horse?"

"Would I ever!"

What had she done? She'd given the minister and Alex the impression that they might remain here, but she hadn't the slightest idea how long Drake Rutledge meant to keep her on as his housekeeper. When he'd hired her, he'd told her that she could stay only until Becca was well.

Listening now as Alex regaled Reverend Arnold with his aspirations of being a wrangler when he was older, Faith comforted herself by remembering the changes she'd observed in her employer. He no longer seemed so angry at having Faith and her children in his home. Perhaps he would decide he needed a housekeeper for more than a few weeks or months.

Becca tugged at her skirt. "Mama?"

"What is it, dear?"

"I'm hungry."

The minister chuckled. "Your daughter has the right idea. I'm rather hungry myself. I'm sure the good women of Dead Horse have prepared a fine feast for this day. Mind if I walk with you, Mrs. Butler?"

She shook her head. "Of course not."

Alex ran ahead as Faith, Reverend Arnold, and Becca moved at a more sedate speed toward the picnic area near the river, where long planks had been set up on sawhorses and covered with sheets. Men stood in small groups beneath the shade of the trees, talking and laughing, while the women loaded the makeshift tables with food, their voices rising in a friendly hum.

Faith excused herself and, with Becca close beside her, went to claim the picnic basket from the back of the Rutledge buggy. Then they approached the tables.

Sadie Gold greeted Faith with enthusiasm, giving her a hug and treating her as if they were lifelong friends. Hooking her arm through Faith's, Sadie drew her into the midst of the other women. "I'm sure you saw most everyone at your church service, but let me introduce you again."

Faith felt uncertain and shy. And hopeful. She wanted to fit in, to belong. She didn't want to be judged and found wanting, as had happened so often in her past—an actress *and* a divorcée. How scandalous!

Unmindful of Faith's trepidation, Sadie began, "This is Claire O'Connell. Claire runs the hotel restaurant. But of course the two of you must have met when you were staying there. This is Mary O'Rourke. Mary and her husband have a farm south of town. These are my daughters. Ruth here is my oldest, then Naomi, Esther, and Tamar. My two sons are off somewhere. Getting into mischief, no doubt." She grinned and gave a small shrug. "But then, when aren't young boys into mischief, I'd like to know?"

Names swirled in Faith's head, but she didn't have a chance to respond or hardly draw a breath before Sadie continued the whirlwind introductions.

"This is Madge Ashley. Madge here makes the prettiest dresses and hats. Prettiest you've ever seen." Sadie swept the picnic area with her gaze. "Where's Agnes? She was here a minute ago. Hmm. I guess she went to nurse her baby. You'll have to meet her later."

Faith braced herself for rejection, but it never came. The women of Dead Horse made her feel welcome.

I'd like to stay in this place, Father. Is it possible that could be Your plan for us? To stay here?

For Faith, the day was a complete delight.

Alex found a couple of soul mates in Samuel and David Gold. When they weren't busy stuffing themselves with the vast array of food the women of Dead Horse had prepared, they were capturing grasshoppers or climbing trees or tossing a ball.

Becca made friends with three-year-old Alice Horne. The two of them sat quietly on a blanket and played with their rag dolls. It did Faith's heart good to see the rosy color in her daughter's cheeks and hear her laughter. Today it was possible to believe the doctor was wrong about Becca's fragile health. Today it was possible to believe only the best of everything.

Faith was delighted by the stir caused when Gertie arrived. She stifled the laughter rising in her throat as the female wrangler, riding astride her horse in her dress, swung down from the saddle, giving one and all a generous glimpse of her knees and calves.

But Rick Telford saved Gertie from complete embarrassment by hurrying to welcome her. Faith hoped the doctor would look beyond the awkward exterior and see the warmhearted woman beneath.

There were moments when Faith thought about Drake, all alone in his big house on the ridge. Sometimes she felt his aloneness as if it were her own. She wished he were here with her, sitting on the same blanket, eating the picnic lunch she'd prepared. She knew she was dancing too close to a dangerous flame. Love and marriage weren't in her future. She'd learned her lesson. Yet she couldn't help but think of him.

After everyone had eaten their fill, the town's celebration continued with a parade, followed by three-legged races. Parker joined with Alex, and the two of them won the first race, much to Faith's delight. There were also horse races, ring tosses, and a pie-eating contest.

As the day waned, Matt Horne brought out his harmonica and Lon O'Rourke his banjo, and everyone sang along to familiar tunes such as "Darling Nellie Gray" and "I'll Take You Home Again, Kathleen." Even though some folks sang a trifle off-key, the warm camaraderie more than made up for a few sour notes.

With the approach of twilight came the time for Faith's performance. A makeshift stage had been constructed near the general store, and torches had been lit, bathing the boards in a flickering light. The townsfolk stood in the street in a wide semicircle.

Faith was surprised to discover she was more nervous before this small audience than she had been in years. She drew a deep breath to calm herself, then began.

" 'Thou know'st the mask of night is on my face, / Else would a maiden blush bepaint my cheek. . . .' "

Again she thought of Drake, thought of the feelings he'd stirred to life within her. She imagined herself saying these same words to him, and she felt Juliet's blush rise in her cheeks.

" 'Dost thou love me?' "

She imagined him there, in the midst of the audience. He would stand a head above the crowd. She imagined the breadth of his shoulders, his long, raven-black hair, his scarred but handsome face.

" 'O gentle Romeo, / If thou dost love, pronounce it faithfully. . . .' "

Her voice faltered slightly, and it was that which drove Drake's image from her mind. She reminded herself silently not to confuse the play with reality and forced herself to concentrate on her lines.

When she was finished with Juliet's monologue, there was a long hush. Then the silence was broken by riotous applause, shouts, and cheers.

"Faith Butler, that was the most beautiful thing I've heard in all my born days!" Sadie exclaimed as she came forward, taking Faith by the hand. "I was spellbound, pure and simple. Simply spellbound."

"Thank you, Mrs. Gold," she responded, even as her thoughts betrayed her with the wish that Drake could have seen her, too.

Gertie let out a long sigh and cast a sideways glance at the man beside her. Rick was grinning from ear to ear, still staring at the stage, still captivated by Faith's presentation. It was as plain as the nose on Gertie's face that he didn't even remember she was there.

She couldn't blame him. She'd been enthralled, too. She'd listened to Faith practice a time or two at the ranch, but she'd never expected to feel as though she'd been transported somewhere else, as if by magic. Faith had almost had Gertie understanding what that Shakespeare fellow was saying with his *knowest*s and *dost*s and *thou*s and whatnots.

And there sure wasn't nobody nowhere as pretty as Faith Butler. No wonder every jack-man present was acting like he'd been kicked in the head by a wild mustang.

Gertie looked down at the skirt of her dress and knew she'd been acting as loco as any of the men. What had ever made her think Rick would notice her? Oh, he'd been a right nice gentleman all afternoon long. He'd never so much as snickered at her like some of the Jagged R cowpokes had. They'd be ribbing her for weeks to come. It would have been worth it if Rick had acted as though he might take a cotton to her. But, of course, he hadn't.

"Faith was wonderful." The doctor turned to look at Gertie.

"Yeah, she was."

"We won't any of us forget this Fourth of July anytime soon."

"No, I don't reckon we will." She knew she wasn't going to forget it. Not when she'd made such an idiot out of herself.

He took hold of her arm. "I'll escort you back to the blanket. Then I've promised to help with the fireworks."

"I can take care of myself just fine. You go on and do what you gotta do."

"I wouldn't think of it, Miss Duncan." He began walking, drawing her along with him.

Oh mercy, how her heart did hammer!

A fool. That's what I am. A loco, crazy fool.

"I'd like to thank you, Gertie."

"Thank me? Whatever for?"

"For inviting me to join you today, for making certain I wasn't alone while James and Nancy are away." He patted her hand where it rested in the crook of his arm. "And for putting on that dress. I know how you must hate it."

It was the first time he'd mentioned what she was wearing. She'd begun to wonder if he'd even noticed.

"It was very kind of you to do that for an old man like me."

I wasn't bein' kind, Doc, and you're not old.

"I imagine you've turned a few heads today," he continued.

But not yours. Her heart sank.

"James and Nancy will be sorry they didn't return in time when they hear all about today."

"Yeah," she whispered, "I reckon they will."

They reached the blanket, where earlier in the day the two of them had sat together, eating fried chicken and biscuits with honey, and cake with frosting, and more.

As Rick let go of her arm, he placed a fatherly kiss on her cheek. "It's been a great Fourth. Thanks again for spending it with me. I know you would rather have been racing your horse with the other cowboys."

"I . . . I wanted t'spend it with you, Doc."

He patted her shoulder. "You're a thoughtful young woman, Gertie Duncan."

"Oh, bother," she muttered.

Then, thinking she couldn't make things much worse than they already were, she grabbed him by the upper arms and yanked him toward her, kissing him square on the mouth.

When she let him go, she said, "You ain't old and I ain't your daughter, and if you can't figure out what's goin' on, then you're … you're …" She left the sentence unfinished. With a strangled sound of frustration, she whirled around and strode toward the horses as she held the skirt of her dress up to her knees to keep the bothersome thing out of her way.

Drake watched Faith's performance from a distance, staying far back from the rest of the crowd, hidden from view by the night. He was mesmerized by her voice, her movements, her expressions. She became Juliet, an innocent young girl in the first flush of love. He heard the lines she recited and wanted to make his own reply.

" 'But trust me, gentleman, I'll prove more true / Than those that have more cunning to be strange. …' "

His heart missed a beat. Once before he'd heard her speak that line, and he'd been angered by the words. But not this time. This time he believed they could be true. He believed *she* could be true.

The soliloquy ended. The good folks of Dead Horse pressed forward, congratulating and praising Faith. Drake fell back farther into the darkness and observed the adulation while mulling his unsettling thoughts.

Faith had her profession as an actress, and he recognized now what a talent God had given her. He had no reason to hope she might want to stay in Dead Horse.

Or that she might want to stay with him.

Still he hoped it.

The crowd began to disperse, moving toward the river for the fireworks display. Drake turned to slip away, to return to the Jagged R before he was seen. He was too late.

"Mr. Rutledge? Is that you?"

He glanced over his shoulder and saw Faith walking toward him, that exquisite smile lighting her face.

How had she seen him? How had she known it was he in the shadows? "You came. You saw the performance." Her voice was as sweet as nectar, lulling him, holding him there, staying his departure.

"I saw it."

"I didn't think you were coming."

"How could I not come to see you, Mrs. Butler?" He asked the question softly, knowing he shouldn't ask it at all.

Her smile vanished. Her eyes widened.

Drake took a step forward, drawn toward her by some invisible cord. Their eyes held and Drake moved closer. She was so beautiful, so—

"Ma, hurry up!" Alex called from just behind Drake. "The fireworks are gonna start!"

Drake whirled toward the sound even as Faith jumped backward. Not more than half a dozen yards away stood Alex and Becca, waiting for their mother.

"Come on, Mama," Becca added.

"I think you'd better go with your children, Mrs. Butler," Drake said.

She hesitated a moment, and he wondered if she might ask him to stay with her.

"Yes." The word was barely more than a whisper. "I must go."

He didn't move. He simply watched as she hurried away from him, took hold of her children's hands, then walked into the darkness of night, leaving Drake alone once again.

11

FAITH spent a restless night, tossing and turning in her bed, unable to sleep. Whenever she closed her eyes, she envisioned Drake at the precise moment he'd stepped toward her, light from the flickering torches dancing across his handsome face.

He'd been going to embrace her, kiss her. She'd known it. Worse still, she'd wanted it. If Alex and Becca hadn't called for her, she would have allowed it to happen.

With a groan, she sat up and shoved her tangled mass of hair from her face.

Hadn't she trouble enough? she wondered. It was only by the grace of God that she was here. She could be serving drinks in a saloon right now instead of having a decent job and a home for her children. What would happen to them if she forgot her proper place?

She rose and walked to the window to watch the coming of dawn. A moment later Drake and Parker strode into view. They walked to the corral, then led their horses out and began saddling them. Soon the rest of the cowpokes joined them.

Faith felt a flicker of joy at seeing Drake with the men of the Jagged R. He belonged there. She could feel it. She could see it in the way he moved. Confident. Strong. At peace. She knew she'd been witness to a small miracle over the past few days. She didn't understand what had caused the rage within him to cool; she only knew it had been there and now it was gone.

Thank You, Lord.

Suddenly Drake twisted in the saddle, his head turning toward her third-story window. His gaze was shadowed by the brim of his hat, but she knew he'd seen her. Her pulse quickened as she raised her hand in a wave, unable to stop herself.

Then common sense forced her to step back from the window, where she remained until she heard the men riding away.

Guard your heart, Faith. Guard it well.

For years, the Jagged R had been nothing more to Drake than a place to hide from the world. He had left the operation of the ranch to Parker, and his friend had done a good job of it. Rutledge cattle grazed thousands of acres of grasslands, a land free of fences, where feed and water were plentiful.

As he and the men rode across the range, Drake thought how good it was to be with them. It was good to be riding in the daylight, too. No one spoke, but it was a companionable silence. A shared silence among men who understood each other, men who were comfortable with themselves and their work.

The years fell away, taking Drake back to the carefree time of his youth when he'd been like these cowboys, when he'd been a whole man, able to see and to ride and to rope. He wouldn't ever be that young cowboy again, but he could be something different, God willing.

Perhaps he *could* make a difference, for himself and for the people who lived in Dead Horse.

With sudden clarity, Drake realized that if it hadn't been for his accident, he would be trapped in an office in Philadelphia instead of sitting astride a horse, surrounded by majestic mountains and the range land he loved. If he'd married Larissa, he would be handling dull, boring cases for Rutledge and Seever during the day and escorting his beautiful, spoiled wife to staid suppers and musicales in the evenings. He would have been imprisoned by that life as surely as he had been imprisoned by his partial blindness, by his guilt.

Drake was pulled from his private musings by Dan Greer's voice.

"We'll be back by the end of next week," the cowboy told Parker. His gaze shifted to Drake. Then he tugged on his hat brim in a friendly salute, turned his horse, and cantered south, accompanied by Swede Swenson on his ugly white gelding. Moments later, Will Kidd and Johnny Coltrain rode east.

"Come on, Drake." Parker turned his mount in the opposite direction. "We'll check on the line shack up on Cougar Creek."

They moved out at a walk, giving their horses a brief rest.

"You should have come into town with us yesterday," the foreman said. "We had quite the holiday."

"Another time. Folks aren't used to seeing a scar like ..."

"It's not so bad. Your face, I mean."

Drake shrugged, not wanting to remember the way he'd felt when Larissa had turned away from him, as if he were some sort of freak.

Faith doesn't turn away.

No, Faith didn't turn away. She hadn't when she first met him, and she hadn't last night. But Faith was different from Larissa in countless ways. She was wary of him, yes, but not because of his scar. Her reasons were different, something to do with her own past. He could sense it, perhaps because he'd carried a similar hurt for so long. If only he could get her to talk about it. Then maybe he could convince her to stay in Wyoming....

He gave his head a slight shake, as if to dislodge the persistent thoughts. Then he asked, "Did you hear any more news about the railroad?"

"Nope."

"Is Telford expected back soon?"

"Rick seemed to think James and his wife would return by the end of the week."

Drake nodded thoughtfully. "Ask him to come see me."

Parker didn't grin, but there was something in the look he shot Drake that suggested one. "I'll do it."

The two men nudged their horses and cantered toward the mountains in the west.

Gertie glared at the wild-eyed mare. "We can do this the easy way, or we can do this the hard way. But we *are* going to do it."

To be honest, she halfway hoped the mare would give her a rough ride. It would match the turmoil going on inside her.

This woman nonsense was likely to drive Gertie plumb loco. She'd been better off before she'd started feeling all soft and fluttery inside whenever she looked at Doc. What did she think it was gonna get her, anyway? Did she think she was suddenly gonna be as pretty as Faith or something?

She muttered a mild oath, then slowly placed her foot in the stirrup and stepped up onto the saddle.

The mare stood docilely for several heartbeats before exploding into motion. Back arched, the horse rose above the ground, landing with a harsh thump as she twisted and jerked, trying to dislodge Gertie and the hated saddle.

Gertie grinned. "Go on!" she shouted. "Give me what fer!"

Time and again the mare bucked and hopped, spun and whirled. Dirt clods flew into the air, pelting Gertie's cheeks. The only sounds she heard were grunts, both her own and those of the horse. Sweat soaked her hatband. More streamed down her spine. She felt the jarring in her back with every landing, but she kept her seat.

She knew the moment the fight went out of the horse, even though the bucking didn't stop at once. Seconds later, the mare quieted.

Gertie felt both satisfied and saddened. She reached out and stroked the animal's sweat-coated neck. "It won't be so bad next time, girl."

"That was mighty impressive, Miss Duncan."

She looked up suddenly. The horse shied and dislodged Gertie from the saddle. Gertie fell with a thump to the ground. Her hat landed near her feet.

Before she could get up, Rick Telford was inside the corral, kneeling beside her. "Are you hurt?"

Disgusted and embarrassed, she didn't look at him. "No."

"Here." He placed a hand against her back and took hold of her arm with the other one. "Let me help you up." Gently Rick drew her to her feet. "Are you certain you're not hurt?"

"I'm all right."

"Gertie."

She felt heat rising up her neck to her cheeks. "Doc, I—"

"Gertie, look at me."

She knew her face must be covered with dirt and streaked with sweat. Her hair would be sticking flat against her scalp. Her shirt was damp under her arms and along her spine.

Why'd he have to come when she was looking like this?

She pulled her arm away. "What're you doin' here, Doc?"

Screwing up her courage, she looked him straight in the eye and waited for his answer.

"I came to see you."

"Listen, Doc, I'm sorry about last night. I don't know what come over me." She looked away again. "Must've been that stupid dress I was wearin'." She walked after the mare, now standing quietly in a far corner, reins dragging along the ground, head hung low. Gertie figured she knew just how the poor critter felt.

"Gertie, we *need* to discuss what happened." He followed her across the corral.

"What fer?"

"Well, for one thing, I'm old enough to be your father."

"But you *ain't* my father."

"Gertie." He touched her shoulder, urging her to face him. "Take a good look at me."

She did. And she liked what she saw. She knew if she didn't do something plenty quick, she'd wind up throwing herself at him like she'd done the night before. She'd just about die if that happened again. Especially since she knew he had no hankering for her kisses.

Before she could make a complete and utter fool of herself, she stepped around to the other side of the mare and began to loosen the cinch. "Let's just pretend it never happened. Okay, Doc?"

There was a long silence; then he said, "I think that would be wise."

She didn't want to be wise. She wanted him to hold her and kiss her. She hadn't lived with a bunch of cowpokes for the better part of her twenty-five years without learning a thing or two. She might still be as green as grass when it came to actual experience, but she knew what was supposed to happen when a man and woman cared for each other. And she cared for him, all right. Loved him, if truth be told.

She wished she could tell him how she felt, but pride kept her silent. After all, Doc didn't want a sweaty, smelly, bronc-busting wrangler for a wife. She couldn't very well blame him for it, any more than she could change the way she looked or what she was.

"I'd better tend to my business, Doc."

"Gertie," he said her name softly, as if in regret.

She didn't dare look at him. She felt a suspicious lump in her throat, and she feared she might burst into tears, something she'd rather die than do. "You go on now. I can't be standin' around all day jawin' with you."

She yanked the saddle from the mare's back, then turned and slung it over the top rail of the corral. She didn't turn back until she knew he was gone.

Laundry basket in hand, Faith stepped out the back door in time to see the doctor get in his buggy and drive away. Quickly she glanced toward the corral, where she saw Gertie leaning her head against a saddle on the fence.

"Wait here," she told Becca as she set the basket on the porch.

She hurried around the circumference of the corral, stopping when she reached Gertie. "Are you all right?"

Gertie didn't even lift her head. "Can't say as I am."

Faith covered the other woman's hand with her own. "I'm sorry, Gertie."

"I busted my first bronc when I was fourteen. Got my first job on a ranch down in Texas when I was sixteen. They didn't even know I was a girl." She straightened, drawing her hand out from under Faith's, then turned and retrieved her hat from the dirt. She slapped it against her thigh a few times, raising a cloud of dust, before putting it on her head.

Faith remained silent.

Gertie's gaze swung to meet Faith's. "Don't know why I thought Doc'd know I was a woman when every other cowpoke I ever worked with didn't notice."

"Oh, Gertie, I think you're wrong. I think Dr. Telford noticed."

"Lotta good it does me if he did." Her blue eyes were filled with sadness.

Faith offered a slight smile of encouragement. "Sometimes these things take time."

"I better stick with broncs. Even with the wild ones, you've got a good idea what they're gonna do next." She shrugged. "Never know what a man's gonna do." Gertie jerked the saddle off the corral rail, bracing it against her back with her hand on her shoulder. "Reckon I'd best get back to work."

Faith wished she could give Gertie a hug, but she knew such a gesture wouldn't be welcomed.

Never know what a man's gonna do.

Faith thought of last night, of Drake, of the moment when she'd known he wanted to kiss her. She hadn't expected him to come to town. She hadn't expected him to watch her performance. Yet there he'd been. And her heart . . . oh, her heart was a traitor she feared.

With a slight shake of her head, she returned to the house, picked up the laundry basket, and walked to the clothesline, Becca following in her wake.

"If I had any sense," she muttered to herself as she pinned a sheet to the line, "we'd pack up and leave."

"But I like it here, Mama."

She glanced over her shoulder, surprised that her daughter had heard her. The girl was seated in the shade, rocking her rag doll in her arms. Despite herself, Faith smiled. "I know. I like it here, too."

"I think we oughta stay forever."

Faith didn't reply to that. What could she say? That this wasn't their home? That they didn't belong here? That God didn't know what He was doing when He brought them here?

She sighed as she grabbed another sheet from the basket, allowing herself to daydream, if only for a moment. Imagining what it would be like if this were their home, if they did belong here.

As if to complicate matters, Drake and Parker chose that moment to return. Faith glanced up at the sound of horses trotting into the yard. Over the top of the clothesline, her eyes met with Drake's. Without breaking the fragile contact between them, he slowed his pinto to a walk, then stopped.

She felt the familiar flutter of her heart and bent down behind the cover of the sheet, ostensibly to pull another item from the basket. She tried to ignore the way her hands shook as she dropped more clothespins into her apron pocket.

"Would you like some help, Mrs. Butler?"

She gasped softly at the sound of his voice so near. She straightened quickly, making her head swim. She swayed unsteadily. In an instant he reached between the two sheets on the line and grabbed hold of her elbow.

"Faith?"

She drew in a deep breath. "Goodness. I don't know what came over me."

She felt the warmth of his hand on her arm. It made her skin tingle. The dizziness worsened.

"Why don't you sit down with Becca for a moment?" Drake suggested.

She pulled free of his touch. "I need to hang the laundry to dry."

"I can do it."

Her pulse hammered in her ears as she looked at him. "I wouldn't think of it, Mr. Rutledge." She thought she sounded breathless, but she couldn't be certain because of the loud beating of her heart.

"I've managed to hang laundry out in the past. I think I remember how to do it."

His teasing words appealed to her. So did his smile. She smiled in return. "I'm quite all right now. I simply straightened too fast."

"Then let me help you."

Drake knew Faith was struggling for the proper response to his offer. He could see her wavering between refusal and acceptance. Before she could decide that it would be better to send him away, he reached down and picked up another bedsheet from the basket. "Pins?"

Her expressive eyes widened. "Here." She dropped several into his outstretched hand.

"Thanks."

He'd thought about Faith often while he and Parker had been out on the range. Even when Drake had been asking questions and gleaning information about the ranch from his foreman, a part of him had been thinking about her. When he'd ridden into the yard and seen her standing beside the clothesline, he'd known he had to talk to her, had to spend time with her.

He looked at Faith now and saw nothing but perfection. She was wearing a gown of spring-leaf green. Her hands and throat were unadorned by jewelry. Her abundant red hair was captured in a bun at the nape, and he thought how beautiful it would look falling in a cascade over her shoulders.

She turned and found him watching her. She stilled, her wariness reminding him of a doe caught grazing in a meadow. He expected her to bolt, so he stopped her by saying the first words that popped into his head. "I've never been more impressed by Shakespeare than I was last night."

She remained silent, still.

He remembered her standing on the stage, the light from the torches flickering in her fiery hair. He remembered the wistfulness of her expression and the graceful gestures of her hands. "You make a beautiful Juliet. Did you always want to be an actress?"

She shook her head, then nodded, then shrugged. Finally she said, "I don't know. I suppose so. My parents were actors. The theater is the only life I ever knew." She sighed and her voice lowered. "That's where I met my ... my children's father."

Her sadness was like an oppressive presence, and Drake hated her ex-husband in that moment. He didn't know what the man had done to her or why they'd divorced, but he knew she'd been hurt by the man who had been her husband. Deeply hurt. That was all Drake needed to know to hate him.

"Becca's looking well." He hoped the comment would drive away the sadness in her eyes.

A gentle smile curved the corners of her mouth as she turned toward her daughter. "Yes, she does, doesn't she?"

"Where's Alex today?"

"He's visiting at the Golds'. I hope he doesn't get into too much mischief."

Drake decided now was not the time to mention the boy's escapades on the banister or by the river.

"Alex has never had any friends his own age before," she added, her smile already fading.

He couldn't bear to see it go. "Faith ..."

She lifted her eyes.

"You're welcome to stay on at the Jagged R for as long as you want. You needn't leave just because Becca is well."

She didn't respond for some time, only continued to look at him, a kaleidoscope of emotions shimmering in her eyes ... emotions he couldn't quite name. He wasn't sure he wanted to name them for fear he might be wrong.

Finally she said, "Thank you, Mr. Rutledge."

Not knowing what to do or say next, feeling unsure of himself, he turned and walked away.

12

I T was sure hot.

Alex sat on the corral fence, staring at the rangy mustang within, wishing for a breeze to stir things up. Not a blade of grass, not a leaf on a tree moved.

Bored silly, Alex let out a long sigh. There wasn't even the sound of flies buzzing to break the stillness. All the cowboys were out on the range, and he didn't know where Gertie had disappeared to. His mother had lain down with Becca to rest during the heat of the day. Mr. Rutledge was shut up in his library again, going over his ledgers, and Mr. McCall had ridden into town earlier in the morning.

Too blamed quiet.

Too blamed hot.

Nothing to do.

He swung his feet over the top rail of the corral and dropped to the ground, sending up a cloud of dust. Looking toward the river, he could see the tops of the cottonwoods above the ridge. He thought how nice it would be to take off his shoes and plunge his feet into the water, but Mr. Rutledge had made it clear Alex would catch the dick-ens if he went down to the river without his mother or another adult.

Alex thought about saddling the little mare Gertie let him ride, but he knew he'd get in trouble for that, too. Gertie had told him he wasn't ready to ride alone yet. He thought she was wrong, but he didn't want to make her mad at him.

He'd had a lot of fun with Samuel and David Gold yesterday. Maybe he could go play with them again. But it was quite a piece to Dead Horse. Not much of a ride, but too long for a walk.

He shook his head, eliminating the idea. He'd have to ask his mother, and she'd already told him he had chores to do once it started to cool off. She wouldn't let him go into town. And if he bothered her now, she'd probably tell him to lie down and rest with her and Becca. He didn't want to spend the afternoon sleeping, that was for sure.

He picked up a small stone, turning it over and over with his fin-gers. Then he hurled it at the side of the bunkhouse. It hit the sun-bleached wall with a *thwunk*. He picked up several more stones and gave each a toss, one at a time.

That wasn't much fun either.

Squinting against the glare that reflected off the hard-packed dirt of the yard, Alex headed toward the barn, thinking that he'd look in on Sugar. He'd cleaned the buckskin's stall that morning and led her around the yard a bit, the way Gertie had instructed him to do. She'd said Sugar's leg was almost healed and the mare could be turned out with the other horses before too long.

The barn was cooler than outside, but not by much. Alex paused a moment inside the doorway, giving his eyes a second to adjust be-fore walking toward the stall. Then he heard a sound overhead. Looking up, he saw a mangy-looking gray tabby hurrying across a thick beam. The cat disappeared into the hayloft, but not before a clamor of high-pitched meows arose.

Diverted from his former objective, Alex veered toward the ladder, climbing the rungs as quickly as possible. The meowing had diminished by the time he reached the loft, but there was still enough noise to guide him to the cat's bed of hay in the corner. The tabby had already stretched out, and several kittens were attached to her belly. Three others were seeking a place to nurse.

Alex squatted for a better look. The cat eyed him warily, but she didn't move.

"It's okay. I'm not gonna hurt 'em." He leaned forward slightly. "Their eyes aren't even open yet."

He reached to stroke one. The tabby hissed and swiped at him with a front paw. Alex jerked back, sending up a flurry of hayseed and dust as he landed on his behind. He sent the cat an angry glare, and the tabby growled in response.

"Okay, I'm going," he grumbled as he got to his feet. "Too hot up here anyway." More softly he added, "Stupid cat."

Turning, he noticed light filtering around the edges of the loft doors. He walked over to them and lifted the latch, letting the doors swing open.

"Wow!"

He had a great view of the house from here. He could see his mother's bedroom window with its gabled roof. If he leaned farther out, he bet he could see clear to Dead Horse.

He bent at the waist and looked.

Almost. He could almost see the town.

He slid a little to the right and leaned out a bit more.

He heard an angry hiss from behind him, then felt claws sink into his leg through his trousers. He yelped and tried to kick free of the cat. As quickly as that, he lost his balance. Pitching forward, he grabbed for anything to hold on to, but all he found was air.

He wondered how bad it was going to hurt when he hit the ground.

Suddenly, the wind was jerked out of him as something stopped his downward plunge. Before he could wonder what, he found himself swinging sideways in a wild arc.

In the past, Drake had preferred days like this. Days when all the Jagged R ranch hands were out with the cattle. Days when silence settled over the house like the curtain of night. There'd been comfort in the solitude. That was, after all, why he'd come to this place.

But today all it felt was lonely.

He left his library and walked toward the back door, his footsteps booming in the absolute stillness of the house. He wondered where Faith was. Would he find her outside, sitting in the shade of the trees?

He hoped so.

He paused on the porch, his gaze sweeping the lawn, but he found no one there. Then he heard the boy's cry.

"Ma!" The single word was laced with fear.

Drake bolted off the porch, running in the direction of the voice. What he saw when he cleared the shade trees caused his heart to trip.

Alex hung from a rope outside the loft doors of the barn, a large hook caught in the back of his trousers. He swung from side to side. His security was tenuous. Even as Drake watched, the rope slipped on the pulley, causing the boy to drop a few inches before halting abruptly.

Alex yelped in fright.

"Try not to move!" Drake shouted.

"M-Mr. R-Rutledge, I'm s-scared."

He tried to sound calm. "I know you are, Alex, but it's going to be all right. Just try not to move."

Drake didn't know how long either the waistband or the loop in the rope would hold. If either gave, Alex was going to drop like a rock to the hard-packed earth below. With a critical gaze, he judged the distance from the rope to the hay doors. He might be able to reach it and pull the boy toward him, into the loft.

"H-hurry, M-Mr. R-Rutledge. I... I th-think it's sl-slippin' again."

Drake ran into the barn, climbing the ladder into the loft as fast as he could. "Hang on, boy. I'm coming."

A thick beam protruded from above the loft doors about eight or ten feet out from the front of the barn. The pulley itself was attached to the beam close to three-quarters of the way out. Just inside the doors, the end of the rope was looped and secured around a metal bracket in the wall.

It took only a quick glance for Drake to know his original plan wasn't safe. The hook, normally used for lifting bales of hay into the loft, had only a precarious grip on the boy's trousers. There seemed to be only one option, and Drake decided to take it.

"Alex, I'm going to lower you to the ground. I'm going to go slowly. All right? I want you to hold real still. Don't try to help. You stay still. Understand?"

"Uh-huh."

"Good. Here we go."

Praying for strength and a steady hand, Drake loosened the rope from the bracket, gripping it tightly and bracing himself against the boy's weight.

"All right. I'm going to start lowering you now."

"O-okay."

Drake's gaze didn't waver from the tip of the large hook where it disappeared beneath Alex's waistband, as if he believed he could keep the hook from slipping free by sheer willpower alone. He sent up a prayer, and then slowly he allowed the hemp rope to ease through his hands, all the while holding his breath. Every inch seemed to take an eternity.

Since his depth perception was less than perfect, it was difficult to gauge how close to the ground Alex was when the cloth of his trousers ripped and the boy dropped. Drake fell backward into the hay, the hook whipping upward until it clanged against the pulley. Drake was up on his feet in an instant, rushing toward the hay doors and looking downward. Alex lay, unmoving, on the ground.

"Alex!"

A heartbeat passed. Then another. Then the boy sat up, turning a dazed look toward Drake.

"Alex, are you hurt?"

"I . . . I don't think so."

Drake rushed to the ladder. By the time he'd climbed down and reached the barn entrance, Alex was standing.

It was on the tip of Drake's tongue to give the boy a scolding he wouldn't soon forget. He had every intention of offering a lecture about safety and precautions and keeping out of places where a boy didn't belong. But before he could begin, he caught a glimpse of Alex's expression, remnants of fear lingering in suspiciously misty eyes and quivering lips.

Drawing a deep breath, Drake started forward again. "You sure you're not hurt?"

Alex drew a forearm beneath his nose. "I'm okay."

"You're lucky." He glanced up at the pulley. "You might have broken your neck." Looking once more at the boy, he asked, "What happened?"

The last vestiges of misgiving vanished, replaced by youthful indignation. "Your cat scratched and bit me. That's why I fell."

"*My* cat?"

"Well, she lives in your barn. That makes her yours, don't it?"

Drake considered the question, then answered, "Yes, I suppose it does."

Alex nodded. "That's what I thought." He peeked at the loft doors. "Sir?"

"Yes?"

"Am I going to have to tell Ma about this?"

"Don't you think she should know?"

"It'd only make her worry."

"True." Amused now, Drake fought the urge to smile. He remembered how often he'd hidden his own childhood high jinks from his mother. More than once, he'd coerced the cooperation of one of the housemaids or the butler to keep his mother from discovering how close he'd come to breaking his fool neck. Sometimes a boy needed an ally. "Where is your mother now?" he asked, trying to sound appropriately stern.

"Upstairs. She said it was too hot, and she and Becca were going to rest awhile."

"She's right about it being hot." He glanced up into the glare of the sun. "What do you say the two of us go fishing?"

Alex brightened. "Fishing? Really? I've never been fishing before."

Drake felt his own spirits brighten. He hadn't dropped a line in the water in years, not since he was a lad of about Alex's age. "Every boy needs to know how to fish. Maybe, if we're lucky, we can have trout for supper." He placed his hand on Alex's shoulder. "Come on. We'll see if we can find some poles."

Faith awakened slowly from her nap, feeling drugged by the still heat in her third-story room. She bathed her face in tepid water from the pitcher on her washstand, but it did little to lift her lethargy. The idea of firing the kitchen stove and preparing supper was repulsive, and yet she knew it was unavoidable.

She checked her watch and was surprised to see she'd slept the better part of three hours. She hadn't realized she was so tired.

Becca continued to sleep soundly, and Faith decided not to awaken her. She slipped from the bedroom and descended the back staircase. The ground floor of the house was cooler than the third story, but not by much. After propping open the kitchen door, she stepped onto the porch, hoping to find a breeze there.

She didn't.

Faith shaded her eyes with one hand as she swept the area for a glimpse of Alex. Her son knew he wasn't supposed to leave the yard without asking. He was usually obedient, but there were many things on this ranch to tempt him. Today, however, things were quiet.

Too quiet.

She stepped off the porch. "Alex?"

No response.

She walked toward the barn. "Alex?"

Still no response.

An old dog lying beneath a wagon near the barn doorway lifted its head when Faith walked by but made no sound. The buckskin mare Alex was helping Gertie tend stood with drooping head in her stall.

"Alex?"

She felt a quiver of concern.

Where could he be? He wasn't with Gertie, and all the cowboys were out with the cattle. Parker had gone to town that morning, and since his horse wasn't tethered to the hitching post or standing in the corral, she knew he hadn't returned yet.

"Alex!"

Faith lifted her skirts a few inches above the ground and quickened her steps, hurrying back into the house, hoping he wasn't bothering her employer. But the library door stood open. The room was empty.

Alex wasn't in the house. He wasn't in the yard or in the barn. Where could he be?

Fear churned in her stomach as countless possibilities raced through her head.

Why hadn't she made him lie down with them? What kind of mother allowed her seven-year-old son to run about unsupervised? Alex was a changed boy since coming to the Jagged R. It had always been easy to keep an eye on him in the theater or in the wagons or in the cramped quarters of a hotel or rooming house. He'd never enjoyed so much wide-open space before. Now it seemed he was always getting into mischief. Faith had grown lax, allowing Gertie or Parker or one of the other cowpokes—who all seemed so willing—to take the boy under their wing.

If something happened to him ...

Laughter reached her ears. Alex's laughter.

She ran to the door and looked out.

There they came, the two of them, fishing poles slung over their shoulders. Alex's feet were bare. His shoelaces were tied together, his shoes riding on the opposite shoulder from the fishing pole. Her son looked at the man beside him with what was clearly adoration.

Something in Faith's chest gave, then broke. Wistful tears sprang to her eyes, but she wiped them away, not wanting the image of her son to blur, not wanting to miss memorizing the expression on his face.

In that moment she loved Drake, if for no other reason than for what he'd given her son.

She let the teardrops fall.

That night, as once again Faith tossed and turned in her bed, she regretted taking a nap in the middle of the day. At least that was the reason she gave herself for her inability to fall asleep.

With a groan of frustration, she rose and padded on bare feet across the room to the window. A sliver of moon rocked in the sky above the treetops. The night was still and untroubled. She rather liked the silence. For too many years she had endured either the bustle of the big cities or the rowdy saloon noises of frontier towns. This peacefulness was refreshing to her soul.

Now, if only her thoughts were equally serene.

But the image of Drake Rutledge with Alex wouldn't be shaken. It had stayed with her throughout their supper of fried trout. It had stayed with her as she'd tucked her children into bed for the night. It had stayed with her as she'd tossed restlessly in her own bed.

What was it that drew her to him?

Tis one thing to be tempted, Escalus,
Another thing to fall. . . .

Truer words had not been written, yet she couldn't seem to stop herself from falling.

"'This love will undo us all,'" she whispered, and felt a chill, as if a cold breeze had entered through the window.

But must it be love? Couldn't it be simple gratitude? Love was so risky.

"Father," she began to pray, "I'm so confused. I want what's best for my children. I want to do what You want me to do. Help me to know what that is."

That was when she heard the music floating up from the lower level of the house. Plaintive notes that clutched at her heart. She knew she would find Drake in the parlor. She knew she should not go.

But go she did. She put a robe over her nightgown and followed the music.

He played in the dark. No lamps brightened the room. He didn't seem to need them. His fingers flowed over the keys with a sureness that proved he needed no light.

Faith paused in the doorway. She closed her eyes and listened, seeing Drake more clearly with her heart than she had when her eyes were open. As time passed, the melody changed from mournful to wistful and then suddenly to a song of joy. The music rose to a final crescendo, then stopped abruptly.

"Did I awaken you, Faith?"

She opened her eyes. "No, I couldn't sleep."

"Neither could I."

She heard the piano bench slide across the floor and sensed he'd risen. "You play beautifully."

"Surprised?"

"A little."

"It was my mother's fondest wish that I learn to play. She hoped I would become a virtuoso. My father demanded I be an attorney." Footsteps brought him toward her. "I haven't played in a very long time. I'm amazed I still remember how." He was silent a moment, unmoving. When he continued, his voice was low and thoughtful. "I guess most people wouldn't think of me as the musical sort. My father certainly didn't."

It seemed she could feel her own heartbeat pulsing throughout the room. "I doubt most people know the real you."

I think I know you, Drake. I think I know you in my heart. Why is that?

"You've changed in these past weeks," Faith said.

Drake smiled. "You had something to do with that."

"Me?"

"You reminded me of someone. She told me once that no matter what I did, I was forgiven. I'd forgotten about that."

Faith felt her heart soar at his words.

A match scratched. A flame burst to life. Light flickered across Drake's face as he lifted the glass and lit the lamp's wick. When he was done, he turned toward her. He inclined his head toward the piano. "Do you play?"

"No."

"But you sing." He moved a step closer.

"Yes." She felt breathless. "Sometimes I sing."

"I've heard you when you're in the kitchen. Your voice is clear." He paused, then added, "And lovely."

She feared her heart might stop beating.

"Faith," he whispered her name as he lifted his hand to stroke her cheek with his fingertips.

For a moment, she closed her eyes and leaned into his touch. For a moment, she pretended she belonged here with him. When he pulled his hand away, she looked at him and knew, before he could speak, what he was about to ask of her.

"Tell me what happened to you, Faith."

She felt ashamed. "I wasn't enough."

"Enough?"

Faith turned away, not wanting to meet his gaze. She hugged herself, feeling strangely cold despite the warmth of the night. "George left me for his mistress."

"Then he must be a fool," Drake whispered.

She smiled sadly. "After he divorced me, he married again."

"Do you still love him?"

"Still love him?" she echoed with a note of surprise. "No. No, I don't still love him."

Drake's hand alighted on her shoulder. "Are you certain?"

She could turn and step into his embrace. She knew it. Wanted it. But she held still. "I'm quite certain." *I know it's true because I love you.*

"Faith?"

With only a slight pressure, he turned her toward him. He lifted her chin with his index finger, forcing her to look up. He stared into her eyes with an unwavering gaze, looking down deep inside her. She felt as if he could see into the deepest secrets of her soul.

"You're safe here," he said at last.

Safe? She felt anything but safe when she was standing so close to him.

"Faith ... I'm going to kiss you now."

He pulled her close and lowered his head with an agonizing slowness. The chill she'd felt only a short time before was forgotten, replaced by a languid heat that radiated through her the moment their lips touched. The kiss was infinitely sweet, immeasurably tender, and far too brief.

It was dangerous to feel what she felt, dangerous to hope for things she shouldn't want. Loving him would surely end in heartbreak, like all Shakespearean tragedies. It was the pattern of her life. Love and loss.

"You shouldn't have done that," she said softly as she stepped back from him.

"Why not? Faith, I—"

"No. Please don't say anything. Please." She turned and fled.

Drake watched as Faith rushed up the stairs. When she'd disappeared from view, he extinguished the lamp and sat once again on the piano bench. But he didn't resume playing. Not while Faith's faint cologne lingered in the air. Not while he remembered the way she'd felt in his arms. Not while he could still taste her sweetness on his lips.

It had been years since he'd believed a woman could look at him without horror and revulsion. But Faith did. Faith Butler made him feel whole again.

And he'd fallen in love with her. Against his better judgment, he'd fallen in love, and he had every intention of making sure Faith learned to love him, too.

13

RICK guided his mare through Dead Horse. The heat and the silence were both thick enough to cut with a knife. It was hard to believe the town's Fourth of July celebration, attended by every living soul within a half day's ride, had been only three days ago. Today Dead Horse looked as dead as its name.

He was returning from Matt and Agnes Horne's farm, where six-week-old Emma was suffering from the colic. Rick knew the baby's condition wasn't serious. He was more concerned about Agnes. He'd spent the better portion of his visit telling her she needed to get adequate rest. He'd also hinted that she should avoid getting pregnant again anytime soon. The young mother of four children under the age of five had dark circles under her eyes, and she was far too thin. Rick was afraid Matt would find himself a widower if Agnes didn't take better care of herself.

He shook his head as he drew his horse to a halt beside the

barn. Too many babies too soon. He'd seen it time and again during his years as a doctor.

Rick unhooked the mare from her traces and led her into the stall. He made certain there was plenty of water and hay, then walked toward the house. He was looking forward to sitting in the shade on the porch and remaining idle until nightfall. It was too hot to do anything else.

He heard a knock at the front door as he entered through the back one. Dreading the idea of hitching the horse to the buggy again, he went to answer the door.

He was surprised to find Jed Smith, the town's postmaster, standing on the porch. Jed rarely left the bench in front of the post office because he refused to wear his peg leg. As for crutches, they made his arms sore. He much preferred to let folks come to him, he always said.

"Saw you ride into town, Doc. Thought maybe you should have this right away. Looked important."

Rick had the strange feeling the postmaster already knew what was inside the envelope with a return address marked Union Pacific Railroad.

Jed made no move to leave.

"Maybe it's news from James and Nancy." Rick tore open the top of the envelope and withdrew the folded letter within.

... train derailment ...

... regret to inform you ...

... Mr. and Mrs. James Telford died instantly ...

The words jumped off the page and seared into his brain. James dead? He read the brief missive again, trying to make it say something else, anything else, but it was always the same.

He shook his head. It couldn't be true.

But it was. James and Nancy were dead. His son wasn't coming home. He was dead.

The paper slipped from his hands as he staggered backward, then sank onto a cane-back chair.

James was dead. He wasn't coming home.

"Rick?"

He tried to focus his gaze but failed.

"You all right?" Jed stepped into the house.

"James and Nancy are dead."

The other man cleared his throat. "I feared as much. Heard about the train wreck. Lotta folks died."

A lot of folks died, but only one was his son; only one was his daughter-in-law. "They never had children. They were still so young. So much ahead of them."

"I'm real sorry," Jed murmured. "Real sorry."

Rick stared at his hands, palms turned up. A physician's hands, meant to heal. For years these same hands had trembled, shaken by the effects of whiskey. Today they'd been steady and sure, but what good had it done him? They hadn't been able to help his son. They hadn't been able to help Nancy.

"Well…" Jed sounded uncomfortable. "Guess I'll be gettin' back to the post office. You be all right?"

Rick nodded.

"Okay then. You need anythin', you let me know."

"Thanks," he replied, still staring at his hands.

A moment later the door closed, and Rick was alone with the silence of the house. Alone.

"It didn't make any difference, Esther," he whispered to his long-dead wife. "Stopping my drinking didn't change a thing."

Gertie heard about the accident as soon as she returned from rounding up a small herd of horses on the Jagged R's south range.

She didn't take time to wash off the trail dust. Something in her heart told her there wasn't time. She just turned her weary horse around and galloped toward Dead Horse.

Instinct caused her to rein in at the saloon. "Ah, Doc," she whispered as she swung down from the saddle and looped the reins over the hitching post. "Sure hope you haven't gone and done somethin' stupid."

But her instincts proved true. She found him slumped at a table in the far corner of the smoke-hazy room, an empty bottle of whiskey in front of him. His head was tilted forward, his chin nearly resting on his chest.

Gertie crossed to the table with quick strides. Once there, she turned a chair around and straddled it, leaning her forearms on the chair back. "Why'd you do it, Doc? Gettin' all liquored up ain't gonna bring 'em back."

Rick glanced up with alcohol-glazed eyes. He made no reply.

"This town needs you, Doc. What if Faith's boy was t'get hurt? You wouldn't be able t'help none."

"I don't want to help. It doesn't change a thing."

"'Course it does."

Rick straightened slightly and looked toward the bar. "Stretch, bring me another bottle."

"Doc..." Gertie covered his hand with her own.

He yanked it away. "Thish isn't any of your concern, Mish Duncan. Go back to your horses where you belong."

His words hurt, but she figured he had a right to hurt her if he wanted, what with James and Nancy being killed. She figured he had a right to strike out at anybody who tried to get close. She'd felt that way a time or two herself. She could take it 'cause she loved him.

"All right, Doc. You just sink to the bottom of that bottle. I'll be here when you're done."

He slammed his palms down on the table. "I don't want you here!"

She tipped her hat back on her forehead. "It's a free country. I think I'll stay anyways."

"Go to the devil." He grabbed the bottle Stretch Barns brought, filled his glass, and tossed the liquid down his throat.

"Looks like you beat me to it, Doc," Gertie said, feeling as if she was going to cry.

The deaths of James and Nancy Telford shook the tiny community. The young couple's bodies arrived two days later, but Rick didn't bother to leave the saloon to claim them or make arrangements for their burial. Gertie did it for him. Rick didn't attend the funeral either. Nothing seemed important to him except the next drink. Nothing seemed important except escaping the pain.

Drake hadn't known James and Nancy and thus was spared the grief himself. However, he knew that James Telford's journey to Cheyenne had been important to the townsfolk, and he wondered whether or not James had convinced railroad officials to authorize a spur through Dead Horse. He knew, once the time of mourning had passed, that others would be wondering the same thing. He figured he would try to find out for them.

The day after the funeral, Drake was writing a letter to the railroad when Gertie knocked on the open library door.

"Come in." He leaned back in his chair.

Her expression was grim as she walked toward his desk. "Mr. Rutledge, you're gonna have to hire yourself a new wrangler."

He raised an eyebrow. "Why's that?"

"Well, sir . . ." She paused as she removed her dusty Stetson. "Truth is, I haven't been tendin' to my duties. Not since what happened to the Telfords."

"Sit down, Gertie."

She hesitated a moment, then did as he'd asked.

Drake swiveled his chair to face her. With a note of compassion in his voice, he said, "I think this has more to do with the doctor than with his son's death. Am I right?"

"Yes, sir, you are."

"I hear he's taking it hard."

Gertie nodded, and her gaze fell to the floor between them.

"What is it you think you can do for him?"

She looked up again. This time there was a spark of determination in her blue eyes. "I'm gonna help him dry out again."

"You can't help unless he wants you to."

"He'll want me to," she answered stubbornly.

Drake knew there was no changing Gertie's mind. He could see it in the set of her shoulders, hear it in the tone of her voice, read it in her eyes.

He hated to see her get hurt. He'd come to like the outspoken wrangler in her trousers and boots. After a few moments of silence, Drake said, "I won't accept your resignation, Gertie, but you can take off whatever time you need. Your job will be waiting when you get back."

"Mr. Rutledge, I can't—"

He stopped her with a raised hand. "If you can help out a friend, so can I."

He saw her surprise and understood it. Only in the past couple of weeks had he actively participated in the management of the ranch. Only recently had he become a familiar sight in the yard or out on the range. Gertie had no reason to believe that her employer was also her friend.

He rose and stepped toward her, holding out his hand. She stood, too, and clasped it with her own, giving it a hard shake.

"I mean what I said," he told her. "Your job will be here when you're ready to come back."

"Thanks, Mr. Rutledge. I ... I don't know what to say."

"You don't have to say anything. Helping others is what the gospel's about."

Gertie raised an eyebrow. "I don't know too much about that," she admitted, "but I know my ma always said everyone deserved another chance."

"She sounds like a wise woman."

She nodded, then turned and walked toward the door.

"God help you, Gertie," he added as she disappeared into the hallway.

He went to the window and stared out at the yard. It was Monday—wash day—and he hoped he would find Faith hanging clothes on the line. He was disappointed. She was nowhere in sight. Then he heard the rear porch door close, and moments later, Faith and Gertie appeared near the corner of the house.

Faith balanced a basket of clean clothes on her hip. Her fiery hair was caught at the nape in a net, but red-gold strands had pulled free to curl against her neck. His fingers itched to brush the hair away so he could kiss the pale flesh beneath her ear.

He shook his head to drive off the image, at the same time shifting his gaze to Gertie.

The wrangler still held her Stetson in her left hand, as she had when she'd left Drake's library minutes before. She bounced the hat against her thigh, speaking to Faith, her eyes downcast. Finally, Faith set down the clothes basket and hugged the taller woman, standing on her tiptoes to do so. Even from here he could feel Faith's love and concern for her friend.

Would she someday be able to love him, too? Not as a friend but as a man?

He remembered the way she had responded to him the night before, when she'd found him playing the piano. He remembered the swirl of emotions in her eyes. She didn't judge him. She didn't see him as a wretched man or a monster, the way Larissa and even his own father had seen him.

But would she be able to love him?

Old doubts surged to life.

Maybe he was only fooling himself, wanting more than he could have. Maybe Larissa had been right.

Maybe no woman could love him.

"I CANNOT MARRY YOU, DRAKE." *Larissa paced restlessly from one side of his bedchamber to the other.*

It hurt to watch her, made his head pound. He closed his left eye. "I won't be in this bed for long. The doctor says I'll—"

"You don't understand me. I said I cannot marry you. Not ever."

The pain behind his right eye intensified as he tried to look at her once again. "Why not?"

"Why not?" Her echoing words were edged with disbelief. "Dear heavens, look at you."

They had been the glittering couple of the season, the darlings of every party. Everyone had known Drake Rutledge and Larissa Dearborne—the darkly handsome lawyer and the golden-haired beauty. Everyone said they'd been destined to marry. He'd heard it said time and again, and he'd believed it. After all, Larissa had told him how much she loved him. He'd given up his dreams of the West. He'd been willing to stay at Rutledge and Seever for the rest of his life in order to please her.

"You can't expect me to be shackled to half a man for the rest of my life," she went on, unaware of his thoughts.

"I've lost the sight in one eye, Larissa. I'm partially blind. Not emasculated."

She gasped. "You needn't be crude."

He closed his eye again. "Sorry." Maybe she was right. Maybe he was only half a man. "What will you tell people? They'll expect you to stand by me."

"I'll say we postponed the wedding because of your mother's death. After a while, it will become apparent we have no intention of setting another date." She paused a moment, then added, "I know you love me. I hope you'll get over the pain in time."

He laughed softly, bitterly. "That's very kind of you, Larissa, to be so caring."

He hated her. Hated her and all she stood for. Even half blind, he saw her more clearly in that moment than he'd ever seen her before. He wondered what he had once found to love. She was shallow and vain and selfish.

And he was no better. Larissa hadn't changed because of his accident, because of his scars or his blindness. She was who she'd always been. He had loved her because she was beautiful, because she'd made his blood boil with desire.

"It's not my fault, Drake. No woman wants to . . . no woman could . . ."

"Love me?" he finished for her, staring at her blurred image.

"Well, you aren't exactly the man I accepted the proposal from, now, are you?"

"No, I'm not." He sighed and let his head fall back against the pillows. "Consider the engagement broken. You needn't come to see me again."

He heard the door open.

"This is for the best, Drake."

"Yes."

"You'll get over me in time."

I'm already over you, he wanted to say, but the words wouldn't form. They were strangled by a bitter fury toward beautiful women who lied with ease, who said they loved when there was no love in them....

George Butler despised riding in the emigrant car among those too poor to buy a decent seat in the passenger car. When he'd come west with Jane, they had traveled in the *Silver Palace* with their own private berths, with rich crimson curtains trimmed in gold that hung from the ceiling and trailed on the soft Axminster carpet.

In contrast with those earlier accommodations, the emigrant car had only a coal stove, a single convenience for both men and women, and rows of benches too short for anyone but a young child. That was all. No berths. No curtains. No carpets. No comfort.

After leaving a sweltering Sacramento—105 degrees at midday—the train had arrived in Truckee near midnight. The temperature had fallen to nineteen degrees above zero, and George had thought he might freeze to death before they finally left.

Now, two days later, after departing the Mormon town of Ogden, the train was once again traversing the plains of Utah, the land white and glaring. By mutual agreement among the passengers, the windows had been left closed to shut out the fine alkaline grit that irritated their eyes and nostrils.

Dust and heat. Heat and dust. Dust and heat.

There was little to see outside to break the monotony of travel, but George chose to stare out the window rather than respond to the chatter of the old crone with the two blackened front teeth who sat beside him. Hour after hour he watched as the train chugged its way through desolate country—muddy streams and rough, arid valleys that occasionally narrowed into canyons, sudden buttes and sage-brush, jackrabbits and antelope.

The only thing that improved his spirits was anticipation of the surprise he would see on Faith's face when he showed up in Dead Horse, Wyoming.

It was by sheer luck that he'd run into Raymond Drew last week and learned of his first wife's whereabouts. He'd learned that the little girl—what was the brat's name?—had been too sick to travel, and so Faith had been forced to remain behind when the theater troupe moved on. The timing of this information couldn't have been better since a few days later George had needed to depart San Francisco with some haste.

He hadn't meant to kill that woman. They'd both been drinking hard, and things had gotten out of hand. That was all. But who would listen to him? He'd had more than his fair share of troubles lately, and he wasn't exactly on good terms with the law.

But nobody would be looking for a man with a family in tow. With Faith and her brats, he could make his way out of the country undetected. The fact that he'd divorced Faith, then married and divorced again, mattered little. It would be easy enough to convince her to return to him. After all, hadn't she begged him to stay? She'd always been so quick to forgive him before. And even if she wasn't, he could at least be certain no one would think to look for him in a place called Dead Horse.

Drake watched as Faith walked toward the clothesline and began the task of hanging sheets and clothes to dry. Across the distance he heard her singing softly to herself, and the melody brought a smile to his lips.

Faith was beautiful. Perhaps even more beautiful than Larissa.

But there was far more to her than mere comeliness. She had a heart full of love, and she showered it upon those around her with pure honesty of spirit.

One day he hoped she would shower her love upon him.

A summer storm blew in during the night. Roiling clouds filled the heavens, hiding the full moon from view, turning the night as black as pitch. Tall trees bent before the wind, leaves crackling and clapping, branches snapping. Minutes later, spikes of lightning, jumping from cloud to cloud, flashed brightly. Thunder pounded like an Indian's drum, rolling before the wind until it faded in the distance. In the yard, one of the dogs bayed. The horses whinnied and snorted as they circled the corral, the sound of their hooves on the hard-packed earth adding to the din of the storm. From somewhere in the mountains came the shriek of a mountain lion.

Faith observed nature's dramatic display from her bedroom window, feeling the storm mirrored in her soul.

Something was about to happen. Something was about to change. She could feel it as distinctly as she could feel the summer wind upon her cheeks. It was as electrifying as the lightning. Her skin tingled with it.

"'For now, these hot days, is the mad blood stirring,'" she whispered.

She felt as mad as some of Shakespeare's characters. For wasn't it madness to fall in love again? Tennyson said it was better to have loved and lost than never to have loved at all. But was that true? Wasn't it pure madness to love Drake? Wasn't it madness to dream, even a little, that she might have a future with him?

Lovers and madmen hav e such seething brains,
Such shaping fantasies, that appr ehend
More than cool r eason ev er compr ehends.

Lovers and madmen indeed! To risk one's heart. To risk one's all. It was truly an act of madness.

For God so loved the world . . .

Sheets of rain began to fall on the heat-parched earth, soaking the ground and freshening the air. The wind grew cool as it whipped her nightgown and tossed her hair.

Greater love hath no man . . .

Lightning flashed directly overhead, followed immediately by a deafening clap of thunder.

"Let me love him," she whispered. "Please, God, if You have called me to love others as You love us, then let me love Drake freely. If it is a sin for me to want to marry again, take us away from here now."

14

THE morning sky was silvered by clouds, the temperature cooled by the previous night's storm. Everything seemed fresh and new.

A suitable day for new beginnings.

Drake looked for Faith in the kitchen and found her standing at the stove, turning bacon in the frying pan. Loose strands of fiery red hair curled along her nape like tiny fishhooks. Her dress was simple, yet she looked beautiful. She moved with the ease of someone who was comfortable in her surroundings. The thought pleased him immensely.

As he stepped up behind her, he noticed the batter in the stone crock, waiting to be poured onto the hot skillet. "Smells good. I love hotcakes."

She gasped at the sound of his voice, whirling to face him, fork in hand, wielded like a sword. "Drake!" Her free hand flew up to smooth her hair.

He grinned, thinking that he'd like to kiss her. "Good morning."

"I didn't hear you come in." Her eyes were wide, her cheeks flushed.

"Quite a storm we had last night," he said conversationally, remaining close even though he could see she was flustered by his nearness. It made him want to kiss her even more. "Did it wake you?"

"Yes." The flush in her cheeks grew more pronounced.

He loved the way wisps of hair curled around her face. He enjoyed the gentle arch of her dark brows, the lush fullness of her mouth, the perfection of her small, shell-shaped ears. He caught a faint whiff of her cologne, a clean, sweet scent that would forever remind him of Faith.

She broke the connection between them by turning back to the stove. "It's almost chilly today."

"A good day for a ride." He waited for a response. When none came, he asked, "Would you go for a ride with me after breakfast? I'd like to show you more of the ranch."

Her hand stilled above the frying pan, then continued to lift crisp slices of bacon onto a plate.

"Faith?"

The silence lengthened before she replied. "Yes, Drake." She still didn't look at him. "I'll go for a ride with you."

"Maybe you could pack us a picnic lunch."

This time she glanced over her shoulder. "I shouldn't be gone so long. The children—"

"Parker will keep an eye on Alex and Becca while we're gone."

"The ironing—"

"Can wait."

She looked away a second time. "All right. I'll pack us a lunch."

Drake felt a lightness in his heart such as he hadn't felt in years. "Good. You see to the food. I'll saddle the horses." He headed for the back door.

"Saddle?"

The note of surprise in her voice caused him to stop and turn. She was looking at him with wide eyes.

"Drake, I'm not much of a horsewoman. I thought . . . I thought you meant in the buggy."

He stared at her in wonder, hardly noticing what she'd said. How miraculous it was that she'd come to live in this house. She'd let in so much light and laughter in the short time she'd been at the Jagged R. She'd reminded him of God's goodness by her own sweet kindness. Gently she'd forced him to face life again. Incredibly, unexpectedly, he'd grown to love her.

"Maybe we shouldn't—," she began.

"I think a woman who makes her *home* on *my* ranch should get used to riding horseback. Don't you?"

It was her turn to be silent and stare. He saw how she weighed his words and knew she was wondering if he meant them the way they sounded.

I do, Faith. I mean them exactly as they sounded. I want you to stay here with me forever, and not as my housekeeper.

"I suppose you're right," she said softly.

"We won't go too fast."

There was something fragile about the look in her eyes. "No, not too fast."

Drake didn't think they were talking about horses any longer. "I promise." He wished he could hold her in his arms and promise her more. Much more.

And when the time was right, he would.

Faith studied Drake from beneath the brim of her straw bonnet. Even though she knew little about riding herself, she could tell a man who was comfortable in the saddle. He looked like someone who belonged where he was.

"This is the westernmost border of the Jagged R," he said, interrupting her musings. "I thought we'd eat our lunch up on the ridge. Above the line shack."

"What's a line shack?"

He pointed. "There."

She saw it then, a dismal-looking dwelling hewed out of the side of the hill. "Who lives there?"

"The men when they're riding line."

"The men? You mean Parker and Swede and the others?"

Drake laughed. "All the comforts of home. Come on. I'll show you."

He had a wonderful laugh, she thought as she followed him. And a beautiful smile.

He glanced over his shoulder. "I lived in a shack like this one winter up in Montana. That's where Parker and I got to be friends. You learn a lot about a person when you've got to live with him in a place no bigger than this. Especially when you're snowed in for weeks at a time."

In front of the shack, they reined in. Drake dismounted, then stepped over to her horse. His hands spanned her waist as he helped her to the ground. Her heart tapped a riotous beat in response to his touch, but Drake seemed completely unaware of the effect his nearness had on her. He released her almost at once, then opened the door of the shack, motioning for her to look inside. Faith stepped forward and glanced around, glad for a moment to calm her raging senses.

The dugout's back wall and part of the two side walls were formed by the rich brown earth. The remainder was made of logs chinked with mud. A flat roof made of dirt-covered logs butted up against the hillside. A couple of cots stood against opposite walls, and a small woodstove, for cooking and heating, was nestled in the front right corner.

Faith had stayed in some undesirable places in her life, but this was more miserable than anything she had ever imagined.

Drake knocked on the door. "All the Jagged R line shacks have wooden doors. Usually there's just a blanket or an old cowhide."

Faith didn't find much comfort in a wooden door. Quickly she stepped outside and drew a breath of fresh, clean air. "You didn't mind living like this?"

"It *is* a bit different from the ranch house." He chuckled as he raked his fingers through his long black hair, then resettled his Stetson on his head as he answered her question. "No, I didn't mind it. I brought along plenty of books to read. Of course, summer's a better time to draw line duty." He stared into the distance. "A man can learn a lot in this country. You learn to read the signs of the seasons. You appreciate sunsets and flowers. You enjoy a serenade by an old hoot owl or a howling coyote. And you get to know your horse mighty well." He paused, looking slightly embarrassed at having admitted so much. With a shrug he added, "I guess I was born to be a cowboy. I dreamed about coming west from the time I was a boy. It was all I ever wanted to do." He frowned. "My parents didn't approve."

More questions swirled in her head—about his parents, about his schooling, about Larissa. Most of all, about Larissa. But she held her tongue. He took hold of her arm. "Come on. We'll lead the horses from here."

She smiled, relieved not to have to get back in the saddle just yet. "Thank you."

"You'll get used to it. You'll be able to ride as well as anyone on the ranch in no time at all."

How long will I be here? Will it be long enough?

Once up the hillside, Drake spread a blanket on the ground beneath some tall pines. Then he tethered the horses while Faith set out the sandwiches she'd wrapped in cloth napkins. Moments later he sat down beside her, and both of them turned their eyes upon the pastoral scene below.

"It's beautiful," Faith said reverently.

"Yes, it is." He turned and met her gaze. "But I'd forgotten it until you came."

Her heart beat madly in her chest. She felt the strange curling sensation in her stomach that always happened when he was near.

Tentatively she reached out and touched the scar on his cheek. "Does it hurt you still?"

His jaw tightened. "No."

"Except for the memories," she whispered.

"Except for the memories." He took hold of her hand, drew it slowly away from his face. Then he turned it and kissed her palm.

"Would you tell me about it?"

He stared into her eyes for a long time, and she knew he was remembering, knew he was deciding whether or not to trust her with that part of himself. Her heart ached for him, for she felt the unseen scars as if they were her own. She knew they went deeper than the visible scar on his face.

"I was living in Philadelphia then," he began, his decision obviously made. "I was practicing law in my father's firm."

Faith listened as he recalled the day that had changed the course of his life. She relived the accident with him and then each moment, each hurt, that had followed. The guilt he'd borne over his mother's death and the added weight of his father's blame. The physical pain of his injuries. The rejection from Larissa. The frustration that had come with his partial blindness. She understood his doubts, his rage, his bitterness, and she longed to be able to make him forget them all.

As if he knew what she was thinking, he tightened his hold on her hand. "I don't know what would have become of me if you hadn't come to the Jagged R."

"I haven't done anything."

"But you have, Faith. You brought light into my house. You made me remember things I'd forgotten. Without even knowing you were doing it, you reminded me to forgive and to accept forgiveness." He leaned toward her. "You helped me remember the good things God has for us if we're smart enough to look for them and to trust in Him."

Drake took Faith in his arms then, drew her close against him. He pressed his face, his lips, against the sensitive curve of her neck. "I love you, Faith," he whispered. "Marry me?"

She drew back so she could look into his eyes, not certain she had heard correctly.

"Marry me, Faith."

"Are you sure that's want you want, Drake? To marry a divorced woman? To marry an actress. There would be people who—"

"Never mind them." He pulled her back into his arms, pressing her close against his chest. "It's only you who matters. Do *you* want to marry *me?*"

Did she *want* to marry him? She'd never wanted anything more in her life. From the moment she'd met him, she had felt a bond between them. She had tried to deny it. She had tried to withstand it. But that bond had remained, an invisible cord drawing her to him. Closer, ever closer.

Only last night she'd prayed she would be allowed to love. Now that prayer had been answered. Now Drake had offered the chance to her. She couldn't run from it.

"I love you." Drake held out his hand toward her. "I'll take care of you and the children. They'll be *our* children. You'll never have cause to regret loving me."

She shook her head. Tears shimmered in her eyes. "But what if I make you unhappy? What if you find you were wrong about me?"

He wanted to hold her. He wanted to crush her to him and drive away the last shred of doubt from her heart. He wanted to brush away her tears. He wanted to shelter her and care for her.

"Dearest Faith."

He saw a tear trickle down her cheek.

Softer this time, "Darling Faith."

She raised her head. Her blue-green eyes were luminous.

A different, more pleasant memory came to him, prompting him to ask, "Do you know the story of Ruth and Boaz from the Old Testament?"

She shook her head.

"It was a favorite of my mother's. Ruth, a stranger in the land, goes to glean in the fields, and as it happened, the field belonged to Boaz, the man who would become her husband, her family re-deemer. It was God's providence that placed Ruth there."

"What has that—"

"Don't you see God's providence in this moment, Faith? What do you think the chances were that you would end up in Dead Horse, working for me? You're an actress. Why are you employed as a housekeeper? *My* housekeeper? Out of all the cities and towns in this country, what were the odds that we would find each other?"

She gave a small shrug.

"A hundred? A thousand?"

Again she shrugged.

"A million?" It took all his resolve not to hold her and kiss her and force her to agree to marry him. "After the accident, I stopped believing in a God who cared. But He didn't give up on me. It took Him a lot of years to get through to me. I put up all kinds of barriers to try to stop Him. But in His mercy, He brought you here so I could hope again, trust again, live again."

"Oh, Drake."

"So I could love again."

Now he did take hold of her, drawing her tenderly into his arms. He pressed her head against his chest and stroked her hair. He loved her. He would always love her.

She still hadn't said yes, but he wasn't worried. God hadn't brought them this far only to let them fail. Drake would just have to be patient.

15

GERTIE took Rick to her hunting shack high in the mountains.

After the word came about James and Nancy, Gertie had spent several days sitting with Rick in the saloon, trying to convince him to stop his drinking. In the end, he'd been too drunk to argue with her anymore. He'd simply passed out cold, and she'd dragged him from the saloon, tossed him over the back of a spare horse, and brought him into the mountains, far from the nearest bottle of whiskey.

More than once in the hours that followed their arrival at the shack, Gertie wondered if she'd made a mistake. She'd never seen anybody talk to folks who weren't there. But Rick did plenty of talking. Occasionally he made sense. Most of the time he didn't. When he finally drifted into sleep, she was afraid he wouldn't ever wake up. She spent the time reading a Bible Faith had given her. She'd come a long way in learning to read, and she was grateful to Faith for teaching her. She'd never had much call to read the Bible before, but she knew she was gonna need help from someone more powerful than herself if Doc was gonna get better. He'd struggled with whiskey before, and she figured it was about time he found some answers that would really help him. She'd found that the words of the book touched her own heart, too, words about bein' loved just as she was, without havin' to try to impress anyone. She wondered why she'd never heard that before.

Just after dawn of their third day in the mountains, she sat beside the bed on a rickety, spindle-backed chair, her legs, crossed at the ankles, stretched in front of her.

You've done some fool things in your life, Gertie Duncan, but this surefire takes the cake. A crazy way to catch a man. Truss him up like some calf ready for brandin' and make sure he can't get away. He's more like t'hate you now.

"Pitiful," she added with an unladylike snort.

"Gertie?"

She straightened with a start to find Rick watching her with blurry eyes.

"Where are we?" His voice was weak and scratchy.

"My cabin. Well, you're stayin' here; I've got a tent pitched outside for me . . . so you won't get no ideas." She let her gaze sweep the small room. "This is where I come to get away when I've had enough of them cowpokes at the ranch. Nobody knows about it but me. And now you." She looked at Rick again. "How you feelin'?"

He groaned as he lay back against the pillow and closed his eyes.

"Can't say that I'm surprised. You near killed yourself, Doc."

"You should have let me."

She leaned toward him. "Yeah, maybe I shoulda, but I didn't. Listen here, Doc. I'm real sorry about what happened to James and Nancy. Just like I'm real sorry about the way you lost your wife awhile back. But drownin' yourself in whiskey ain't gonna bring any of 'em back."

"I need a drink."

"Sure thing." Gertie rose and went to a side table, returning a short while later with a tin cup filled to the brim. "Here ya go, Doc."

He raised his head, covered her hand with his own quivering fingers, and took a swallow. He gagged and spit it out. "Good heavens, woman! What are you trying to do to me?" He stared at her with accusing eyes.

"Givin' you a drink, like you asked for."

"I meant whiskey, not water!"

"Well, you're outta luck. There ain't any."

He looked around the room again. "Where are my things?"

"I don't recall where I put 'em."

His eyes flashed with anger. "Listen, Miss Duncan, you can't keep me prisoner here."

His breath was foul, and he was in dire need of a bath. She didn't suppose there was much about him to love at the moment, but love him she did.

"Sorry, Doc. I can't."

"Then I'll just go as I am." He shoved aside the sheet.

Gertie turned her back toward him. "It shouldn't take you more'n about five or six days to walk to town. You'd best take care of your feet. They're likely t'get mighty sore 'fore you get there, bein's you got no shoes to wear. Oh, and you oughta keep an eye out for bears. I've seen some signs of a grizzly round these parts." She strode across the room.

"Where's my horse?"

"Can't recall that either, Doc. Sorry." With that, she was out the door and headed into the hills.

It wasn't long before she heard Rick yank open the cabin door and stomp outside. Fool man.

She let him go. She figured he wouldn't go far. He hadn't eaten anything solid for more than a week now. There wasn't a lot of strength left in his legs. She'd give him time to walk off steam, then go looking for him. She knew he didn't have a chance of finding the horses on his own.

"Like it or not, Doc, we're gonna see this through."

On her hands and knees, Faith attacked the kitchen floor with scrub brush and soapy water. It was as if she were trying to rub Drake from her thoughts with elbow grease and soapsuds. But it was a useless effort. He was firmly entrenched in her mind. She'd thought of nothing else but him since the moment he'd told her he loved her, since the moment he'd said he wanted to marry her.

What's wrong with me?

She'd asked God to let her love Drake, and when her prayer was answered, she'd been afraid to say yes.

She sloshed more water onto the floor and scrubbed with extra vigor.

But what if I can't make him happy? He says he loves me, but what if he stops after we're married?

She'd been left before. There had been something missing in her. She'd been unable to keep her husband. What if she failed again?

On the other hand, if Drake was right, if it was God who brought them together, how could she run away? How could she refuse if this was God's plan for her? for them? And wasn't love worth the risk?

As if summoned by her tumultuous thoughts, Drake appeared in the kitchen doorway, looking strikingly handsome. He wore black trousers, vest, and suit coat, with a white shirt beneath. He carried a black Stetson in his right hand. A gold watch chain disappeared into a watch pocket.

Her breath caught in her chest at the sight of him. She'd scarcely seen him yesterday. She'd known he'd left her alone to work through her thoughts and doubts, which were legion. Now he was there before her, and all she could think of was throwing herself into his arms.

"I'm going to be gone for a few days," he said.

"Gone?"

"Parker and I are going to meet with a man from the railroad."

She stared at him, her mind harkening back to the day—not so very long ago—that she'd determined to help Drake start living again. And now it had happened. He was going to help bring the railroad into Dead Horse.

"Faith? You're making this much harder than it needs to be."

"I know."

He crossed the room with slow, deliberate strides. She thought for a moment that he might reach out and draw her to her feet. Instead he knelt, bringing his eyes level with hers, unmindful of the soapy water dampening his trousers. Then he lifted his hand as if to touch her before letting it fall again to rest upon his thigh. "What are you afraid of?"

Surprisingly, she didn't hesitate to answer. "I'm afraid your love for me isn't real, or if it is, that it won't last. I'm afraid I'll take a chance on loving you and only get hurt. How can you possibly know if you love me or not? I've been here such a short time. You don't really know me, Drake. You don't know who I am."

"I know you, Faith," he answered softly. "I've been observing you from the day you first arrived. You love your children, would do anything for them. I've seen your patience, your joy, your tenderness, your concern for others ... even your faith in God." He reached out again, this time fingering a strand of her hair. "I know you're beautiful but never vain ... because you have even more beauty in your soul."

His image blurred as tears filled her eyes.

"I know when I hear your voice, my heart comes alive. I know when I hear you singing, I feel like singing, too. I know that even when you're afraid, you do what you need to do." He moved his hand to the side of her face, pressing his palm against her cheek, cupping it gently.

She leaned into it and closed her eyes. Always his touch had been gentle.

He continued in a whisper, "I know that when you kiss me you make me feel whole again instead of like half a man."

Faith felt the words pierce her heart. She lifted her head from his hand and opened her eyes to stare at him. Half a man? Is that what Larissa had seen? If so, then she'd been the one blinded in Drake's accident. When Faith looked at him, she saw a man who took her breath away.

"I know I want you for my wife, Faith. I know I love you. And I'll love your children as if they were my own. We could be a family, if you'll only take the chance."

Take the chance....

Her heart beat like a tom-tom.

Take the chance.... Take the chance.... Take the chance....

Drake rose from the floor, towering above her, tall and strong and splendid. "Please think about what I've said while I'm away."

Think about what he'd said? She knew she would think of little else. How could she do otherwise, loving him as she did?

"I've asked Faith to marry me," Drake told Parker after they'd been riding in silence for about an hour.

His friend reined in his horse, coming to a dead stop. "You've asked ..." Eyebrows raised, he stared at Drake, mouth slack. Finally he said, "Well, I'll be. When you got back to livin', Drake, you did it up right and in a hurry."

"She hasn't said yes yet."

"You think she won't?"

Drake stared toward the horizon. "I don't know."

He remembered the way she'd looked at him, her pretty eyes brimming with unshed tears. She loved him. He was sure of it. What he wasn't so sure of was whether or not she would ever risk admitting it—to herself or to him.

But she must, for losing Faith now would be a hundred times worse than the blindness that had changed his life seven years ago.

Faith went for a stroll with the children after supper. The house seemed unpleasantly quiet and empty without Drake there.

They walked down from the ridge to the river below and sat in the shade of the tall cottonwoods, pines, and aspens. Alex recounted the day Mr. Rutledge had taken him fishing here, pointing out the place where he'd caught his very first fish.

Becca was suitably impressed with her brother's adventure. "Do you think Mr. Rutledge will take me fishing, Mama?"

Before Faith could open her mouth, Alex said, "'Course not. You're a girl."

Becca's eyes filled with tears of disappointment as she looked at her mother for confirmation.

"Alexander Butler," Faith said sternly, "I've never heard such nonsense. Becca is perfectly capable of going fishing."

"Well, she wouldn't catch nothin'."

"Perhaps not. But perhaps you won't catch anything the next time you go, either."

"Becca couldn't toss in her line the way Mr. Rutledge showed me. She's not strong enough."

"Then maybe you'll have to help her."

Becca rubbed her eyes with her knuckles. "I wish Mr. Rutledge was here right now."

"So do I," Faith admitted. She drew up her legs, hugging them to her chest as she rested her chin on her knees. "So do I."

"Ma?"

"What is it, Alex?"

"Are we gonna stay here forever?"

Marry me, Faith.

"I don't know."

"Won't Mr. Rutledge let you keep workin' as his housekeeper?"

She glanced at her son. "Don't you miss traveling? Think of all the cities we've seen. And remember all our friends in Mr. Drew's company. Don't you miss them?"

"I'd rather stay here with Mr. Rutledge."

Marry me, Faith.

"So would I, Mama," Becca chimed in.

Marry me, Faith.

She reached out and stroked Becca's strawberry blond hair, then glanced toward her towheaded son. It had been the three of them against the world for so long now.

Wife and child,
Those precious motives, those strong knots of love.

She turned her gaze once more upon the swift-running river, but it was Drake she envisioned standing before her.

We could be a family, if you'll only take the chance. . . .

"All right, Drake," she whispered. "I'll take the chance."

16

GREGORY Shoemaker, the railroad's representative, a corpulent man in his late fifties, was fastidiously dressed in a tweed suit, white shirt, and stiff collar. What hair was left to him had turned yellow gray and was trimmed close to his scalp. Smoking a fat cigar, he leaned back on his leather-upholstered chair with the air of a man used to commanding immediate agreement from those around him.

Drake disliked him instantly.

"As I told Mr. Telford a few weeks ago, I'm afraid I can promise nothing for Dead Horse." Shoemaker's nose wrinkled, as if the very name of the town caused a bad taste in his mouth. He tapped the ashes from the cigar into an ashtray on the table. His gaze drifted to the window of the opulently decorated hotel room that served as his office.

Drake wasn't so easily dismissed. "It's my understanding James Telford went to Cheyenne to meet with other people in your company. It sounded as if there might have been another opinion expressed there."

Shoemaker's round face turned red, and his eyes narrowed as he directed them toward Drake again. "I can assure you, you're mistaken, Mr. Rutledge. I make these decisions."

Drake rose from his chair, his gaze never wavering. He set his Stetson on his head, then leaned forward, resting his knuckles on the table. "Let me help you understand a few things. I am not some cowpoke just off the Chisholm Trail with only two bits in his pocket to show for it. I have enough money to buy and sell you, and if you want me to prove it, I'll be happy to get myself a ticket to Cheyenne so I can have a talk with your superiors. Maybe they'll be interested in the number of cattle I'd be shipping out of Dead Horse."

The large man's Adam's apple bobbed as he swallowed nervously.

Drake straightened. He tugged the brim of his black hat, settling it more securely on his head, shading his eyes from view. "Now, why don't you check into this a little more thoroughly and find out what it will take to get that line up to Dead Horse. I'll come back tomorrow. Shall we say about nine o'clock?"

"Now see here—"

"Or shall I simply send a telegram to arrange a meeting in Cheyenne?"

Shoemaker scowled. "All right. Be here at nine. I'll look into it for you."

Drake left without another word. When he stepped onto the boardwalk outside the hotel, he paused and drew a deep breath, then smiled. It felt good to care about something beyond himself. He might not know the townsfolk of Dead Horse that well, but he was going to do his best to help them save their town. It was his town, too, even if he had realized it late.

Then he wondered what Faith was doing at that same moment. Breakfast would be over by this time and the dishes already washed and put away. What had she fixed the cowboys to eat this morning? Hotcakes? Eggs? Porridge?

She'd never been confident of her cooking abilities. He'd seen her reading that cookbook, poring over the recipes, then watching the men as they ate, trying to judge if she'd succeeded or failed. But she'd done her best. Faith always did her best. She deserved the best in return.

He glanced across the street at the row of shops. Before he went back, he meant to find Faith the perfect gift. Something that would prove how much he loved her.

Whistling beneath his breath, he stepped off the boardwalk and headed toward the shop marked "Millinery." It seemed a good place to start.

Gertie wondered if she was crazy for bringing Rick into these hills to sober up. He surefire wasn't appreciative of what she was doing for him. She figured she'd rather bust fifty broncs in one day than knock heads with the doctor for another ten minutes.

It wouldn't be so bad if she knew what to expect from him half the time. But she didn't. One minute he was as docile as a newborn kitten. The next he was as cantankerous as a bronc with a burr stuck in his haunches.

That first day he was sober enough to know what she'd done, he'd set out walking, thinking he could find Dead Horse on his own. She'd let him wander around lost until an hour before sundown; then she'd gone for him. They'd ridden double on her dun-colored mare back to the hunting shack, but he hadn't been particularly grateful for the rescue.

Just like now. She sent up a prayer for help, as she'd taken to doing of late.

Rick stared at the fried eggs and bacon on his plate as if they were poison. Much of the time "poison" was a fair description of Gertie's cooking, and she was the first to admit it. But even she could fry up eggs and bacon without doing them too much damage.

"There's enough grease here to float a warship," Rick grumbled.

"Eat it anyway." She sat down on a chair opposite him. "You need t'get your strength back."

"Why are you doing this, Gertie?"

"We been over that already."

"I'm not worth your time and trouble."

"I think you're wrong, Doc."

He sighed as he moved the food around his plate with his fork. "Take me back to Dead Horse."

"I don't think you're ready."

He glanced up. His eyes were clearer today, but all that did was make it easier for Gertie to read the misery behind them.

"Doc, what're you punishin' yourself for?"

He ignored her question as he got up from the table and walked to the door. He opened it and stepped outside.

"Drinkin' won't bring 'em back." She followed him. "Won't bring your wife back neither. It'll only make you feel worse about yourself."

He let out a humorless laugh. "Don't you *ever* let up, woman?"

"Guess not."

"It must be why you're a good wrangler." He glanced over his shoulder, a mixture of resentment and admiration in his eyes. "You just hang on until you wear those wild horses down, don't you?"

"Yeah, I expect that's a fair description of what I do. But you ain't no wild horse."

"No. I'm not."

It near broke her heart to see him suffering this way. She didn't reckon it was going to make him love her in return, but she'd move heaven and earth to see him make it through this rough patch.

"Tell me about your wife," she instructed softly.

Her request was followed by a lengthy silence.

She waited. After all, she wasn't going anywhere. She was staying right here, stuck to Rick Telford like a tick on a hound dog. And that was where she meant to stay until he'd come to terms with himself and what life had handed him.

"Her name was Esther."

Gertie stared down at the mountain meadow, quiet in the mid-afternoon sunshine.

"She was the daughter of a doctor and the granddaughter of a doctor. I suppose that was one reason she agreed to marry me. I studied under her father. That was how we first met." He paused a moment. When he continued, his voice had softened. "Esther was pretty in a gentle sort of way. James looked a lot like her. She was a caring woman. Worked beside me throughout our marriage, helping me with my patients. Even after James was born, she still found ways to help." He fell silent again.

"You loved her a lot."

"Yes, I did."

Gertie turned. Rick was leaning against the wall of the cabin, his head bent forward, his arms crossed over his chest.

She wondered if her heart might break, right here and now. "Esther was mighty lucky."

"Lucky?" He let out a sharp laugh. "Not hardly."

"Why not?"

"Because I couldn't stay away from my liquor. Not even when I saw how unhappy it made her. Not even when my drinking affected my work. Not even when she became ill and needed me more than ever."

"My guess is she loved you anyway."

"Why are you doing this?"

"It's simple, Doc. You see, I understand why your Esther fell in love with you 'cause I feel the same way."

He opened his mouth to protest, but she stopped him with a raised hand.

"Don't say nothin', 'cause you ain't gonna change what I feel by tellin' me I don't really feel it." She took a step forward. "Now I know you think you're too old for me, but you're wrong there, too. You ain't too old. 'Sides, age ain't got nothin' t'do with love. Nothin' at all. Feelin's are just feelin's. They just are what they are. See?"

"I've lived a good deal longer than you, Gertie, and I—"

"There you go again, talkin' about how old you are."

"I'm a drunk. An old drunk."

She shortened the distance between them with a few quick strides. She didn't stop until their noses were mere inches apart. "Is that what you *want* to be?"

She waited for an answer, but he didn't give her one. Suddenly angry, she thought she might haul off and punch him. To keep from it, she spun around and marched off into the trees.

Let him stew in his own juices and fry his own eggs.

Waiting for Drake's return from Green River City was torturous. Minutes seemed like hours, hours like days.

Faith gave the house another thorough cleaning, washing and dusting, polishing and scrubbing. She went riding with Alex and found that her son was now the teacher and she the pupil. She made a new rag doll for Becca, sewing at night by lamplight.

She avoided her bedroom until forced there by exhaustion. She knew when she closed her eyes it would be Drake's face she saw. He haunted her dreams, made her restless with yearnings that had lain dormant for years.

With each new day she greeted the rising sun with a prayer that Drake would return soon. She prayed he would meet with success. She prayed he would still love her, still want her, when he came home. Then she prayed again he would return soon, before his absence alone broke her heart in two.

A full week passed before her prayers were answered.

Faith wasn't certain what had drawn her to the corner of the barn, but there she stood, staring toward the road. She'd stood there for a good ten minutes before she caught a glimpse of something. Nothing more than a blur at first, and then she made out two riders. They were cantering their horses.

Was one a black-and-white pinto?

She strained to see more clearly, walking forward, hardly mindful that she was moving at all.

Yes! Yes, one was a pinto.

She pressed the palm of one hand against her chest, as if to still the racing of her heart. She felt a wave of weakness wash over her and feared for a moment that she might faint from joy.

He's home!

Home. What a wonderful word it was. She'd never understood what it meant to have a home. She'd always thought it meant nothing more than having a house of one's own. But it didn't. A home was a place where people loved one another. Home was here, with Drake.

Hurry!

She saw the pinto break into a gallop, pulling away from the other horse. She knew Drake had seen her; she felt it in her heart. She wanted to lift her arm and wave. She wanted to pick up her skirts and run to meet him. Yet, feeling suddenly shy and unsure of herself, she did neither.

I love you.

Scarcely breathing, she waited for him to arrive. She strained to see his face, to read his expression, wondering if she would see her own feelings in his eyes.

And then he was there, sliding his horse to a stop, vaulting from the saddle. She saw his smile as he stepped toward her. She laughed, unable to contain her joy. A moment later she was in his arms, and he was whirling her around in a circle, his laughter joining hers.

"I love you, Drake." The words came with ease, as if she'd been speaking them for years.

He stopped, set her feet on the ground, cradled her head between his hands, stared deep into her eyes. "What?"

"I love you."

"Say it again."

"I . . . love . . . you." She rose on tiptoe and kissed him.

When their lips parted, he whispered, "Say it one more time."

"You first."

He kissed her forehead. "I . . ."

He kissed her earlobe. "Love . . ."

He kissed the tip of her nose. "You."

He kissed her lips, hungrily this time.

It was the sound of Parker clearing his throat that finally pulled them apart. Faith flushed as she met the foreman's gaze, then looked at Drake.

"Well?" Drake said. "Wasn't there something else you wanted to say?"

"I already told you." She smiled, despite her embarrassment over Parker's presence. "I love you, Mr. Rutledge."

"And?"

With mock innocence she echoed, "And?"

"And what else?"

Teasing humor vanished, and she answered him in earnest. "And I'll marry you."

He drew her to him with an agonizing tenderness. "You'll never regret it, Faith. I swear, you'll never regret it for a moment."

"I know." She pressed her head against his chest and closed her eyes.

This time Parker coughed. "Why don't I take care of your horse while you tell Faith about the railroad?" Without waiting for a reply, he led the pinto away.

Faith drew back and looked up. "The railroad. What happened?"

He grinned. "The trains are coming."

"Truly?"

"Truly."

She threw her arms around his neck. "We must go into town today. At once. We must tell everyone. They've been waiting so long for good news. You should be the one to tell them."

He stared down at her. She felt his gaze, as soft as the caress of his fingertips. It warmed her skin, quickened her pulse. With sudden insight she understood his hesitation. It had been one thing to go to Green River City and meet with strangers. It was something else entirely to face the people who were his neighbors, the people he'd avoided for so many years.

"I'll be with you," she said softly, tightening her arms around his neck. "I'll be with you always."

17

───────◆───────

GEORGE splayed the cards on the green felt surface of the table. "Three aces. Read 'em and weep." The other players grumbled as he swept his winnings toward the edge of the table with both hands.

It had been a good few hours with the cards, but George knew it was time to stop. He had the money he needed to buy a horse and a few supplies. It was time to move on. More than a week ago, he'd gotten off the train in this two-bit town on the Utah-Wyoming border. Something in his belly had warned him he'd fallen under the scrutiny of the conductor. Taking no chances, he'd disembarked at the next stop and lain low for a few days, using the last of his meager funds to rent a room at the local boardinghouse.

"Well, gentlemen." He stood. "It's been a real pleasure. I hope we'll have the opportunity to do this again."

He left the saloon and made his way to the boardinghouse at the edge of town.

Faith had better appreciate all I'm doing to come see her, he thought. *She'd better be glad to see her long-lost husband.*

Word about the railroad spread like a prairie fire. It warmed Faith's heart to see Drake standing with the other men of the community. In a matter of minutes he'd become a leader, someone to look up to, a man of authority. As for the women of Dead Horse, they seemed in awe of the mysterious Drake Rutledge. His long black hair, his broad shoulders, his height, and what Faith had always thought of as his pirate's patch seemed to have a dangerously appealing impact on the fairer sex.

I can't believe it. I'm jealous!

Every time Drake looked or smiled at another woman, Faith wanted to object, to stand between them and let it be known that he belonged to her. It wasn't a particularly pleasant feeling, and she was glad when they finally returned to the ranch.

While in town, they stayed apart, maintaining the illusion of employer and housekeeper, hiding their true feelings. They decided that until Reverend Arnold returned to Dead Horse and they could marry, it was best to share the news only with those closest to them. But once they were home, the children fed and put to bed, and the cowboys gone to the bunkhouse for the night, there was nothing to separate them any longer.

Drake led Faith into the parlor. Soft light spilled from a single lamp, lending a golden glow to everything within its reach. Outside, crickets chirped, and in the distance, the hoot of a night owl could be heard.

Drake turned and drew Faith into the circle of his arms. He pulled her close, then rested his cheek on the crown of her head.

"Was I imagining it," he asked, "or did you tell me earlier today that you'd marry me?"

She laughed softly as she nestled more closely against him. "You weren't imagining it."

"Say it one more time."

"I'll marry you, Drake."

She tipped her head back, and he kissed her sweetly. When their mouths parted, he stared down into her eyes. "The reverend better return to town soon."

They kissed again. Kissed until Faith was left limp and breathless. Then Drake guided her to the sofa and settled her there.

"I have something for you. Wait here." He strode from the room.

Was this really happening to her? she wondered as she stared at the empty doorway. Was any of it truly possible? Could she be so blessed to have found this happiness?

Drake stepped back into the parlor doorway, his arms laden with packages. "I brought you a few things from Green River City."

Faith laughed aloud. "A *few* things?"

"You think I got carried away?"

"Perhaps a little."

He knelt on the floor in front of the sofa and set the packages beside him. All signs of teasing disappeared as he met her gaze. "I've never done this before."

She leaned forward at the waist, wanting to be closer to him. "No one has ever done this *for* me."

Drake heard volumes in the truth of that simple statement. She'd never been cherished as she deserved, never treated as the gift from God that she was. He wanted to cradle her in his arms and promise her that nothing would ever hurt her again. He wanted to find George Butler and break his neck.

He picked up one of the packages and handed it to her. "Open it."

Faith's eyes sparkled as she untied the string and tore back the tissue paper. It was a dress, the same blue-green color as her eyes. She held it against her, gazing down as she rubbed the palm of one hand over the fabric. "It's beautiful."

"*You're* beautiful." He set the next package on her lap, eager for her to continue.

She raised her eyes to meet his. Warm color infused her cheeks.

"Go on. Open it."

She loosened the string, lifted the lid off the hatbox, and drew out a straw bonnet decorated with ribbons that matched her new dress. "Drake, it's lovely." She rose from the sofa and went to a gilded mirror on the opposite side of the room.

He watched as she set the bonnet on her head at a jaunty angle, tying the ribbons beneath her chin in a perfect bow. When she turned, she gave him a saucy smile. "What do you think?"

"I think you'd better open the rest of your gifts."

He couldn't recall anything he'd ever enjoyed more than watching Faith open one package after another. There was a second dress in one, matching shoes, gloves, and pocketbook in another.

Finally he placed a small box in her upturned hands and waited anxiously as she lifted the lid and pushed aside the tissue paper. He heard her sudden intake of breath.

Her gaze darted up to meet his. "Oh, Drake."

"Does it fit?"

She shook her head, seemingly unable to speak.

He took the narrow, solid gold ring—filigreed and set with three sparkling diamonds—from the box and slipped it onto her finger. "It does fit."

"You shouldn't have."

"Why not? I want my wife to have a beautiful wedding ring. This was the finest I could buy in Green River City.".

"Oh, Drake. I want to be a good wife."

He heard what she didn't say: *What if I fail you?*

Tears glittered in her eyes. "'Our wills and fates do so contrary run / That our devices still are overthrown; / Our thoughts are ours, their ends none of our own.'"

"*Hamlet?*"

She nodded.

With his finger beneath her chin, he tilted her head and gazed at her until she looked at him. "'Men at some time are masters of their fates.'"

A hesitant smile curved her mouth. "*Julius Caesar.*"

"Trust me, Faith. You've already made me the happiest man alive."

<hr/>

By moonlight, Gertie walked to the hot springs alone. The small, warm-water pool wasn't far from the cabin. It was one of the reasons she'd selected this site on which to build her hunting shack. She hadn't told Rick about the springs. Perversely, she'd forced him to make do with heating his water on the stove and filling the small washtub whenever he wanted to bathe.

As she sank into the hot water, her tension eased and the taut muscles in her shoulders relaxed. She let out a long sigh, closed her eyes, then slipped beneath the water. When she resurfaced, she rested the back of her head on a smooth stone and stared up through the trees and rising steam at the star-studded heavens.

What now? she asked God. *What am I supposed to do next?*

She hadn't returned to the cabin since she'd stalked off in anger earlier in the day. She'd gone to where she'd hidden the horses and taken her mare for a long ride, trying to settle her thoughts. It hadn't worked, of course.

"This lovin' business sure is a problem."

She'd been better off when she'd just had her work to tend to. She wasn't any good at bein' a woman, never had been, never would be. She should have known that and kept herself away from Rick from the start.

At least he was sober again. He might not stay that way once he was back in town, but for now he was sober. If only she could get him to see what she'd come to know—that a person was loved by God no matter what they did to try to push Him away. He was loved just as he was, drunk or sober. It was why Jesus came—to show His love to men by dyin' on that cross. Rick was just too stubborn to see it.

"Maybe I oughta keep him here. Never let him go back at all."

She shook her head. Even she didn't want a man by making a prisoner out of him. She'd rather dry up inside than get him that way, no matter how much she loved him.

She would have to take him back to Dead Horse soon. He'd have to make the decision about what he'd do then. He'd have to make his choice to stay sober or go back to drinking until he killed himself.

She straightened and reached for the soap sitting on the ground. She lathered her hair and skin, then rinsed herself clean. Next she pulled her dirty clothes into the water for a thorough scrubbing. When she was finished, she got out of the pool and dried herself off, then dressed in clean clothing before laying the just-washed items on two large boulders not far from the water's edge. She would come for them tomorrow afternoon once they'd had a chance to dry in the sun.

She took her time walking back to her tent. Rick would be asleep by now. He'd spent a great deal of time sleeping since she'd brought him here. She didn't know whether or not that was good for him.

She combed her fingers through her short, damp hair as she let out a long sigh.

She guessed she didn't know much about anything except horses. She most always knew what a horse was going to do. She could read things by the twitch of an ear or the flick of a tail. But folks were different. It was hard to know what they were thinking or feeling.

The cabin came into view, and Gertie stopped to stare at it. She wanted Rick well. She wanted him to look at her and see that she was a woman.

She silently scolded herself as she started forward again. She might as well wish to be the queen of England. It was just about as likely to come true.

The cabin door creaked softly as she opened it to peek inside. Pale moonlight spilled in with her, falling across Rick's bed.

He was sitting on the edge, staring at her. "I wondered if you were coming back," he said as he stood.

"You oughta know I wouldn't just leave you here."

"Yes, I guess I ought to know that."

She entered and turned as she pushed the door closed.

"I've been doing some thinking," Rick said.

She heard him step toward her, felt herself grow tense at his sudden nearness.

"You were right about me, Gertie. You were right about a lot of things."

She wasn't quite certain how to reply, so she remained silent.

"I owe you a debt of gratitude."

"You don't owe me nothin', Doc." She moved away from the door, slipping away from him, too.

Behind her, she heard a match strike, saw the flicker of light intrude on the darkness, followed by the glow of the lantern as the wick caught fire. A moment later Rick's shadow joined hers on the wall of the cabin.

"Gertie?"

"What?"

"Will you look at me?"

She drew in a deep breath, then did as he'd asked.

He touched her cheek. "I apologize."

"Don't want your apologies, Doc, or your gratitude."

"Nonetheless, you have them both."

"I just done what I thought was right."

"Gertie, I think it's time you take me back to Dead Horse."

Sadly, she agreed. "I reckon you're right, Doc. We'll ride out at first light." With that, she left the cabin, returning to her tent where she could let her heart break in solitude.

18

AUGUST arrived, ushered in by another heat wave. The sun burned the grasslands to the color of sand and shrank the streams and rivers from their banks. The house on the bluff above Dead Horse blistered in the summer sun. Late-afternoon thunderstorms blew through nearly every day, exploding with spectacular displays of lightning but no rain.

Short-tempered cowboys snapped at each other. Even the ever-affable Gertie scarcely had a good word to say to anyone. Alex and Becca were no better than the others; they fought with each other constantly.

Only Faith and Drake seemed immune to the effects of the high temperatures that blasted the valley like a furnace. Each moment they were together was a joy, and they made an unspoken pact not to allow anything to mar the newly discovered pleasure of loving each other as they impatiently awaited word of the good reverend's return to Dead Horse so they could marry.

When each day was done, they rendezvoused in the parlor.

Drake frequently played the piano, and Faith would sing in the still of an evening. They talked about their childhoods, acquainting each other with the pasts that had shaped them. Drake told Faith about his parents, about his schooling, about his years of travel. He even told her about Larissa. And Faith talked about the cities she'd visited and lived in, about the life of an actress, about her dreams and aspirations.

They had covered nearly everything imaginable, had come to know each other better than either had thought possible, when Drake broached the one topic they'd been avoiding. "Tell me about George."

She looked up and met his gaze. "What would you like to know?"

"How you met. Start there."

"The company was in Boston," she said softly, looking back in time as she returned her head to his shoulder. "We were performing *The Taming of the Shrew,* and I had the role of Bianca. I was seventeen. I don't know how George came to be backstage that night." She gave her head a slight shake, realizing she'd never asked and wondering why she hadn't. "I don't remember who introduced us. Just suddenly there he was, telling me how marvelous my performance had been, that I should have had the lead part, that I would be famous and wealthy one day, that I was a great beauty."

"You *are* a great beauty."

Again she shook her head. "No, he was the beautiful one. I always thought he looked like an archangel with his golden hair and blue eyes. He had the most disarming smile. I'd never met anyone else like him. His tongue was glib, and I often said he could make a river run upstream with just a few sweet words."

"You loved him."

"Yes. At least I thought I did." She stopped and considered her answer, then said, "No, I know I loved George. But it was the man I thought he was whom I loved. We were married a few months later, right after my eighteenth birthday."

She paused again, wondering what to say next. Her marriage had been unhappy and disappointing from the start. George had so often hurled cruel words at her, and once he had hit her with the back of his hand. She'd been pregnant with Alex and unable to work. They'd had little money left, and George had flown into a rage, blaming her for all the things they'd lacked. It was the one and only time he'd struck her physically, but not the last or only time she was in pain because of him.

Drake's fingertips stroked slowly over her hair. "He hurt you."

"George expected life to be easy. He expected everything to be given to him on a silver platter. It often was, but not by me. I failed to do what I was supposed to do. I was supposed to make him rich or, at the very least, to support him while he pursued other pleasures." She pressed her mouth closed, not wanting to hear the bitterness that had crept into her voice.

"But he gave you Alex and Becca."

Drake amazed her sometimes, the way he knew the right thing to say.

"Yes, he gave me Alex and Becca."

He tilted her head, forcing her to look up. "If they'll let me, I'll be a father to them. You know I love them."

Her heart felt as if it would burst. She'd never thought she would be able to trust again. She'd never thought she would be willing to risk her heart, her love, again. But she trusted Drake. She'd risk anything for him.

"I'll love them as much as the children I hope we'll create together." He kissed her temple. "I hope we'll give Alex and Becca many brothers and sisters."

A firestorm ignited within her as his mouth claimed hers with a kiss made more furious by controlled passions.

When their lips parted, Faith glanced up again, staring at the man she loved beyond reason, shaken by the depths of her feelings.

He kissed her again, tenderly this time, then rose from the couch and lifted her in his arms. He carried her to the stairs and set her on her feet, one step above him. "You'd best go to your room, Faith." His smile was tense. "I'm a man, not a saint."

Oddly, she felt like laughing for joy.

Rick stared at his reflection in the mirror. The face of a forty-three-year-old man stared back at him. A forty-three-year-old dry-drunk who had no business thinking about a girl of twenty-five the way he kept thinking about Gertie Duncan.

He swirled the brush in his shaving mug, then applied the soap lather to his face and began the morning ritual of scraping away the dark gray bristles.

Gertie hadn't come into Dead Horse since the day they'd returned from the mountains. For all he knew, she'd left the Jagged R Ranch. For all he knew, he'd never see her again.

Finished shaving, he splashed his face with water and dried it with a towel, glancing one last time in the mirror.

Gertie might be a tough, no-nonsense wrangler around her horses, but she was an innocent when it came to men. She thought she was in love with him, and her infatuation appealed to his ego, made him feel younger, stronger. There wasn't anything more to it than that.

Was there?

"You're an old fool," he muttered. "Just an old fool."

But he still couldn't stop thinking about Gertie.

Gertie leaned on the corral gate, staring dismally at the horse inside. She hadn't worked the gelding today. She hadn't felt like it. All she wanted to do was lie down someplace cool—wherever that might be—and sleep.

"Gertie?"

She glanced over her shoulder and watched Faith's approach.

"I haven't seen much of you since your return. How is Dr. Telford?"

"He's okay, I guess. Haven't seen him lately."

"And what about you?"

"I'm okay, too." She turned her gaze to the horse in the corral, hoping Faith hadn't seen the truth in her eyes. She was anything *but* okay.

Faith touched Gertie's arm. "We just learned that Reverend Arnold will be in Dead Horse at the end of the week. I was hoping you would do me a favor."

"If I can, you know I'd be glad to."

"I'd like you to stand up with me at our wedding."

Gertie gaped at Faith.

Faith's smile was serene. "Please."

"Shootfire! I'm no good at stuff like that. I proved that back on Independence Day. I got me no business in a dress. I look plumb foolish."

"You don't have to wear a dress."

This time the laughter ripped right out of her chest. "You want me there in my Sunday-best buckskins?"

"If that's what you want to wear."

Her laughter died abruptly. "You're serious."

"Gertie, you were kind to me from the first day I came to the

Jagged R. You've taken an interest in Alex, helped occupy his time while I did my work, taught him all about horses."

"Wasn't nothing."

"You've been my friend. I want you to be my witness when I marry Drake."

Her friend. A lump formed in Gertie's throat, making it hard to reply. She could use a friend right about now.

"Gertie? Are you certain you're all right?"

She shoved away from the corral. "'Course I am," she snapped, suddenly irritable. "What do you think's wrong with me?"

Faith raised an eyebrow but said nothing.

Gertie wished she could confide in Faith about her love for Doc, but she didn't know how. She'd always been tight-lipped about her own business. Always had thought it best to keep her private matters private.

"You can talk to me anytime about anything, Gertie. Just remember that."

She shrugged, as if Faith's offer didn't mean the world to her.

"We're planning the wedding for right after Sunday service. You'll be there?"

"I'll be there."

"Thank you." Faith stepped forward and kissed Gertie's cheek, then hurried back to the house.

I wish it was us gettin' hitched, Doc. Why couldn't you let it be us?

19

FAITH awoke with a start. She sat up, placing one hand over her rapidly beating heart. The details of the nightmare had already been swallowed into some dark place in her mind, leaving only remnants of terror.

She rose and went to the window, hoping for a cool breeze to soothe her, but the night was still. A sliver of moon was overhead, halfway on its trek across the sky.

It was the heat, she told herself. She was feeling oppressed by too many hot days in a row. That was what caused the nightmare. There was nothing to fear.

Feeling restless and fearful, she left the bedroom, descended the stairs, went outside, and walked across the swath of lawn toward the bluff. Here at last she found a light breeze rising from the valley below.

She forced her breathing to slow, forced her jangled nerves to calm. The nightmare had been the result of exhaustion, she told herself. Sadie Gold had once again organized the women of Dead

Horse, this time to help with Faith's wedding. Sadie had them baking and sewing and heaven only knew what else. It was all the work and planning for the wedding and not enough sleep. That was all. Nothing more.

The days since learning of the reverend's imminent return—allowing them to at last announce their intention to wed—had been happy, contented ones. Alex idolized Drake, and Becca was completely under his spell, too. At the ranch, there had been plenty of good-natured ribbing to go hand in hand with the congratulations. Faith had enjoyed every moment of it. They were all her family, she'd realized—Parker, Gertie, Swede, Johnny, Dan, Will, and Roy. She'd grown to care for each and every one of them. This was her home. She had everything she would ever need or want right here.

In truth, her life on the stage seemed faraway and long ago. It seemed to have happened to someone else. Her new life was harder in many ways, the work never-ending. But it was infinitely more satisfying to her at the end of the day when she tucked her children into their beds and saw the healthy glow on their cheeks, heard the laughter in their voices.

And moments with Drake were always pure bliss. Her love for him increased by the minute, as did her happiness.

As those thoughts filled her head, the effects of the nightmare drained away, and she felt once again the rightness of what lay before her. She let out a contented sigh as she combed back her long hair with her fingers, the night air cooling her scalp. She turned and looked at the house, the roof rising above the treetops. She could see the window to her room—only it wouldn't be hers for much longer. In a few short days she would move her things into the master bedchamber. In a few short days she would be Drake's bride. In a few short days . . .

She shivered again, but not because of the nightmare or the cooler air.

"Just a few more days," she whispered. "Just a few."

Rick glanced at the clear blue sky. An eagle soared overhead, winging its way west. The sun, still early in its daily trek, had already evaporated the morning dew from the range, and the summer air smelled fresh and clean. From up on the ridge, he heard a young boy's shouts of pleasure.

Not long ago, he wouldn't have taken note of any of these simple things, not even when he'd been sober. He'd been too busy wishing he could drink again, resenting the pull the bottle had on him. But no more.

He had Gertie to thank for so much, but his thanks wouldn't be welcomed. Gertie didn't understand he could still be grateful for the help and support she'd given without confusing it with the love that had taken hold of his heart. He was sure of it now. He'd found a new freedom and God had also given him this love.

His horse and buggy topped the rise, and the Jagged R came into view. A moment later he saw Gertie on horseback in the field beyond the barn. She called something to Alex as the boy guided his mount through a maze of poles stuck in the ground.

He steered the buggy in her direction. He still didn't know what he was going to say. Whatever he came up with, she would probably dismiss it. He'd hurt her by rejecting her declaration of love, and for that he was immensely sorry.

She turned her head and saw him. The smile left her face.

When he drew near, Rick reined in, then got out of the buggy. "Good morning, Gertie." He waved at the boy. "Morning, Alex."

Alex waved back but didn't stop riding.

Rick returned his gaze to Gertie. Her hat hung from its leather string against her back. Her chestnut hair gleamed in the morning sunlight. Her complexion was tanned, but even so, he could see the splash of pink in her cheeks as he walked toward her. He loved it when she blushed like that.

"You haven't been back to town, Gertie."

She glanced toward Alex. "Been busy."

"Too busy to see me?"

She ignored him.

"I've missed you."

That caused her to look over.

"I'd like to talk."

"Don't know that we have anything more t'say to each other, Doc. I think maybe we said it all."

"I wish you'd call me Rick."

She cocked an eyebrow.

"Would you mind dismounting? Just for a moment? I'm going to get a crick in my neck from looking up at you."

She shrugged, then did as he'd asked.

Rick took a deep breath, searching his mind for the right words to say. "Gertie, I've made a lot of mistakes in my life. Through the years, I failed Esther and James, my friends, and my patients. I don't want to make another mistake with you."

Hurt flashed in her eyes.

He took hold of her hand, squeezing tightly so she wouldn't pull away. "No. You've misunderstood. The mistake I mean would be losing you." His grip tightened even more. "Common sense says I'm too old for you, but I don't care. I want you with me, Gertie. I want you to marry me."

After a long silence, she asked, "Why?"

"Not because I'm grateful for what you've done for me, for saving my life when I didn't think it was worth anything, although I'm glad you did."

"Then why, Doc?"

"Because I've come to care for you."

Gertie took a step back, jamming her thumbs into the waistband of her trousers as she turned her head to stare at Alex. The boy was still riding through the training course.

Rick took hold of her arm and drew her back around, forcing her to face him again. "Do you still care for me?"

"Look at me, Doc. I ain't wife material. I wear trousers and bust broncs and work with a bunch of sweaty, smelly cowpokes. I don't speak proper. I can't read no better than Alex over there. I'd make a mighty poor doctor's wife."

"Then you shouldn't have set out to make a doctor fall in love with you."

✦

Gertie felt like crying, something she tried never to do, even on the worst of days. Wranglers didn't cry. Not if they were going to be accepted by the other cowpokes on a ranch. She'd learned that a long time ago.

"I'm all confused," she mumbled, speaking the truth before she could stop herself.

"I know." He drew her close. "So was I for a while. But I'm not any longer." He kissed her. "Be my wife, Gertie."

Her heart pounded so hard she could scarcely hear herself think. She went all weak in the knees, and her throat was choked with tears. Somehow she managed to say, "I reckon you'll be plenty sorry if we marry."

Rick laughed. "I doubt it." Then he kissed her again, and the last of her resistance went out of her.

"All right, Doc—," she began when the kiss ended.

"Rick," he interrupted.

She sighed. "All right, Rick. We'll get hitched, but not 'til next week, not 'til after all the hullabaloo for Faith and Mr. Rutledge is over. And don't say I never warned you how sorry you'd be."

"I won't."

"Remember, we ain't sayin' nothin' until next week. Agreed?"

"Agreed." He was grinning as though he'd won first prize at the state fair.

She scowled at him. "Don't be so blamed agreeable."

His smile broadened. "Okay."

"Men," she muttered as she strode to her horse, feeling happy and confused at the same time. She ignored the stirrup and swung up onto the saddle using only the saddle horn. Gathering the reins in one hand, she returned her gaze to Rick one final time. "Don't think I'll be changin' for you. I am who I am."

Something subtle altered his smile into a look of tenderness. "I wouldn't change a single hair on your head, Gertie," he answered softly. "Not one single strand."

20

TODAY IS MY WEDDING DAY.

It is early morning as I sit at the table in my room on the third floor of this house. The sun has yet to peek over the horizon. The sky is slate gray, in that half state between dark and light. Alex and Becca are asleep in the adjoining room. The house is quiet. It seems only I am awake and eager for this day to begin.

It has been more than a year since my last entry into this journal. I don't know why I awakened this morning, wanting to put my thoughts down. Perhaps one day when I am old and gray, I will read these words and smile in memory of the young woman, so in love, so happy. And that is what I am.

So in love.

So happy.

Do I, Faith Butler, deserve such a wealth of joy as Drake has given me?

There has been so much to do in preparation for the wedding, and I am impatient for it to be over, impatient for the moment to arrive when I am Drake's wife.

*Time goes on cr utches till
Love have all his rites.*

I did not understand the truth of those lines ever so much as I do now. I could scarcely sleep last night. Time crawls.

Never once had I thought to love again. Certainly never did I expect to give my heart so completely as I have given it now. This is, I think, simply another form of madness, but if so, I am willingly mad. It is tremendously freeing to be able to trust someone again, not to hold others at bay for fear of what hurt might be incurred later.

Today marks the beginning of a new life for all of us. Not just the children and me, but Drake, too. I look at him now and cannot remember the angry man whom I met in his darkened library. I know he was once so, but I cannot remember him. God has so transformed him. And only within these pages can I confess that I am glad Larissa Dearborne was a stupid woman. If not, I would never have met Drake. If not, I would not know such bliss.

Yes, I am glad Larissa was a fool. Selfish of me, I know. Drake suffered because of her, but out of his hurt came the man I love, the man who loves me.

The day has arrived. The first rays of sunshine are spilling through my window onto the floor. The robins have begun to sing in the trees, as if rejoicing for me.

It is going to be a glorious day. I can feel it.

I altered my favorite dress, the gold-and-brown stripe with the silk polonaise. Sadie made me a gift of a felt hat with an aigrette in front that matches the gown perfectly. A new pair of tan suede gloves completes my wedding attire.

Will Drake think me beautiful?

Silly question. It has always meant nothing to me when people complimented my looks, yet I long for Drake's approval. I want him to think me beautiful, to desire me as I desire him.

I hear sounds in the next room. The children must be waking. It is time for me to close this entry.

Today is my wedding day.

Drake mounted the stairs to the third floor, glad that after today it wouldn't be necessary to do so. After today, when he went looking for Faith, he would find her in his own bedchamber.

Pausing at her door, he rapped softly. "Faith?"

"Come in."

He twisted the knob and pushed the door open before him. His gaze immediately sought and found her. She was standing in front of the looking glass, her hands near her head as she secured her hat into place. As he entered the room, her arms lowered and she turned slowly to face him.

He stopped abruptly, whispering her name. Never had he seen her look more enchanting than she did at this moment. It wasn't her clothes, although they were lovely, the gold color flattering to her complexion. It was more the expression she wore and what it did to his heart. She was beautiful in countless ways, ways that mere words failed to define.

He held out the small box in his right hand. "I brought you something."

"Not another gift." She smiled as she shook her head. "You've spoiled me enough already."

He moved farther into the room. "I could never spoil you enough." He stopped, took one of her hands, and placed the small box in it. "Go on. Open it."

She lifted the lid, and a gasp slipped through her parted lips. "Drake…"

"It was my mother's."

She gave her head a slow shake. "I can't—"

"I want you to have it."

She lifted the gold necklace, set with teardrop-shaped topaz stones, from the box.

"It matches your dress," he said, stating the obvious.

"As if it were planned," she whispered, more to herself than to him.

"It was planned." His hands on her shoulders, he turned her to face the mirror, then met her gaze in the reflection. "Only not by us. God brought us together. I know it's true."

"Drake?" She turned, a sudden urgency in her voice. "You've made me wonderfully happy. I didn't know I could feel this way." The words rushed out of her, like water bursting through an earthen dam. "I never hoped I would find a love like this. Sometimes, I'm afraid I'll wake up and find it's all been a dream and that you were only someone I imagined. Or that I'm too happy and you'll be taken from me." She swallowed hard. "I wasn't a good wife to George. I didn't know how to make him happy. He turned to other women for his pleasures. He said I was … cold."

Drake's heart tightened in his chest as he drew her into his embrace. "Ah, Faith, you're anything but cold." He brushed his lips against her temple, lowering his voice. "You don't have to be afraid that I'll disappear. I won't ever leave you, no matter what. You taught me how to trust again. How to trust God and how to trust others. You can trust me, too." He stepped back and took hold of her arm. "Come along, Faith Butler. I want to change your last name to match my own."

A smile brightened her face. "I want that, too."

Everyone was there. Gertie Duncan and all the Jagged R cowboys. Sadie and Joseph Gold and their children. Rick Telford. The O'Rourkes and the Hornes. The widows O'Connell and Ashley. Jed Smith, wearing his false leg in honor of the occasion.

Benches had been placed in the shade of the trees. Most people had come directly from church, but even those who didn't attend services, like the Golds and Stretch Barns, were dressed in their Sunday best.

Standing nearest the river, talking to the reverend, was Drake. He looked dashing in his black coat and trousers, white shirt, and gloves. In all Faith's years in the theater, she'd never seen anyone who looked more handsome, anyone who commanded more respect or attention.

"Is it truly possible he wants to marry me?" she whispered to herself as she stared out the back door of the hotel.

"What?" Gertie asked.

Faith gave her head a slight shake as she turned to look at the woman beside her.

Gertie had indeed worn her fancy buckskins, and Faith thought she looked wonderful. The soft clothing had fringe along the outside seam of the trousers as well as across the back of the jacket. In honor of the special occasion, Gertie's dark curls were freshly washed. Her eyes sparkled with pleasure, and there was a look about her that made Faith wonder if Gertie was keeping some sort of secret.

She might have asked, but just then Becca skipped through the doorway. "Mama, Reverend Arnold says it's time to begin. You're to come out now."

Faith's stomach fluttered, and her mouth went dry. It was time. It was about to happen. It was real.

"Ready?" Gertie asked.

Faith reached for the bouquet of late-summer wildflowers Becca had picked that morning on the way into town. "I'm ready."

Gertie and Becca led the way out of the hotel. Faith hesitated a moment, then followed them into the sunlight.

Her gaze was locked on Drake.

Drake...

Her future...

Her happiness...

Her all.

From the window of his hotel room, George Butler watched as Faith came into view. He knew it was Faith, even though he couldn't see her face. No other woman he'd ever seen had hair quite that color.

So, she thinks she's going to marry another man, does she? He grunted. *Not likely.*

And to think he might have arrived in this two-bit town too late. When he'd registered last night, he'd asked the proprietress if she knew Faith Butler.

"Of course," the woman had answered. "Are you here for the wedding? I'll confess I was very surprised when I heard the news. Mr. Rutledge was such a mystery to us all. Actually, he frightens me a little to look at him, but I guess the same can't be said for Faith. Of course, he *is* the wealthiest man in the state, from what I hear. We can be thankful he's decided to help this town. Once the railroad comes through, we'll all prosper. I was afraid I would be forced out before too long. Thank heavens it won't happen now."

George had been going to sign his last name as "Harvard," the alias he'd been using since leaving San Francisco, but then he thought better of it. Quickly he'd scrawled his real name across the registration book.

"Butler?" the proprietress had asked upon seeing his signature. "Are you family?"

"Yes," he'd replied evenly, "but Faith isn't expecting me. I'd like to keep my presence a secret until tomorrow." He gave her one of his most charming smiles. "Will you help me do that, Mrs. O'Connell?"

Last night, he hadn't known for sure what he intended to do. He'd only known that Faith's wealthy intended would somehow be his ticket out of his present troubles with the law. Now, as he watched Faith walk down the aisle between the rough wooden benches, a plan formed in his mind.

He slipped his arms into the sleeves of his suit coat, then tried to brush the travel dust from it. Afterward he smoothed his hair back with a dab of water on the palms of his hands. A quick glance in the mirror told him he looked as presentable as possible.

"Good enough for a long-lost husband."

"Dearly beloved ..."

Faith was only vaguely aware of Reverend Arnold's exhortations regarding the union between man and wife. Her pulse was racing too fast for her to concentrate on anything except wishing it to be over. In a few minutes she would be transformed into Mrs. Drake Rutledge. It mattered little to her what the reverend said or how long or short the ceremony was. She just wished it to be over.

"If any man has just cause why these two ..."

Her heart was happy, her soul content. Only a few months ago, if someone had told her what would be happening today, she would have scoffed. But look at her now. It was—

"I believe I have just cause."

There was a collective sucking in of breath from the wedding guests. For one terrible moment, Faith's gaze locked with Drake's. Then he turned around. But Faith couldn't seem to move. Even her heart threatened to cease its beating.

In a disapproving voice the reverend asked, "And who are you, sir?"

"I am the bride's husband. George Butler."

More gasps followed the statement; then a buzz of whispers began.

Faith felt as if she were starving for air. *No! No, it can't be true. It can't be.*

"Am I not your husband, Faith, my dear?"

She turned slowly.

He stood behind the wedding guests. He was thin, and his clothes looked worn. Yet he still had an air of assurance.

"You left us," she whispered. "You divorced me."

"Actually, I never got around to that small detail."

How very like him, she thought, feeling the insane urge to laugh.

She became aware of Drake's fingers tightening on her arm. She glanced up, wanting nothing more than to take hold of him and never let go. Then she saw something in his eyes that calmed her fears. He was here. He was with her, and so was God.

George strolled confidently down the break between the benches, drawing her gaze back to him. "It's fortunate I arrived when I did, my dear. It would have been rather messy to find yourself with two husbands. Don't you think?"

Drake stepped forward. "What do you want, Butler?"

"Ah, an enraged bridegroom." George smirked as he lifted an eyebrow. "How positively quaint."

"You're divorced," Drake challenged. "You married another woman."

"I never married Jane." George waved a hand at the onlookers. "But perhaps we should find someplace more private to continue this discussion."

Faith tried to think of something to say but she came up blank.

George gave her a cheerless smile, then turned toward the front bench where Alex and Becca were sitting. "Are these my children? Look how they've grown." He hunkered down and motioned them to approach him. "Come here and give your loving father a welcome back."

True terror sluiced through Faith. This was what she'd feared most of all. She understood the workings of George's mind, and she knew exactly how he meant to hurt her.

She moved quickly to place herself between him and her children. "Leave them alone, George," she whispered urgently. "Please."

"I don't understand." He rose from the ground. "I'm simply returning to my family."

"Whatever it is you want, you may have."

He looked genuinely surprised. "Whatever I want? But, my dearest wife, it is you and the children I want. Nothing more. Just you."

Her eyes filled with tears, and her throat was tight. "You're lying," she said, but only George was close enough to hear the words.

"You wound me to the quick." He covered his heart with the palm of his hand. "To the quick, my love."

She felt herself being sucked into some horrible vortex from which there was no escape. She wondered if she were about to faint. Drake's hand on her elbow saved her from finding out.

"I believe Mr. Butler is right," Drake said. "We should talk in private." He glanced over his shoulder. "Sorry, Reverend Arnold, but the ceremony is over. Alex. Becca. Get in the buggy."

Faith felt a sense of relief as the children hurried to do as they'd been told. *Run!* she wanted to scream. *Run away!*

"Come along, Faith," Drake said more softly.

"I beg your pardon, but—," George began.

Drake stopped him with a glare. "You may follow us to my house."

"See here—"

"I said to follow us, Mr. Butler." With a firm grasp, he drew Faith toward the waiting buggy.

"Mama," Becca said when Faith was settled on the front seat, "is that really my papa, like Alex says?" She hesitated, then continued, "I thought Mr. Rutledge was going to be my papa?"

Faith choked on a sob.

"I am, Becca," Drake responded firmly. "Just not today." He slapped the reins, and the horse shot forward.

No one spoke during the ride home. Faith didn't know if George followed, didn't have the courage to look behind her to find out.

He'll take my children. He'll take my children.

It wouldn't happen. Drake wouldn't allow it to happen.

But how could Drake stop George? George was the children's father. If he—

No, it wasn't going to happen that way. Surely this day would not end this way. Not today. Not today of all days.

Today was to have been her wedding day.

21

GEORGE Butler might never have performed on the stage, but Drake recognized immediately that he was a consummate actor.

"So, this is where you've been living," George said to Faith as his gaze swept the parlor. "My dear, I always thought you had the beauty and even the talent to make a name for yourself. I just never imagined that your talent lay outside the theater." His insinuation was clear in his expression and the inflection of his voice.

Drake would have struck him then and there, but Faith's hand on his arm stopped him. She stepped forward, her head held high, her shoulders rigid. "What is it you want?"

George offered a smile. "I believe I explained quite clearly in front of your wedding guests. I've seen the error of my ways and have returned for my wife and children. Thankfully I arrived when I did. Two husbands would have been illegal." His gaze shifted to Drake. "I believe I heard you're an attorney, Mr. Rutledge. Isn't it illegal to marry another man's wife?"

Faith didn't give Drake a chance to reply. "You married your mistress. I heard so from others."

"We lied." He shrugged. "Can't marry a second wife when you haven't divorced the first. Besides, Jane and I were never suited. We parted company a long time ago. I realized I'd made a tragic mistake in leaving you, Faith. You're my wife. My place is with you and the children." He glanced toward the hallway. "By the way, where *are* the children?"

Drake answered, "In their room. We thought it best if we spoke to you alone."

"*You* thought it was best?" George's voice showed his contempt. "You have no right to decide what's best for my children."

Sheer willpower kept Drake from tearing the man limb from limb.

Faith sank onto the sofa. Her gaze fell to her hands, folded in her lap. "I don't love you, George. The children and I ... we've made a new life for ourselves."

George wore a pained expression, but Drake saw right through it. He'd met others like him through the years, petty dictators of their own little worlds who took joy in hurting those weaker than they. George Butler wasn't here because he cared about his family. He was here for himself and only for himself.

Faith looked up, tears swimming in her eyes.

George shook his head. "If you won't change your mind and go with me, I suppose the children and I must go alone. But they'll miss you, I'm sure."

"George," she whispered hoarsely.

Drake couldn't bear it. He saw Faith's heart breaking, and he couldn't take it any longer. He stepped over to stand beside her, placing his hand on her shoulder. "I think it's time you left my house, Butler."

Without flinching, George answered, "As soon as the children are ready to go with me."

"You aren't taking Alex and Becca anywhere." Drake clenched and unclenched a fist.

"I *will* take them. You may be an important man in this town, Mr. Rutledge, but that won't stop me. Faith has been living with you. It's apparent to anyone what's been going on here. That won't sit well with a judge. He'll take those kids from her, and she'll never be allowed to see them again."

"Faith is my housekeeper."

"And I'm her husband and their father." He sneered as his gaze shifted to Faith. "You may have a divorce, my dear wife, if that's what you choose, but you'll never see your children again. The law will see to that."

Faith was crying softly now, tears streaming down her face. "Why are you doing this, George? Why?"

His expression turned once again to innocent concern. "Why? Because I love you, of course. I love you and the children, and I want us to be together again."

"Get out," Drake growled, his patience snapping. "Now."

"The childr—"

Drake took a threatening step forward. "Get out!"

Some of George's arrogance drained from his face. "Very well. I'll go. But I'll be back tomorrow." He picked up his hat. "Make up your mind what you're going to do, Faith. If I must, I'll send for the marshal to take them from here. The children are going to be with me. If you want to be with them, you'll be ready to leave, too."

Drake followed George into the entry hall and watched as he left the house. His chest tightened. His mind raced. He dreaded returning to the parlor. He knew Faith would look up at him, tears streaking her cheeks, and expect him to tell her everything would be all right.

He couldn't do that.

The law was on George's side. Even if George had divorced Faith and married another, according to a long-established tenet of the American legal system, fathers were the natural guardians of their children.

Drake raked his fingers through his hair, still wanting to do bodily harm to the man. George was lying. Drake was certain of it. He suspected Faith's husband—if indeed that was what he still was— was after something more than his family. Drake felt it in his gut.

"Drake?"

He turned and found Faith standing in the parlor archway.

"He can take the children. We can't stop him, can we?"

He said nothing. He'd rather be silent than lie to her.

Faith moved through the remainder of the day by rote. While Drake closeted himself in his library, searching for answers in his law books, Faith saw that her children changed out of their Sunday clothes. She answered their questions with words that explained nothing, but they were the best she could do. She prepared the noon meal for the subdued ranch hands, ignoring their looks of concern. She felt numb—and was grateful for it.

At supper, where all tried to pretend this was just a normal day, conversation was nearly nonexistent. By the time it was over, Becca was close to tears and Alex was mutinous.

"Can I be excused, Mama?" Becca whispered in a choked voice.

"Yes, you may."

Her daughter slipped from the table and ran up the back staircase. After a rebellious look at Faith, Alex followed close behind his sister. One by one, the cowboys likewise excused themselves, and within moments only Faith and Drake remained at the table.

She felt a strange panic squeezing her chest. She didn't want to be alone with Drake. She didn't want to face what had to be faced. Not yet. She kept her gaze locked on her untouched supper plate, pretending Drake wasn't there.

"Faith?"

Reluctantly she lifted her eyes. "The law is still on his side, isn't it? Simply because he's their father."

Drake was silent for a long time, his gaze unwavering. She could see his own heartache, which only increased her panic. Finally, in a gentle voice he replied, "Yes." He paused, then added, "But he won't succeed in keeping them."

"We can't be sure of that, can we?"

"Faith—"

"Please, Drake." She rose from her chair. "I can't talk about it now. I need some time alone." She fled, leaving the house, swift footsteps carrying her down the hillside and toward the river. She'd found comfort and answers there before. Surely she would find them again.

She followed the riverbank. She had no idea how long she walked. Time had no meaning to her. Finally, when she became tired, she sank to the ground, drew up her knees, and hugged them against her chest while she stared at the river.

Her thoughts slipped backward. Like faded photographs, memories flashed in her head. The first time she'd met George. Their courtship. The day he'd proposed to her. Their wedding day. The hopes that had filled her heart. The disappointments that had followed. Small apartments. Dingy hotel rooms. Fights, lots of fights. Alex's birth. Becca's birth. The night she'd found George with his mistress. The hard and lonely times that had followed.

George didn't love the children. He'd scarcely known they were alive when he'd lived with them. They had been an inconvenience to him. If he were to take them, he would neglect them. And if Becca should fall ill again …

She shivered as the sun sank behind the mountain peaks.

She remembered the first time she'd met Drake. She remembered the way her heart had been drawn to him. Had she begun to love him as early as that first meeting, when he'd snarled at her? She thought perhaps she had.

More memories of Drake filled her mind, and she pondered them, wanting to hold them close to her heart. Drake, turning up the lamp in his library, expecting her to run in horror from the room. Drake, standing on the porch in the moonlight, bitter and alone. Drake, carrying Becca down to the lawn, his touch so gentle. Drake, in town the night of her performance. Drake, with Alex's hand in his, the two walking side by side.

Drake, holding her.

Drake, kissing her.

Drake, loving her.

"What's the right thing to do, Lord? I'm confused. I'm frightened. What am I to do? I believed he divorced me. I thought I was released to marry because of his adultery. But what now? What now?"

If God had an answer, she didn't hear it.

Tears slipped down her cheeks. She didn't sob, not even when she realized she was bidding Drake farewell in her heart.

Like it nor not, George was legally her husband and the father of her children. She could refuse to go back to him. In time, she could probably obtain a divorce. But Alex and Becca would be awarded to George. His threat was not an idle one. She had seen it happen often enough among her acquaintances and fellow performers. She had seen it happen to her own parents. Actors and actresses were notorious for their disastrous marriages and their divorces, and the courts were not kind to them.

Dusk fell over the valley, turning the sky to pewter and the earth to ash. A short while later, Faith was surrounded by the earnest darkness of night. Stars twinkled overhead in a moonless sky. The song of the night creatures began—the chirruping of bullfrogs, the howl of a timber wolf, the hoot of an owl—but Faith was oblivious to it all.

She laid her cheek against her knees, closed her eyes, and began to rock back and forth. Soft, whimpering sounds rose in her throat but were strangled there.

That was how Drake found her, and if he lived forever, he would never forget the sight of her at that moment.

He dismounted and went to stand behind her, then sank to his knees. He drew her back against his chest and buried his face in her hair. "Faith," he whispered. "Don't. Don't cry. It's going to be all right."

"No, it isn't going to be all right. It's never going to be all right. I've loved you with everything in me. I never wanted to fall in love again. It hurts too much when it fails. But I loved you. Loved you more than I thought possible. And now I can't have you. Can't ever have you."

"You're giving up?"

"What else am I to do?"

He stood, drawing her with him, turning her toward him. He wished he could see her eyes, wished he could read what was written on her face. "Listen to me, Faith. I quit living seven years ago. I gave up. I turned my back on the world and wallowed in my own bitterness." He cupped her chin with his right hand. "You didn't quit. You rose above everything. You went on, no matter what. You gave your children whatever they needed. You didn't give up when George left you." His voice softened. "You can't just give up now."

She pulled away from him. "I'm not giving up. I'm being practical."

"Faith—"

"I'm still his wife."

Impotent rage welled in his chest. "He's lying. I can feel it. We'll prove it."

"And in the meantime, he'll take Alex and Becca away."

"Faith, you've got to trust me."

Her reply was small, almost inaudible. "I can't take the risk."

22

F AITH looked around the sparsely furnished hotel room with a feeling of déjà vu. This was where she and her children had begun their sojourn in Dead Horse. How appropriate that this would be where it ended.

"I don't wanna be here, Mama," Becca wailed plaintively. "I wanna go home."

Home. Faith's heart twisted as she mouthed the word. But she couldn't bring herself to say it aloud, knowing it would hurt too much. Besides, the Jagged R wasn't their home, merely a place where she'd worked. No different from the countless theaters in which she'd performed over the years.

No different at all.

Her shoulders slumped. What a lie that was. She couldn't fool herself or her children. Alex and Becca knew the Jagged R was more than where their mother had worked and more than a temporary place for them to live. In recent weeks it *had* become a home. *Their* home. Theirs and Drake's.

Drake.

She missed him. Missed him beyond even what she had imagined possible. A short time ago, he'd stood on the front porch and watched her drive away in the buggy. He hadn't argued with her this morning, hadn't tried to convince her to stay, but he hadn't made her leaving easy. He'd stood there and watched, his expression grim, his gaze unwavering.

Faith, you've got to trust me. You've got to trust God. . . .

I can't take the risk. I can't lose my children. . . .

You've got to trust me. . . .

Can't take the risk. . . .

Trust me. . . .

I can't. . . .

She sank onto the end of the bed, trying to rid herself of those terrible words playing over and over again in her head. She knew she'd struck Drake a cruel blow with her reply, but there'd been nothing else she could do, nothing else she could say.

"Is there anything you'll be needing, Mrs. Butler?"

Faith heard the curiosity in Claire O'Connell's voice, knew that whatever she did or said would be fodder for today's gossip at the general store. She glanced toward the doorway where the other woman stood. "No, there's nothing."

"I've sent Quinlin O'Rourke to find your husband. He went out half an hour ago."

"Thank you."

"Mr. Butler has the adjoining room. Under the circumstances, I thought—"

"Thank you."

Claire hesitated, looking as if she might say something more. Then, with a slight shake of her head, she hurried out of sight, not bothering to close the door.

Alex turned from his place at the window. "We oughta go back to the ranch, Ma."

"We can't."

"That's not true. Mr. Rutledge said we could stay."

Faith rubbed her eyes, wishing she could wipe away the headache behind them. "He was wrong."

"He wasn't wrong." Alex spoke with all the conviction of an almost-eight-year-old. *"You're* wrong."

"What's this? A tiff between mother and son?"

Faith looked up at the sound of George's voice. Her stomach twisted into a knot.

George closed the door behind him. "Mrs. O'Connell would dearly love to hear what we have to say to each other, but I think I'll leave it to her imagination."

As Faith rose from the bed, Becca hid her face in her mother's skirts. Faith stroked the little girl's head, both seeking and offering comfort.

Yesterday she had been too upset to notice many of the changes in George's appearance. Now she saw them. He had the look of someone who drank too much and ate too little. His clothes, always a source of pride to him, appeared worn and shabby; they hung loosely on his gaunt frame, as if made for someone else. His gold hair looked dull and lifeless. Gray half circles were etched beneath his eyes, and his complexion had turned sallow.

Golden, debonair, handsome George. Once upon a time she had loved him. She remembered it was true, but she couldn't recall the feeling itself. She found nothing appealing about him now. Perhaps because she'd learned how deceiving appearances could be. Perhaps because he was the one who had taught her that lesson.

"You look ill," she said for want of anything else to say.

His mouth tightened. "Sorry, Faith. I'm not going to keel over dead just so you can marry another." He muttered a foul curse as he approached her.

"Mama," Becca whimpered.

"Stop it, George. You're frightening her." Faith sat on the bed again and hugged her daughter. "It's all right, Becca. There's nothing to be afraid of."

"I don't feel good."

"It's okay, sweetheart. You don't have to—"

Becca twisted away suddenly and threw up on the floor. The vomit splattered onto her father's shoes and trousers.

George cursed again, this time shouting a string of words that must have been heard all the way down at the general store. "Clean that up before it makes us all puke," he snapped before storming out of the room.

Becca sobbed softly.

"It doesn't matter, darling." Faith helped her daughter onto the bed. "You didn't do anything wrong. You'll feel better in a minute."

"I hate him," Alex said with real venom.

Faith wondered if she might shatter into a thousand pieces. Her head pounded. Her nerves jangled. But somehow she managed to say, "Alex, it's not right to hate anyone. He's your father. You mustn't say—"

"He's not my father! He's not!" Then, just as George had done moments before, Alex slammed the door behind him as he left.

Gertie didn't need to pick up supplies today, but she hadn't felt much like staying at the Jagged R, where the mood was as unhappy as a woodpecker's in a petrified forest. Everybody was snapping at each other, from the boss to Parker to young Johnny. 'Course, she was as guilty as the rest. Seeing Faith and her kids riding off this morning was about the saddest sight she'd witnessed in years.

She glanced down the street toward the Telford house, wondering if Rick was inside or off on a doctor's visit somewheres. Tomorrow they'd been supposed to announce to one and all that she and Doc were getting married. That was what they'd agreed to on Sunday morning. But then George Butler had showed up, and she didn't know what was going to happen next. She looked over at the hotel, wondering if Faith was all right. It didn't seem fair that Gertie should be able to marry while Faith's heart was breaking. No, it didn't seem fair at all.

Just then Gertie saw Alex come out of the hotel. He ran down the main street, short legs pumping. Gertie didn't know much about kids, but she could tell when somebody was hurting. She'd bet a month's wages Alex was crying. She nudged her mare's ribs and followed the boy.

Alex veered off the road and headed toward the river, stumbling occasionally but never falling. He didn't stop until he reached the riverbank. Once there, he picked up a stick and threw it as hard as he could into the water. Then he picked up another and threw it, too.

Gertie dismounted. "Hey, Alex."

The boy spun around, then quickly rubbed his forearm across his cheeks, trying to erase all sign of tears. "What're you doin' here?"

"I thought you might need a friend."

"I don't need nobody." He turned his back to her and tossed another dried branch into the river.

"We all need somebody sometimes." She stepped up beside him, facing the rushing water but watching the boy out of the corner of her eye. "Want t'tell me what's got you all riled up?"

"I hate him!"

"Your pa?"

"Yes."

"Hatin' don't do you much good." She dragged the toe of her boot in a small circle, leaving a mark in the loose soil.

Alex looked at her. "I hate him anyway, and I'm not gonna stay with him. I'm going back to the Jagged R. Mr. Rutledge said I could be a wrangler for him someday. Well, I'm not gonna wait. I can work with you, just like I've been doing."

Gertie took a deep breath, then squatted beside Alex. As he'd done before her, she picked up a piece of wood and tossed it into the water. "I want you t'think long an' hard about this. I know things ain't easy for you, what with your pa showin' up and all. But things ain't easy for your ma, either. Don't you think she's gonna need you more'n ever?"

He sniffed and wiped his nose with his forearm.

"I know it'd just about break your ma's heart if you were t'go away."

"It isn't fair."

"No, I don't reckon it is."

Alex suddenly threw himself into her arms, knocking her off her heels and landing her backside in the dirt. She put her arms around him and hugged him close, letting him cry it out. At this point she was crying, too.

"It's gonna be all right, little wrangler," she whispered. "You'll see. It'll be all right. God has a way of workin' these things out. Ain't that what your ma always says?"

Gertie didn't know how long she held Alex, letting him weep against her shoulder. It didn't matter much. She just wanted to make the hurt go away. She also pondered a few choice things she'd like to do to that cur who called himself the boy's father. She might not know the whole story about him and Faith, but she knew enough to wish she could run him out of town and away from Faith and her young'ns.

After a long spell, Alex cried himself out. He sniffed noisily as he pulled back. "Sorry, Gertie," he mumbled.

She wiped her eyes, not caring that he was supposed to call her Miss Duncan. "Nothin' t'be sorry for." She got to her feet. "Now I reckon you oughta be gettin' back to your ma 'fore she starts t'worry. You want me t'come along?"

"No." He shook his head. "I'll be okay."

"Sure you will, pardner."

"Gertie?"

"Hmm."

"You won't tell the other cowpokes about... about this, will you?"

She offered an understanding smile. " 'Course not. Us wranglers've gotta stick together."

"Thanks."

She watched him walk away, saw the brave set of his shoulders, and she wanted to cry all over again.

Drake paced the length of his library, then turned. "I want you to go to San Francisco," he told Parker. "There's got to be something we can use against Butler. He didn't turn up here because he missed his family. He's in some kind of trouble. We need to know what."

"I'll do my best."

"Parker?" He stopped pacing and faced his friend. He sought the right words as he handed Parker an envelope containing the necessary funds and all the information he'd managed to compile.

Parker laid a hand on Drake's shoulder. "Don't have to say it. I know how important this is. We won't let him take those kids from Faith or her from you."

Drake nodded.

"I'll send word as soon as I can."

He nodded again as Parker left the library. Then he went to the window and stared out at the lawn. He knew he was looking for Faith, wanted her to be sitting in the grass, reading to Becca, or standing beside the clothesline, wisps of hair curling around her face and neck.

I can't take the risk....

He'd wanted her to trust him. She was supposed to trust him. And now she was at the hotel with the man who called himself her husband, and Drake couldn't do anything about it.

He leaned his forehead against the window frame. He tried not to listen to the small voice in his head whispering that Faith had returned to her husband by choice, that George was a whole man, not a blind one, that she had once loved him and might still. But those doubts were silenced as he remembered the look of defeat Faith had worn. She had left Drake only to protect Alex and Becca. And could he blame her? Wouldn't he have given his own life to protect them all if only he'd been given the chance?

He struck the window frame with his fist. There had to be something he could do. He would never allow that man to take Faith and the children. They were *his* family, not Butler's.

It was nearly midnight before George returned from the saloon. Faith was in bed with the children, Alex on her left, Becca on her right.

Faith heard him enter the adjoining room, heard his footsteps on the bare board floor as he crossed to the connecting doorway, heard him twist the knob. She tensed, uncertain if she heard his curse or only imagined it.

"Open the door, Faith."

She pulled her arms from beneath the children's heads, then slid out of bed and crossed to the locked door, her way lit by a low-burning lamp. Placing her mouth near the door, she said, "Go to bed, George. The children are asleep."

"Unlock the door."

A moment's hesitation, then, "No."

This time she heard his curse and knew she hadn't imagined it.

"I'm staying with the children. They're upset. I'm not leaving them."

"You're my wife and you'll do what I say. Now open this door!" He pounded on it.

"Ma?" Alex called from the bed.

"You're waking the children, George. Sleep it off, and we'll talk in the morning."

She heard a loud noise and barely had time to step back before the doorjamb splintered. The door burst open, striking the wall.

George strode through the doorway and grabbed her by the upper arms, hurting her with his tight grasp. "Next time I tell you to do something, you'll do it."

Even in the dim light, Faith saw something in his eyes she hadn't recognized earlier. Rage. Perhaps even a touch of insanity.

"Don't ever lock me out, Faith. Do you hear?"

She could smell the cheap whiskey on his breath.

"Ma?"

"It's all right, Alex." She drew a quick breath. "Please, George. Let's talk about it in the morning. Please." Fear edged in.

A knock sounded on the outer door. "Everything okay in there?" Claire O'Connell said in the hallway. "I heard a loud crash."

George gave Faith a shove, then said, "We're just fine, ma'am." Then he whispered, "Don't ever lock me out again. You'll regret it if you do."

Faith stood, staring, as he went into the next room. She listened as he moved about the room, dropping his shoes on the floor one at a time. She heard the squeak of the bed as he lay down.

It wasn't until Alex took hold of her hand that she realized she was shaking violently, enough to make her teeth chatter. Now it was her son's turn to say, "It's okay, Ma. I won't let him hurt you. God will take care of us." Then he led her back to the bed.

Drake was halfway to Dead Horse the next morning—on his way to get Faith and the children—when he saw a young boy running along the road from town. He didn't have to get any nearer to know it was Alex. He nudged his pinto into a canter, closing the remaining distance between them. Then he reined in and dismounted.

"Alex, what are you doing out here?"

"I . . . was comin' . . . for you," the boy said between breaths.

Drake grabbed him by the arms and steadied him. "What's wrong?"

"It's *him*. He kicked in the door last night."

"Did he hurt your mother?"

Alex shook his head. "No, but he was going to. I could tell. He was mad 'cause she locked him out. Don't let him hurt Ma. Don't let him take us away."

"I won't." Drake straightened. "Come on. We're going for your mother and Becca. I never should have let any of you leave the Jagged R."

They'd gone down to the hotel restaurant for breakfast. Faith had been thankful there were no other guests. It had been bad enough enduring Claire O'Connell's curious glances.

Only George had actually eaten what he'd ordered. The children and Faith had merely moved their food around on their plates.

Finally George had stood and told the children to go outside and play while their parents had a talk.

Now, as she watched him moving around the hotel room, pausing at the window, then continuing his circuitous route, she shivered with dread. Instinct told her he didn't want to talk—he wanted to strike out and hurt her. She'd never feared him in the years they'd been together, despite the things he'd done. But something inside him had changed.

George stopped and turned toward her. "I need money. How much have you got?"

She stilled her quaking heart. "Only a little."

"Where is it?" He took a threatening step toward her.

"There." She pointed toward her jewelry box on the dresser.

George opened it and removed the paper money and coins Faith had stashed away so carefully. She had intended to use the money to one day leave Dead Horse, but of course that had been before she'd accepted Drake's proposal of marriage.

Her breath caught in her chest when she saw George lift the topaz necklace, letting the gold chain slide through his fingers. "That isn't mine," she said quickly as she rose from her chair. "I must return it."

He cast her a sideways glance. "Not yours?"

"It was a wedding gift from Drake." Her chest hurt. "I must return it to him."

"Not likely."

"I must." Her throat tightened. "I can't marry him, so I must give it back."

"No."

She reached for the necklace. "Give it to me."

His unexpected blow sent her crashing against the wall. Before she could get her bearings, before the ringing in her ears could cease, he had pinned her there, his arm pressed against her throat.

"Don't you cross me, woman. You'll do what I tell you to do." He pressed harder, cutting off her wind. "Do you know how easy it would be for me to kill you? I know. I know how easy it is."

She believed him. She could see it in his eyes. He did know. He'd killed before. *O God, help me!*

"I could kill you now, and then I'd take the children and go. You wouldn't be around to protect them, would you? The girl, she'll be pretty like you. There are men who—"

Faith kneed him in the groin as hard as she could. Hard enough to cause him to stumble back from her, which gave her a chance to draw a breath. He bowed over in pain, and she took advantage of the short reprieve. She grabbed a nearby ladder-back chair and swung it with all her might, landing a solid blow against the side of his head. He fell with a thump to the floor.

She stood shaking, staring at his inert form. "You'll never hurt my children. Never."

The door flew open, and Faith lifted the chair, ready to strike again if necessary. Then she saw a commanding presence standing in the doorway.

Drake.

A tiny cry tore from her throat. A moment later she was in his arms. "I was on my way to rescue you," he said, "but it seems I'm a bit late."

She drew back and looked into his face.

He smiled wryly. "Remind me never to cross you."

Tears pooled in her eyes as she nodded.

"I'm taking you and the children out of here now. Agreed?"

Again she nodded.

"I don't know how or when we'll get it sorted out, Faith. But will you trust me to see that it does?"

"Yes," she whispered.

"Then let's go home."

23

GERTIE leaned forward on the buggy seat, as if that would get them to the Jagged R sooner.

"Hurry, Doc," she whispered.

Her stomach was tied in knots, and she wrung her hands anxiously. She didn't know what was wrong, but something was urgently pulling her to the ranch. She was certain Faith needed something.

As the house came into view, Gertie reached over and covered one of Rick's hands with her own. "I might be loco, Doc, giving into this feelin'. It's probably nothing, but thanks for humorin' me."

"You might be loco, Gertie, but if you are, then that's one of the things I love about you. I'll always try to do what you ask of me if it's in my power to do so."

One of the things I love about you . . .

For a moment, as his words repeated themselves in her head, Gertie forgot about Faith and reveled instead in Rick's confession of love. He'd never used those exact words before, and she hadn't known how much she'd wanted him to until he did.

"I love you, too, Doc." She leaned over and kissed him. Then she hopped out of the buggy as it rolled to a stop and hurried toward the house.

"Mr. Rutledge!" she called as she opened the front door. "Faith!"

A moment later she heard footsteps upstairs. Just as she looked up, Faith leaned over the third-floor railing.

"Gertie. Thank God. We thought you'd gone to town to see Rick."

"I did. We—"

"Please go back and tell him he's needed."

"Don't have to. He's right outside. What's wrong?"

"It's Becca."

Gertie whirled around and rushed through the open doorway. "Doc, git your bag and git in here quick. Becca's sick." She didn't wait for him. Instead she ran up the stairs, taking them two at a time. She found both Faith and Drake in the children's bedroom.

Faith was bending over the bed, smoothing Becca's forehead with her fingertips. "It's all right, Rebecca Ann. Dr. Telford is here. He's going to make you feel better again."

Before Gertie could say anything or ask any questions, Rick entered the bedroom, his black leather bag in hand. His gaze met Drake's for the briefest of moments before he strode to the bed.

"She took sick in the night," Drake said. "We haven't been able to bring her fever down."

"She was doing so much better." Faith's eyes were wide and misty. "She was doing so much better. This is all my fault. She was upset by everything. If I hadn't..." She fell silent and glanced around her as if she'd forgotten what she'd been about to say.

"Gertie," Rick said in a low voice, "take Faith down to the kitchen and see that she eats something."

"I can't leave," Faith protested.

"Gertie, take her now."

Obediently, she took hold of Faith's arm. "Come with me. Let Doc see what he can do for Becca. She'll be all right now that he's here. You said so yourself." She glanced quickly at Rick, and he gave her a slight nod before returning his attention to his patient.

Gertie drew her toward the door, murmuring reassurances that Becca would get better. She wished she knew if anything she said was true.

George paced back and forth across the length of the hotel room, his brows crinkled in an angry frown. He was caged, trapped in this cursed little town, and he didn't like the feeling one bit. He rubbed the side of his head where Faith had struck him with the chair, and spewed obscenities about the woman and all the trouble she'd caused him.

Nothing had gone right for him lately, and this time it was Faith's fault. Faith Butler, his faithful and loving wife. Well, she used to be his wife, and she thought she still was.

He paused and counted the remaining money in his pocket. The money he'd taken from Faith. Not much here. Not enough to get him out of this jerkwater town to a place of safety.

With a sudden fierceness, he kicked the small commode, breaking the porcelain pitcher and spilling water across the floor.

It wasn't fair! He should be living high on the hog in the big city. He should have women at his beck and call, as he had in years past. Why was this happening to him? He didn't deserve this. Why were the fates against him? Wasn't he deserving of at least a little luck?

He strode to the window of the room and stared at the gray house on the ridge. It was an elegant place, built in the middle of nowhere. He could probably live for years on what Rutledge had paid for some of the oil paintings hanging on his walls or for that piano in the Jagged R parlor.

George cursed as he slammed his fist against the window frame. There had to be a way he could get his hands on enough money to take him out of this stinking backwater town and out of the country—far from the law, far from San Francisco and its accompanying ill fortune. To Europe, perhaps, where a man could live like a man was supposed to live. George was the one who should be living in luxury. Not Faith. Never Faith and those brats of hers.

It was evening when Will Kidd delivered the envelope addressed to Drake Rutledge at the Jagged R Ranch. Drake didn't have to open it to know the letter was from George Butler, and he knew Faith didn't have to be told. He could feel her apprehensive gaze upon him as he slid his finger beneath the envelope's flap and broke the seal. He removed the folded sheet of paper and read it in silence, his gaze flicking over the short missive several times.

"What is it?" she whispered.

Drake glanced up. "He wants to meet with me."

"Don't go." She grabbed his wrist. "It's a trap. You mustn't go. He's mad, Drake. I saw it in his eyes."

"I have to go, Faith."

"No. No, you don't."

He cupped her chin, smoothing her skin with his thumb. "We have to settle things with him so we can marry. We belong together—you, me, the children. We can't go forward until we come to terms with the past."

"But—"

"Shh." He kissed her, drawing her close against him. He sought to comfort her with his tender caresses. He wanted only to dispel her fears.

Faith clung to him. Silently he promised he wouldn't fail her. No matter what he had to do, he wouldn't fail her.

The two men met in the hotel restaurant late that night. No one else was present. Even Claire O'Connell had enough sense to remain out of sight.

Drake didn't speak as he took his seat on the chair opposite George. He deliberately kept his expression neutral, hiding the anger that burned in his heart. He didn't know exactly what George wanted, but he was certain it was about money. With a man like George Butler, it almost always was.

He read disdain in George's eyes as their gazes met across the table. It was a look Drake had seen in people's eyes before, but this time he was thankful for it. He saw Drake's blindness as a vulnerability, which was a mistake. But then George had already proven himself a fool in other ways; Drake was not surprised to find his judgment flawed in this instance.

"You used to be a lawyer," George began, breaking the silence.

Drake gave a curt nod.

"Then you should know it won't go well for Faith in a divorce. She's an actress, and she's been living in your house while married to me. You can protest all you want about her position as housekeeper. The fact is, you were going to marry her. No judge will allow her to keep the children after they know that. You know I'm right."

Drake knew it didn't look good, but he didn't say so. He simply waited for the other man to continue.

George glanced quickly toward the doorway, then leaned forward, arms on the table, and spoke in a low voice. "Listen, I'm willing to make it easy on everyone. If I go away, there doesn't have to be a divorce. We'll just pretend I'm dead. You can marry Faith if you want or keep her as your mistress. Who cares?"

Drake's mouth thinned, but he held himself in check. Smashing his fist into George's face wouldn't solve a thing.

"Look, I'm a little short of travel funds right now. And if I have to stay here, I want those kids with me, as is my right. But for, say, ten thousand dollars, I think I'd be able to leave Dead Horse and never trouble any of you again."

"Are you offering to sell Faith and the children to me?" Drake asked.

George had the gall to smile. "I wouldn't put it exactly that way."

Perhaps it would be worth ten thousand dollars to see the last of George Butler, but Drake knew it wouldn't be the last time they would see him. Men like him never stopped looking for an easy dollar. If Drake gave in to his blackmail this time, George would eventually return for more. Besides, even if no one else knew the truth, he couldn't pretend George was dead. Drake wouldn't be able to marry Faith until she was free of him once and for all.

"Listen, Rutledge." George's voice dropped to a whisper. "It's either this or I go for the marshal."

He's bluffing. The knowledge struck Drake with a sudden certainty. George wasn't going to go for the marshal. He was in trouble, probably hiding from someone. He needed money to get away, far away. He was a desperate man, and desperate men made mistakes.

Drake rose from his chair. "Go ahead and send for him."

George's eyes widened in surprise.

"On second thought—" Drake leaned forward, knuckles on the table—"I think I'll send for him myself."

George jumped to his feet. "Why, you—"

Drake's hand around George's throat cut short a foul exclamation. "Come near Faith, Alex, or Becca again, and I'll personally validate your death notice!"

"You can't keep me from my kids," George croaked.

"Watch me."

Faith awakened with a start, surprised she'd fallen asleep on Alex's bed. A lamp, turned low, burned on the table near the window, and the pale light revealed Drake sitting beside Becca's bed, holding the little girl's hand.

"Drake?" Faith sat up.

"The fever's broken."

Faith got up and moved to her daughter's bedside. "How long ago?"

"Not long."

Faith touched Becca's forehead to see for herself. It was cool and dry. "Thank You, God," she whispered.

"You should go back to bed."

"I don't think I could fall asleep again."

Drake came to her. He placed an arm around her shoulders, and together they watched Becca sleep. After several minutes Drake's arm tightened. "Let's go downstairs."

She didn't resist.

Carrying the lamp to light the way, he guided her out of the bedroom, down the stairs, and into the parlor. They settled on the sofa, Faith's cheek against Drake's chest. She felt his lips brush across the top of her head, and warm contentment spread through her.

After a long while she looked up. "What's going to happen now?"

He was silent for several heartbeats before answering. "We can't wait for George to try to take you or the children away again. When Becca's well enough, I want us to go down to Green River City to see the marshal. It's a chance I think we need to take. Will you go with me?"

Ever since George had interrupted the wedding a few days before, Faith had been trapped in a web of her own fears. She'd given up, just as Drake had said, and her lack of trust in God and in Drake had almost cost her the only chance for real happiness she'd ever known. Now, as Drake held her in his arms, she felt the last of her apprehension melting away. His quiet confidence became her own. She believed in him. She trusted him. She loved him.

"Faith?"

"I'll go with you," she replied. "We all will."

"No, you won't."

Faith gasped even as Drake rose from the sofa and shoved her behind him.

George stepped from the shadows of the parlor doorway, a gun pointed at Drake's chest. "Trouble. That's all women are. Trouble."

"Get out of here, Butler," Drake warned.

"You know what she wants from you, Rutledge? Your money. I should've killed her back in New York. Should've killed Jane, too. It's not so hard. I found that out. It's not so hard."

He's mad. O God, George is mad. He really means to kill us. Help us, Father. O God, help us.

"Why don't we go outside and talk about this?" Drake suggested.

George cocked and released the hammer of the gun several times. "Where're the brats?"

"Asleep."

"I should have killed her, you know. Nothing's gone right for me since the day I met her. Let's go to California, she said. Let's go get rich. Faith there, she was supposed to become some great actress. She was supposed to make me rich, too. But all she ever wanted was a passel of brats and a house to raise 'em in. Now look at her. Just like Jane. Lying to me, just like Jane." He cocked the gun. "Well, it's not going to happen again."

"No!" Faith shouted.

Drake lunged forward even as a deafening explosion split the air. Faith saw him fall in midstride, saw the frightening red stain spread across his shirt. A silent scream echoed in her mind. She wanted to run to him but was unable to move.

"Now it's your turn." George cocked his weapon a second time and aimed it at her chest.

It didn't matter if he killed her. Not if Drake was dead. Nothing mattered if he was gone.

Faith heard the blast of the gun and waited to feel the bullet slam into her, waited to fall beside Drake. Instead she saw a look of surprise flash across George's face moments before he crumpled to the floor, his eyes open but sightless.

Then Gertie stepped into view, pistol in hand. Her eyes flicked from the two men on the floor to Faith. "I reckon we'd best see to the boss. There's no help for Butler now."

As if Gertie's words had released her from some invisible bonds, Faith rushed forward, falling to her knees beside the man she loved. "Drake, don't leave me. Please don't leave me."

She didn't expect a reply but heard one anyway, breathless and pain filled as it was.

"Not a chance, Faith. I'm going to stay with you for a long, long time."

24

THEIR wedding day arrived, a crisp autumn afternoon in late October. The leaves on the poplars and aspens had turned to gold; the ones that had already fallen crunched beneath the wheels of the wagons that brought their guests to the Jagged R. The purple mountain peaks had received a dusting of snow the night before, and the promise of winter hung in the air.

The marriage of Drake Rutledge and Faith Butler was to be a quiet affair, held in the parlor of the gray house on the ridge, with only a few witnesses—Alex and Becca, Rick and Gertie Telford, still newlyweds themselves, Sadie and Joseph Gold and their children, and the Jagged R ranch hands. Faith had wanted to keep it small and intimate. After several weeks of caring for Drake as he recovered from the bullet wound in his shoulder and dealing with questions and suspicions from the Green River City marshal, she longed for simplicity.

For a while, she had feared Drake would be accused of George's murder. After all, the marshal had said, Drake wanted to marry the wife of the deceased. Perhaps this had been the easiest way to elimi-nate an inconvenient husband. Faith had responded to the implica-tions with indignant denials. If anyone was to blame, it was she herself, she'd declared. Drake had sought only to protect her, and he had been injured for it.

The marshal then turned his attention to his other suspect. Gertie had admitted she'd seen George Butler enter the house and had followed him, gun in hand, and shot the man after he'd fired at Drake. "I wasn't gonna let him hurt nobody else," she'd said without apology.

Then the marshal had learned Butler was accused of a murder in San Francisco and had also confirmed that George had ob-tained a divorce from Faith long before coming to Dead Horse. At that point, he'd ruled the shooting self-defense and returned to Green River City, leaving the survivors to piece their lives together again.

Now, with Drake recovered and Becca healthier than ever, the horror of that night seemed like a bad dream to Faith. Today she faced the future with gladness and tingling anticipation. She was to be Drake's wife. She would bear his name, and one day she would bear his children, too.

She was, indeed, most blessed among women.

Wearing her gold-and-brown-striped dress, a spray of dried flowers in her hair, Faith descended the front staircase. Her groom awaited her in the entry hall. Her heart leapt at the sight of him—tall and handsome, his ebony hair tied back at the nape with a satin rib-bon. She found the moment unreal, knowing she was bound to this man by a love still undreamed of only last spring.

With a look of adoration in his uncovered eye, Drake reached out and took hold of her hand, squeezing her fingers gently, drawing her toward him.

Toward Drake and all their tomorrows.

She went gladly.

Reverend Arnold smiled at the couple as they entered the parlor, and Faith heard one of the Gold girls whisper how handsome Drake was.

"Dearly beloved..."

Yes, she was beloved. She felt it, like a soft wind caressing her skin. Dearly beloved, indeed.

O spirit of lo ve! ho w quick and fr esh ar t thou.

"...we are gathered here today, in the sight of God, to join this man and this woman..."

He is the half par t of a blessed man,
Left to be finished b y such as she;
And she a fair divided ex cellence,
Whose fullness of per fection lies in him.

"...in the state of holy matrimony..."

Honour, riches, marriage, blessing,
Long continuance, and incr easing,
Hourly jo ys be still upon y ou!

"I, Drake, take thee, Faith..."

Love . . . as sw eet and musical
As bright A pollo s lute, str ung with his hair:
And when Lo ve speaks, the v oice of all the gods
Makes heav en dr owsy with the harmony .

"I, Faith, take thee, Drake..."

Doubt thou the stars ar e fire;
Doubt that the sun doth mo ve;
Doubt tr uth to be a liar;
But nev er doubt I lo ve.

"'The Lord bless thee, and keep thee: The Lord make His face shine upon thee, and be gracious unto thee: The Lord lift up His countenance upon thee, and give thee peace.' Now and forevermore. Amen."

At the end of Reverend Arnold's benediction, Faith opened her eyes. Drake was watching her with a look so filled with love, it nearly stopped her heart.

"You may kiss your bride."

"With pleasure." Drake drew her into his embrace, crushing her bouquet between them. Like a perfumed cloud, a sweet scent rose to tickle their nostrils. Drake smiled, then captured her lips in a kiss both tender and passionate.

I think ther e is not half a kiss to choose
Who lo ves another best.

Faith's heart soared with a joy too marvelous to be contained. When their mouths parted, she threw her arms around Drake's neck in reckless abandon and laughed as she exclaimed, "I love you!"

Applause broke out behind them, reminding Faith they were not alone, that there were guests to greet and food to be served and endless conversations to be held before the afternoon would be over.

Alex was the first to step forward. He held out his hand toward Drake. *"Now* can I call you Pa?"

"Yes, Son. Now you can call me Pa."

Faith's heart fluttered.

"Me, too!" Becca shouted, throwing herself exuberantly into Drake's arms, much as her mother had done moments before.

Drake lifted the girl off the floor. "And you, too." He planted a kiss on Becca's cheek, then met her mother's gaze.

My crown is in my heart, not on my head;
Not decked with diamonds and Indian stones,
Nor to be seen: my crown is called content.
A crown it is that seldom kings enjoy.

Standing side by side on the front porch, their arms around each other, Faith and Drake waved to their children as the Telford wagon rolled down the drive and into the glare of the setting sun.

"Alone at last." Drake drew her around to face him. Unhurriedly he lowered his mouth toward hers, his gaze unwavering. In anticipation of what was to come, she moistened her lips with the tip of her tongue.

"Mrs. Rutledge…" He stretched out the two words, making them a verbal caress. Then he kissed her. His mouth teased, tasted, and sampled, a sweet ending to a wonderful day.

"Drake," she whispered, mingling breath for breath as his mouth still hovered above hers. "Hold me like this forever. Never let me go."

"Never." He plucked the spray of dried flowers from her hair, then removed her hairpins, one after another, each one clicking softly as he dropped them onto the porch. When all such impediments were gone, he combed his fingers through her thick tresses, lifting her hair toward his face and breathing deeply.

"Do you know how often I've longed to do this?" he asked.

She shook her head.

"Forever."

She lifted a hand to caress his cheek, her fingers lingering on his scar. She felt him stiffen and knew a moment of truth had arrived. Without hesitation, she raised her other hand and untied the thongs that held the patch in place. She felt his tension, knew he half expected her to recoil. She didn't. He was beautiful, wondrous, perfect in every way. Rising on tiptoe, she cradled his head between her hands and kissed him again. When their lips parted, she smiled.

"Oh, Faith. You're as warm and inviting as sunshine on a summer day. You've made me the happiest man alive." He paused, then whispered, "'O, she doth teach the torches to burn bright! / It seems she hangs upon the cheek of night / Like a rich jewel in an Ethiop's ear— / Beauty too rich for use, for earth too dear!'"

"'Speak low, if you speak love.'"

Drake lifted her into his arms and carried her inside, into a house no longer dark and shadowed but into a home filled with light and love.

A Note from the Author

Dear Friends:

When I wrote my first novel in 1981, I wanted to prove I could write and sell the type of fiction I liked best without including those things I found personally objectionable. I succeeded in doing so, selling my first book and all that followed. But as time went on, I began to compromise my ideals in the name of success, giving in to the demands of the market and requests from editors until there was little about my books to distinguish them from those written by unbelievers. With each compromise I made, I created—then widened—a chasm between myself and my Savior. But God is faithful even when we're faithless. He never took His hand off me, and little by little and ever so gently, He drew me back into fellowship with Him.

In 1995, in the midst of my drawing-back process, I wrote a novel that I purposed in my heart to be a type of love letter to God. There were threads of the redemption theme throughout the book, but it was flawed because I also included many things that were not God honoring.

In 1997, one year after my "flawed love letter" was published, the Lord placed a story idea in my heart that would eventually become my first novel for the Christian market. And so began a new season in my life, a season of serving Jesus with the creativity and talent He'd given me. What a joy it has been to give my will and my life over to Him with new abandon.

When the opportunity arose to take my previously published "flawed love letter" and rewrite it for HeartQuest, I was thrilled to do so. I love second chances, perhaps because God, in His mercy and grace, has given me so many of them. *Speak to Me of Love* is the end result of those rewrites. May it—and everything I write—be pleasing in His sight. I hope it is now the love letter I intended it to be.

In His grip,
ROBIN LEE HATCHER

About the Author

Author Robin Lee Hatcher, winner of the Christy Award for Excellence in Christian Fiction and the RITA Award for Best Inspirational Romance, has written over thirty-five contemporary and historical novels and novellas. There are more than 5 million copies of her novels in print, and she has been published in fourteen countries. Her first hardcover release, *The Forgiving Hour,* was optioned for film in 1999. Robin is a past president/CEO of Romance Writers of America, a professional writers organization with over eight thousand members worldwide. In recognition of her efforts on behalf of literacy, Laubach Literacy International named the Robin Award in her honor.

Robin and her husband, Jerry, live in Boise, Idaho, where they are active in their church and Robin leads a women's Bible study. Thanks to two grown daughters, Robin is now a grandmother of four ("an extremely young grandmother," she hastens to add). She enjoys travel, the theater, golf, and relaxing in the beautiful Idaho mountains. She and Jerry share their home with Delilah the Persian cat, Tiko the Shetland sheepdog, and Misty the Border collie.

Readers may write to her at

P.O. BOX 4722

BOISE, ID 83711-4722

or visit her Web site at **www.robinleehatcher.com.**

ROBIN LEE HATCHER
From her heart . . . to yours

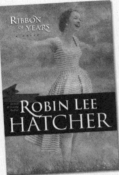

RIBBON
OF YEARS
hardcover ISBN 0-8423-4009-2

Standing at the edge of her dreams, Miriam passionately embraces the future. Through tears and joy her ordinary life becomes a remarkable journey as she impacts others in miraculous ways.

"This poignant view of one woman's life is a superb read, and one I am glad I did not miss!"—**Romance Reader's Connection**

"Keep tissues handy. Miriam's life isn't sugarcoated, but a testament to triumph over adversity."—**CBA Marketplace**

*f*IRSTBORN
hardcover ISBN 0-8423-4010-6 · softcover ISBN 0-8423-5557-X

Erika's worst fear is realized when her well-kept secret shows up on her doorstep. As she reaches out to the daughter she gave up for adoption nearly twenty-two years ago, her husband pulls away, leaving Erika with an impossible choice.

"This is a well-written inspirational novel."
—**Publishers Weekly**

"Robin is a gifted writer whose novels unfailingly stir and challenge readers' hearts."—**Francine Rivers**

Turn the page for an exciting
preview from Robin Lee Hatcher's next
HeartQuest book

CATCHING
KATIE
(ISBN 0-8423-6099-9)

Available in early 2004 at a bookstore near you.

BEN FROWNED as he read over his editorial for the third time. It was boring. The words were as dry as dust, pure and simple. With a sigh he dropped the papers onto his desk, then leaned back in his swivel chair and rubbed his eyes with his knuckles. He wondered if he was ever going to get it right.

Staring at the ceiling, he allowed his thoughts to drift once again to Katie. Only three more days and she would be here. And it was about time, too.

His mother feared that Katie had been gone so long they wouldn't recognize her, but Ben knew that was impossible. He would know Katie no matter how long she stayed away. Eleven years hadn't dimmed his memories of her.

He remembered the little girl with the thick black braids reaching to her waist and the enormous brown eyes that had seemed too big for her face. He remembered the tomboy, often dressed the same as he was, in shirt and trousers, scabs on her knees, scrapes on her hands. He remembered the girl who could swing a baseball bat as hard as any boy in Homestead and who was absolutely fearless as she raced her horse alongside the train. He remembered his childhood pal in a hundred different ways, and all of them made him smile.

Katie Jones was unforgettable.

Grinning, he rose and walked to the large plate-glass window. Main Street was quiet, as usual. Just the way he liked it. But even he had to admit he missed the way Katie could liven up a town. Nobody else was so full of ideas or mischief. She'd gotten Ben in plenty of hot water when they were kids, but he'd always forgiven her. He couldn't help but forgive Katie anything.

Yes, it was going to be great having Katie home again. But she wouldn't be here until Friday's train pulled into the station, and in the meantime he had an article to write for the next edition of the paper. Reluctantly he returned to his desk.

As he sat down, he stared at the editorial. It hadn't changed itself in the last few minutes while he'd been daydreaming. It was still boring, boring, boring. He picked up his pen, promising himself that he would finish it, even if he had to sit there until the wee hours of the night.

Maybe if he added a paragraph right here, and then—

"You're working late, Mr. Rafferty."

He glanced up, surprised someone had entered without his knowing it. The hinge on the front door was badly in need of oiling and creaked abominably whenever it was opened.

The woman smiled. "Haven't you a welcome for an old friend?"

Ben stood. "Katie?" He knew his expression must border on the ridiculous.

"Have I changed so much?"

Had Katie changed? *Yes!* When had she become a woman? A beautiful woman? And despite the flecks of mud on her cheeks and clothes, she *was* beautiful. She hadn't been beautiful before, had she? Ben didn't think so. She'd just been Katie.

A frown replaced her smile. "Well, for pity's sake, say *something.*"

He moved from behind his desk, stepping toward her, studying her face for some sign of the gawky schoolgirl he'd remembered. Her eyes were the same luminous dark brown, but they no longer seemed too big for her face. Her complexion was smooth, her skin the color of honey. She was still tiny, a good foot shorter than he was, but she was noticeably more curvaceous than the girl he'd left behind. The braids were gone, he suspected, but he couldn't be certain because of the broad-brimmed hat and scarf she wore.

"Have I *really* changed so much?" she repeated.

"I can't believe it's you."

Her dazzling smile returned. "It's me all right, Benjie."

Then, without warning, she threw herself into his arms and kissed him on the cheek as she hugged him tightly. Her laughter warmed the office like a fresh ray of sunshine. "Oh, Benjie, it's so good to see you."

Suddenly he laughed with her, all else forgotten. "It's good to see you, too." He set her back from him, his hands still on her upper arms. "How did you get here? You're not expected until Friday."

"I arrived in Boise City yesterday and decided to drive up. My motorcar is out front."

"You *drove?*"

"All the way from Washington. I've been following the Suffrage Special on its tour of the West in the Susan B."

"The Susan B.?"

Katie took hold of his hand and drew him toward the door. "She's my Ford touring car. I named her for Susan B. Anthony. Come take a look at her."

This was Katie all right. Leave it to her to be the first valley resident to own an automobile. Leave it to her to motor clear across the country, and to blazes with the convention that said a woman didn't do such things.

"There she is." Katie waved an arm toward the Model T Ford parked in front of the *Homestead Herald* office. "Isn't she scrumptious?" She squeezed his fingers as she turned toward him. "Will you drive out with me to the Lazy L? I'm sure Papa will loan you a horse to get back to town, and I'd love to talk with you awhile. It's been so long since we've seen one another, and I want to catch up on all the news. Letters aren't the same as hearing things firsthand." She stepped closer, and he caught a whiff of rose water.

When he was twelve and Katie just shy of eleven, Ben had kissed her. They'd been up on the ridge near Tin Horn Pass, and she'd said she didn't know what made grown folks want to get married, but maybe it had something to do with kissing, since her father was always kissing her mother. She'd wondered what all the fuss was about, so they'd decided to find out. Afterward they'd decided kissing wasn't anything special. Certainly nothing they'd cared to try with each other again.

That was a long time ago. Ben had kissed more than a few girls since then. Now he found himself wondering if Katie had discovered, as he had, that kissing wasn't so bad after all.

"Say you will, Benjie. Please?"

Memories of Katie saying those same words rushed over him—*"Say you will, Benjie. Please?"*—and he knew it was useless to argue. She would get her way before she was through. It had always been so between them.

He nodded. "Let me get my hat and lock up."

><+>•<•>•<

While Ben was inside, Katie let her gaze wander the length and breadth of Main Street. She was surprised by the emotions she felt at the sight of her hometown. She hadn't thought she wanted to return to Homestead, to leave her friends and the intense activities of Washington State for the quiet sameness of Idaho. Yet now that she was here, she was glad.

She heard the door close, and she glanced at Ben as he stepped up beside her.

Homestead might not have changed much, but the same couldn't be said for Ben Rafferty. He'd grown tall, and his shoulders were amazingly broad beneath the cut of his suit coat. The angles of his face had sharpened, matured. The boyish good looks had more than fulfilled their promise in the man he'd become. The color of his hair—which brushed his collar, begging to be trimmed—had darkened to a rich shade of gold, and she thought it a shame when he placed his hat on his head, hiding it from view.

"Ready?" he asked, glancing down and meeting her gaze.

She felt a sudden embarrassment, as if she'd been caught doing something inappropriate.

"Katie?"

She saw a teasing good humor in his dark blue eyes, and her embarrassment vanished. This was Benjie. This was her dearest friend in the world.

"I'm ready," she answered.

Ben took hold of her arm and guided her toward the passenger door. "Mind if I do the driving?"

She cast a dubious look in his direction.

"I *know* how to drive, Katie. I went to college, too."

It was on the tip of her tongue to tell him she never allowed anyone else to drive her motorcar, but his next words caused her to swallow the argument unspoken.

"You wouldn't withhold the pleasure from me, would you?" He ran his fingers along the side of the door. "It's been a long time since I've had the opportunity."

"Of course you may drive her, Benjie. Anytime you wish."

Grinning like a schoolboy, Ben reached inside the automobile and pulled the latch, then opened the door with a flourish and assisted Katie onto the running board and into the Susan B. When she was settled and the door once again closed, he went around to the driver's side, reached in, and set the levers. He whistled a tuneless melody as he walked to the front of the motorcar and gave the engine crank a hefty turn. Without a trace of her sometimes temperamental behavior, the Susan B sprang to life.

Straightening, Ben shot Katie a look of pure joy before returning to the driver's side, where he vaulted over the stationary door and settled onto the seat behind the wheel. A few minutes later the two of them were well on their way to the Lazy L Ranch.

▶·┤◈·○·◈┤◀

Ben had forgotten how much he enjoyed driving an automobile. Homestead had a way of making one forget there was a whole other world beyond this valley and the surrounding mountains. Maybe it was good to remind himself of that fact every so often.

Overhead, dusk splashed the smattering of clouds with shades of pink, announcing the coming of night.

"The headlamps are electric," Katie said softly.

Her voice drew Ben's gaze in her direction. She was holding her hat with one hand while the fingers of her other hand fiddled with a button on her duster. He wondered if she was nervous about going home.

Hoping to distract her, he asked, "It hasn't changed much, has it?"

"Homestead?" She shook her head. "No. Not much."

"Surprised?"

"No. Not really." She smiled. "Tell me about the newspaper."

"Nothing much to tell. It's still a weekly. I do everything but the typesetting. Harvey Trent does that. Harv's the best typesetter west of the Mississippi. He used to work for the *Idaho Daily Statesman*, but I lured him away." He chuckled, remembering how hard it had been to convince the man to move to Homestead. Ben had succeeded only after Harvey started sparking Esther Potter, the proprietress of Zoe's Restaurant.

"Do you write all the articles and columns?"

"Yes."

"It must be a great deal of work. Week after week. Maybe you should hire a columnist to help you."

"A columnist?" He had a niggling suspicion.

Katie met his gaze and flashed him another smile. "Don't you think a women's column would be of interest to your readers? Of *course* it would be of interest. Women read your newspaper, too. Don't you think they would enjoy a column from a woman's perspective?"

"And who would write this column?" As if he didn't know.

She twisted on the car's seat, then leaned forward, touching his arm. "Oh, Benjie, there is so much they need to hear. Do you know how fortunate the women of Idaho are to be able to vote? But so many waste that right. It's a right that should be exercised, but they throw it away, leaving it up to men to decide what happens in our country. If only we could make them see—"

"*We?*" He allowed the automobile to roll to a stop.

Katie's eyes danced with excitement. "Yes. *We*. Don't you see how much good we could do? You own the newspaper, and I have so much to share about my work. I've met some of the most distinguished and gifted women in the country. Even now they're calling upon women voters of the enfranchised states to—"

"Hold up a minute, Katie."

Her expression sobered.

Ben searched his mind for the right words. It wasn't that he didn't support suffrage for women. He did. A woman's vote was as valid as any man's. But he wasn't certain Homestead—or the rest of Idaho, for that matter—was ready for Katie's firebrand variety of women's concerns. Katie never did anything halfway. She would stir up a hornet's nest in no time.

And there he'd be, smack-dab in the middle of it.

Visit www.HeartQuest.com for lots of info on
HeartQuest books and authors and more!

HEART QUEST

Coming Soon

FALL 2003

Christmas Homecoming
Diane Noble, Pamela Griffin, and Kathleen Fuller

Tying the Knot
Susan May Warren

Summer's End
Lyn Cote

CURRENT HEARTQUEST RELEASES

- *Magnolia*, Ginny Aiken
- *Lark*, Ginny Aiken
- *Camellia*, Ginny Aiken

- *Letters of the Heart*, Lisa Tawn Bergren, Maureen Pratt, and Lyn Cote

- *Sweet Delights*, Terri Blackstock, Elizabeth White, and Ranee McCollum

- *Awakening Mercy*, Angela Benson
- *Abiding Hope*, Angela Benson

- *Ruth*, Lori Copeland
- *Roses Will Bloom Again*, Lori Copeland
- *Faith*, Lori Copeland
- *Hope*, Lori Copeland
- *June*, Lori Copeland
- *Glory*, Lori Copeland

- *Winter's Secret*, Lyn Cote
- *Autumn's Shadow*, Lyn Cote

- *Freedom's Promise*, Dianna Crawford
- *Freedom's Hope*, Dianna Crawford
- *Freedom's Belle*, Dianna Crawford
- *A Home in the Valley*, Dianna Crawford
- *Lady of the River*, Dianna Crawford

- *Speak to Me of Love*, Robin Lee Hatcher

- *Sunrise Song*, Catherine Palmer
- *Final Proof*, Catherine Palmer
- *English Ivy*, Catherine Palmer
- *A Touch of Betrayal*, Catherine Palmer
- *A Kiss of Adventure*, Catherine Palmer (original title: *The Treasure of Timbuktu*)

- *A Whisper of Danger*, Catherine Palmer (original title: *The Treasure of Zanzibar*)
- *Finders Keepers*, Catherine Palmer
- *Hide & Seek*, Catherine Palmer
- *Prairie Rose*, Catherine Palmer
- *Prairie Fire*, Catherine Palmer
- *Prairie Storm*, Catherine Palmer
- *Prairie Christmas*, Catherine Palmer, Elizabeth White, and Peggy Stoks
- *A Victorian Christmas Keepsake*, Catherine Palmer, Kristin Billerbeck, and Ginny Aiken
- *A Victorian Christmas Cottage*, Catherine Palmer, Debra White Smith, Jeri Odell, and Peggy Stoks
- *A Victorian Christmas Quilt*, Catherine Palmer, Peggy Stoks, Debra White Smith, and Ginny Aiken
- *A Victorian Christmas Tea*, Catherine Palmer, Dianna Crawford, Peggy Stoks, and Katherine Chute

- *A Victorian Christmas Collection*, Peggy Stoks
- *Olivia's Touch*, Peggy Stoks
- *Romy's Walk*, Peggy Stoks
- *Elena's Song*, Peggy Stoks

- *Happily Ever After*, Susan May Warren

- *Chance Encounters of the Heart*, Elizabeth White, Kathleen Fuller, and Susan Warren

MOVING FICTION

OTHER GREAT TYNDALE HOUSE FICTION

- *Safely Home*, Randy Alcorn
- *Out of the Shadows*, Sigmund Brouwer
- *The Leper*, Sigmund Brouwer
- *Crown of Thorns*, Sigmund Brouwer
- *Looking for Cassandra Jane*, Melody Carlson
- *A Case of Bad Taste*, Lori Copeland
- *Child of Grace*, Lori Copeland
- *Into the Nevernight*, Anne de Graaf
- *They Shall See God*, Athol Dickson
- *Ribbon of Years*, Robin Lee Hatcher
- *Firstborn*, Robin Lee Hatcher
- *The Touch*, Patricia Hickman
- *Redemption*, Karen Kingsbury with Gary Smalley
- *Remember*, Karen Kingsbury with Gary Smalley
- *Winter Passing*, Cindy McCormick Martinusen
- *Blue Night*, Cindy McCormick Martinusen
- *North of Tomorrow*, Cindy McCormick Martinusen
- *Embrace the Dawn*, Kathleen Morgan

- *The Sister Circle*, Vonette Bright and Nancy Moser
- *Lullaby*, Jane Orcutt
- *The Happy Room*, Catherine Palmer
- *A Dangerous Silence*, Catherine Palmer
- *Fatal Harvest*, Catherine Palmer
- *Blind Sight*, James Pence
- *And the Shofar Blew*, Francine Rivers
- *Unveiled*, Francine Rivers
- *Unashamed*, Francine Rivers
- *Unshaken*, Francine Rivers
- *Unspoken*, Francine Rivers
- *Unafraid*, Francine Rivers
- *A Voice in the Wind*, Francine Rivers
- *An Echo in the Darkness*, Francine Rivers
- *As Sure As the Dawn*, Francine Rivers
- *Leota's Garden*, Francine Rivers
- *Shaiton's Fire*, Jake Thoene
- *Firefly Blue*, Jake Thoene
- *The Promise Remains*, Travis Thrasher
- *The Watermark*, Travis Thrasher